CYBORG MEETS SEA CREATURE

Just as the Cousteaueans were altered humans, the boka were altered dolphins. Besides speech, they too had been given highly efficient lungs. Unlike the Terran dolphins they were descended from, the boka could extract the oxygen they needed from the water; but when they worked and played near the surface, they took advantage of the opportunity to get the oxygen directly. It was only at depth that they breathed water and their blowholes became exhalatory and vocal orifices alone.

"You guys are too easy," Sam said, smiling.

"Sam swim with us?" one of the returnees asked, while the other two now filled their lungs. Sam knew that a boka could make a lungful of oxygen-rich surface air last a long time.

"Sure," Sam said. "Just try to keep up with me."

Ace Books by Kenneth Von Gunden

The K-9 Corps Series

K-9 CORPS
UNDER FIRE
CRY WOLF
THE LAST RESORT

STARSPAWN
THE SOUNDING STILLNESS

THE
SOUNDING
STILLNESS

KENNETH VON GUNDEN

ACE BOOKS, NEW YORK

This book is an Ace original edition,
and has never been previously published.

THE SOUNDING STILLNESS

An Ace Book / published by arrangement with
the author

PRINTING HISTORY
Ace edition / November 1993

ISBN: 0-441-77598-5

ACE®
Ace Books are published by The Berkley Publishing Group,
200 Madison Avenue, New York, NY 10016.
ACE and the "A" design are trademarks
belonging to Charter Communications, Inc.

PRINTED IN THE UNITED STATES OF AMERICA

10 9 8 7 6 5 4 3 2 1

*This novel is dedicated to the person
who makes it all possible:
my friend, partner, and wife,
Donna.*

PART ONE

SAM

1

GALEN YEAGER HAD ALWAYS LIKED HOUSTON. IT WAS A ROBUST city that seemed both representative of Texas and yet possessed of a distinct cosmopolitan and multicultural atmosphere that suggested the liberal coasts more than the conservative heartland. Yes, Galen had always liked Houston—despite the fact that it was the city where he'd first met his estranged wife Adrianna.

Adrianna. Yeager almost started when the image of her face swam into focus in his mind's eye. He was surprised by how easily he had put her and the memory of their marriage into a sealed compartment at the back of his mind.

It was a compartment he rarely ventured to open these days; Galen Yeager was good at compartmentalizing his life that way. It was necessary to wall off what was unpleasant or inconvenient to confront on a regular basis, he decided. It was necessary, or the memories of his secretive profession would haunt him too much. And he couldn't have that.

Adrianna. Both his family and hers were impossibly complex genealogical entities encompassing scores of kinsfolk zealously protective of the rights and privileges their common ancestry entitled them to. Given such circumstances, marriage was nothing he or she could enter into lightly.

Teams of lawyers expert in contract marriage were called in by both sides and the concluding, binding documents were minutely examined and vetted before they could be signed. No simple bonding of man and wife, their marriage was the joining, if in name only, of two great family fortunes.

"That's why we never got a divorce," Galen Yeager said softly to himself. "Dissolving such a social, legal, and economic compact is neither easy nor inexpensive."

He shrugged. It was time to make his way to the Foundation.

Flush enough to afford a human-driven cab, Yeager flagged down a limousine outside the main terminal of the LBJ Space-port. The luxurious floater's owner/driver glanced in the rearview mirror at Galen's face and commented, "Hey, you sure have a big smile on your face, mister. You must be happy to be home."

"I'm happy to be in Houston again," Galen replied, stretching out in the back seat and turning off the small hol-vee showing sumo matches. "But it's not my home."

"You're not from here and you *like* Houston?"

Galen smiled at the incredulity in the man's voice. Natives always seemed alternately boastful and defensive about their towns. "Can't wait to get some of that gulf shrimp," Galen told him. "And I'm here to meet someone."

"Is *he* a native?"

"No, he . . ." Galen stopped and reconsidered. "Actually, I suppose you could say he was born here."

The driver's eyes in the mirror narrowed as he considered that strange statement. "Did I hear you say '*could* say he was born here,' mister?"

Galen nodded. "He died here. That much I know."

The driver's eyes stared back at him for a long time before he asked, "Hey, mind if I put on a little music?"

"No. Go ahead."

As the music and voice of a newly famous country artist filled the limo, Galen thought, *Guess I've put the nail in the coffin of that conversation. Can't say I blame him for being spooked.*

He remembered an early conversation he'd had with Henri Bussot, the administrator/research M.D. who ran the Voorhees Foundation.

"I presume you've managed to get me one, Dr. Bussot."

"Please, call me Henri."

"Sure. And you can call me Galen," he replied, smiling at the good doctor's holographic image. "But forgive me if I'm impatient to know if you—"

Bussot nodded, his head bobbing up and down enthusiastically. "Yes, we have gotten you the cryo-sleeper you wanted."

Galen slowly released the lungful of air he'd been holding in. "Fantastic." Then he frowned and asked, "He is . . . *was* . . . legally dead?"

"Of course. All the sleepers have been declared dead by the courts, given the lack of measurable brain activity. That is the only reason we have been able to find a suitable candidate for what you wish done." He made a face.

"Is something bothering you, Henri?"

For a moment, the doctor looked like he was going to deny he had second thoughts. Instead, he said, "Yes. It's just that while there is nothing to stop us legally from going ahead with what you propose to do, the moral issues bother me."

"This is the closest he can come to what he was, doc. I think that's very moral."

"Perhaps you are right."

"I am," Galen said with sudden conviction.

"If it works the way we have envisioned it," agreed Bussot, "we might be giving someone his life back." He sounded relieved. Bussot reached out to break the connection. "Forgive me, but I must go. You see, it begins now—all of our experimentation and effort."

"Good luck, Henri."

"Thank you." His image dissolved.

How long ago was that? wondered Galen. Then he answered his own question by remembering it had been eleven months ago last week.

"Here we are, buddy. One Voorhees Square." The limousine deposited him in the plaza in front of the Voorhees Foundation. He used his cashcube to pay the driver, adding a generous tip in actual paper money. Despite cashcubes and debit cards, people still liked getting their hands on actual Prin-creds, on real money.

Standing in the open plaza, Galen's eyes took in the imposing edifice that housed the Voorhees Foundation. The Foundation was a nonprofit arm of the Soweto Corporation established more than fifty years earlier by Galen Yeager's maternal grandfather, Piet Voorhees.

His grandfather, a wealthy South African entrepreneur, had earned his money the old-fashioned way—he'd stolen it. That wasn't entirely true, reflected Galen, but he had been one of the African continent's most successful and larger-than-life twenty-first-century robber barons.

His fortune secured and centered in the massive and powerful Soweto Corporation, Piet Voorhees took as his lifemate a leading black politician, Ghannee Mugambi, cementing his ties with both black and white Africa. Together, they made a formidable team.

The Soweto Corporation spawned a number of Byzantine trusts and endowments to insure that Galen and the other grandchildren would receive healthy annual payments over the course of their adult lives. It was these trusts that had so encumbered his marriage to Adrianna.

In return for the Corporation's largess, Galen did what he could to provide financial intelligence to it. He prided himself on compromising neither his position nor his ideals; while notions of illegality did not much deter him—in that respect, he was very much the grandson of Piet Voorhees—he took care to pass along nothing that could be considered subversive or politically or militarily destabilizing to the world order.

Galen's only goal was to arm the Soweto Corporation with the knowledge it needed to survive in a world hostile to all but the most self-sufficient corporate states.

Since his was one of the more powerful families on Terra, Galen would occasionally take full advantage of his familial connections to have a service done him no one else could provide. This trip involved one of those rare occasions that he asked the Corporation—or in this case the Foundation—for a special favor.

II

"Mr. Yeager," said Dr. Henri Bussot, offering Galen his hand. "It is such a pleasure to finally meet you in person after all our 'phone conversations."

Galen shook the tall and imposing man's hand and allowed

his own to be pumped enthusiastically. "It is good to meet you, too, Henri."

Galen glanced around Bussot's office, seeing that it was furnished to underscore the director's exalted position within the Foundation while simultaneously taking care not to imply unbridled extravagance. Admiring the thought and effort that had gone into the decor, Galen thought that here was a man who knew his way around.

"Is he ready for me yet?" Galen finally asked.

Bussot beamed. "He has progressed through the program with remarkable speed. He gives every indication of being a complete success and a vindication of all our hard work."

"I am pleased to hear that," Galen said.

"Shall I take you to him now?"

"If you would be so kind." Internally, Galen laughed at his own words: *If you would be so kind. Balls, I sound like an actor in a second-rate French farce. Talking to old Henri does that to me every time.*

They entered a small, expensively furnished apartment. *Now this one is clearly too elegant,* thought Galen when he noticed an original Yannetti hanging on one wall. *I'll have to get on Henri's case about how he's spending Granddad's money.*

In addition to the paintings and several exquisite Eridani sculptures, there was a long-legged, raven-haired man sitting expectantly on the edge of a chair. Although he wore pants and slippers, his bare torso perfectly sculpted.

"I take it you are the one I've come to meet?"

The man nodded. He was handsome in a rugged way. Galen thought that he would have looked well in dirty jeans or in a tuxedo and black tie. He could think of no form of attire that might diminish his natural dignity; he held himself with the sort of grace that comes naturally to an athlete or a cat. His eyes, when he looked up, were golden-hued.

"Why are his irises that remarkable color?" Galen asked, turning toward Bussot. Speaking as if the graceful-looking man was not in the room, he said, "They're striking but highly irregular."

Bussot rolled his own eyes and sighed in exasperation. "It is all too silly. It is a reaction to how astonishingly flawless androids have become," he said.

"Could you be a little more specific?"

"Look at him," Bussot said, tilting his head toward the golden-eyed man. "He's perfect. Not one person in a thousand could pick him out as an android."

"Yes?"

"That's the point of his eye color, you see. Some legislators and their constituents got nervous about artificials which could pass for human in the street or workplace. They demanded a sign, a scarlet letter or a mark of Cain, to make them readily identifiable."

"And they decided upon golden eyes?"

"Yes," Bussot said. He picked at the corner of his mouth with his index finger, seemingly bothered by something. "You were unaware of the debates about all this?"

"My work as a xenologist takes me out of the system much of the time. The times I called you were either from offplanet or on one of my increasingly infrequent trips back to Terra." That was at least partially correct, Galen told himself. He had been educated as a xenologist; in reality, however, he'd long been an agent for the Principate's secret police. For Hashem Fedalf.

"I see," said Bussot.

Galen walked toward the android sitting on the edge of its chair. It—he?—watched Galen's approach with interest, his remarkable eyes large with interest in exactly the way a human's would be.

"Do you know who you are?"

The android frowned. "I . . . I can't remember my name."

Galen nodded, then asked Dr. Bussot, "How long has he possessed self-awareness?"

"Nearly a month."

"A whole month!" Galen exclaimed. "And you just called me yesterday!"

"We had to be certain that he was in good health, so to speak. We did not want to allow him to leave with you before he was ready."

That got the android's attention. "I am to leave here with you?"

Instead of answering the android's question, Galen asked one of his own. "Do you know where you are?"

"Inside the Foundation's research laboratories."

Galen nodded. "Yes, but more generally than that. Do you know what city and state we are in?"

"Houston," the android said, looking at Dr. Bussot and back again at Galen. "Houston, Texas."

When neither Galen nor Bussot said anything, the android asked plaintively, "Can you tell me who I am? Dr. Bussot and the others refuse to say anything on the subject."

Dr. Bussot opened his mouth to speak, but Galen silenced him with a raised hand. That impressed the android, who had grown used to seeing everyone kowtowing before the mighty director of the Foundation.

"You truly don't know who you are?" Galen asked.

"They tell me that I am an extremely advanced and sophisticated android, and that I was activated within the past month. Beyond that, I know very little about myself."

The android looked both men in the face and then stared at the floor. "If they are correct in who and what I am, then I am not human. Yet I have . . ." He appeared troubled, and his voice trailed away.

"Go on," said Galen.

"I have . . . memories." The android put his hand to his head as if he was feeling the effects of a migraine headache. "Disturbing memories. Memories of giants bending over me and taking me by the hand—grownups, I suppose. Memories of eating something sweet. Memories of an animal—a dog, I think—licking my face. Bits and pieces."

"That's all?" asked Galen.

The android shook his head sadly. "Yes. Nothing more than that—scattered images and sounds. Impressions, really."

"What do you make of them?"

"I am not sure." Looking down at his chest, he did something with his right hand, pulled back a flap of skin, and revealed his mechanical inner workings. Galen found the sight oddly compelling.

"As you can see, I am irrefutably a machine. But the memories I have . . ."

"Yes?"

The android's golden eyes bored into him like lasers. "They are the memories of a human being."

Galen and Bussot exchanged knowing looks. "I suppose it is time for you to know the truth," Dr. Bussot said. "To hear the whole story."

"Please." The android's hands lay in his lap, the strong yet slender fingers intertwined like two multilimbed arthropods mating.

"You were a wealthy individual who died more than a hundred and twenty-five years ago. As stipulated in your living will, your body was placed into what was called cryogenic suspension."

"Cryogenic suspension?"

"An oversimplified explanation is that you died and your corpse was frozen," explained Galen.

"Yes," said Bussot, making a face as if recalling something distasteful. "Wealthy people who feared death believed that if they preserved their bodies immediately upon cessation of life signs they could be revitalized at some future date, their terminal disease 'cured,' and themselves restored to life."

"Theoretically," Galen said, "your cells and tissues were stabilized and maintained. In reality, your dead body deteriorated. Everyone in your situation shared the same fate: Although you were remarkably preserved, you were for all intents and purposes dead. As dead as a frozen carp." Galen shrugged. "The painful truth is, dead is dead."

"But—"

"I'm getting to that," said Galen, putting up a hand. "But once you and the several thousand others like you were declared legally dead, your carefully preserved bodies little more than inert hunks of flesh, researchers found that some—I repeat, *some*—elements of your core personalities remained within the neural pathways of your brains."

"My mind survived the death of my body?" asked the android.

"Yes. It was possible to retrieve some of the original you." He paused, then added, "Some but not much, really."

Dr. Bussot held up a finger. "It was at this point that challenges were mounted against the ruling that you and the others like you were dead. In one sense, you clearly were not. But, just as clearly, the person you used to be no longer existed. Your body was dead and your personality—your mind—survived only in a piecemeal fashion. The original court rulings were therefore not reversed. You *are* legally dead."

"But you know who I am . . . or was, don't you?"

Bussot shook his head. "So as not to cause undue mental anguish and strain on the descendants, the records were first sealed and then later destroyed."

"I don't even have a name, then," the android said despondently.

"I am about to rectify that," Galen said.

"You?"

"The Foundation has agreed to place you in my custody."

"As if I were nothing but a machine?" cried the android.

"In the eyes of the law, that is exactly what you are," Galen replied. "But Dr. Bussot and I hope to give you a life of your own. Well, a life spent with a friend and a companion." He held out his hand. "I need a partner."

"A partner?" the android said dubiously.

"Sure," said Galen, still extending his hand.

Hesitantly, the android took Galen's hand.

Galen shook it and, still holding it, turned to Dr. Bussot and announced, "Doctor, please meet Sam Houston."

The bar was dark, cool, and reasonably devoid of other customers. That made it perfect, Galen thought. "Come on," he said over his shoulder. "Let's find a table and sit down."

"All right," said Sam Houston amiably. "I warn you, though— I'm a mean drunk."

Pulling out a chair and plopping into it, Galen laughed. "I'm glad you have a sense of humor." He made a rueful face. "Actually, you probably have more of one than I do. My mother used to say I was the only child she ever knew who was born without a 'funny bone.' "

"Funny bone?"

"See, I can't even make a proper joke of that." Galen's brow furrowed. "You know that bone in your elbow—really probably a tendon or a nerve sheath—that tingles and burns when you bump it? Well, my folks used to call that your funny bone."

It was Sam's turn to be rueful. "That's right," he admitted. "I remember that from somewhere."

"I thought it was more universal than just my family."

Mulling over what Galen had said earlier, Sam asked, "Do the others have a sense of humor? Ordinary androids, I mean?"

Galen considered that. "Many models have simulated personalities so close to human you might have a hard time telling them apart. So, I guess they do, but only up to a point."

Sam frowned. "Up to a point?"

"They have a built-in series of humorous or wry responses

they can call upon depending upon the circumstances," Galen told him. "But I don't think they can really create humor."

"And I can?"

"Your personality is intact, ensconced in a Pseudo-Quantum-Gravity android mindpack. You've got the equivalent of a one-and-one-half-kilo meat computer in a plasteel and petropolymer body."

"I guess you could say I'm Prince Albert in a can," Sam joked.

As Galen just nodded at that, unsure what the android was talking about, a servibot rolled up. "Welcome to Mad Mex's Bar and Grill, gents," the 'bot said. "What's your pleasure today?"

"I'll have a Lone Star draft," Galen said.

When the 'bot looked expectantly at Sam, the android said, "What the heck, I'm not driving. Bring me a quart of 10w30."

"I beg your pardon?"

"Just the Lone Star, please," Galen told the little 'bot.

"Yes, sir."

"*It* certainly doesn't have a sense of humor, does it?" said Sam as he watched the little 'bot roll away. He tapped the side of his head with his finger. "Out to lunch."

Galen agreed with that assessment. "Yes, but comparing yourself to that peabrain is like comparing an old biplane to the Tokyo–New York shuttle rocket."

Sam Houston smiled. "You make me sound like something special."

"You are," said Galen.

"I must have been a foolish person when I was . . . well, *before*."

"Why do you say that?"

"Because I believed in something so silly—in the idea that I could be frozen and then revived."

"Thanks, pard," Galen said to the servibot when it placed his beer in front of him. After taking a sip and sighing in pleasure, he responded to Sam by saying, "You did it, though, didn't you? You survived your own death. I mean, not *exactly* the way you envisioned it, but you did it nonetheless. You weren't so silly after all."

Sam brightened at that. "Yeah, I guess I did, didn't I?"

"Sure you did," Galen said.

A pot-bellied man wearing a cowboy hat, blue jeans, and cowboy boots ambled out of a door marked "Stallions" and passed close to their table on his way back to the bar.

"Well, hot damn!" he exclaimed, stopping dead in his tracks.

"What is it, Earl?" one of his three buddies at the bar called over to him.

"I think we got ourselves one o' them damn stinkin' phony-baloney ann-droid fellas sittin' right here as cocky as a bull in Elsie's bedroom. Jes' like he owned the place—when he ain't even got the right ta be in the joint!"

"Shit!" said Galen softly.

"This is not good?" asked Sam Houston.

"This is not good," confirmed Galen.

The bellicose cowboy approached their table, leaned over, and stared in Sam's face. "Yes, sir, boys, he's got hisself some o' them blondie eyes. No doubt about it. Well, if'n the nerve o' this guy don't harelip your old grandpa, I sure as hell don't know what does!"

"Are you for real?" asked Galen.

Instead of responding to Galen's comment, the cowboy now craned over and stared in his face. "Well, leastways this one ain't no machine." He straightened up and pointed a finger at Galen. "Tell me, boy, you and this here machine got some kinda thing goin' on betwixt the two of you? Sumpthin' unnetcheral?"

Galen was aware that the other three were drifting over toward their table.

"Son, didn't you hear me?"

"I heard you."

"Well, you gonna answer my question or not?" the cowboy demanded, his huge beer belly quivering.

"I'm sorry, I forgot the question. Could you repeat it?" Galen said, getting to his feet.

"I think we're gonna have us a party!" the cowboy drawled. " 'Course, the robot feller cain't play, since hurtin' a real human being is agin his mechanical nature."

Galen winked at Sam, then threw the rest of his beer in the cowboy's face, saying, "This one's on me, lard-ass!" He short-armed a hard right in the middle of the cowboy's pinched face.

Galen's punch knocked the cowboy flying, and his friends bellowed like enraged steers and charged.

"You might consider helping," Galen said as he ducked a roundhouse right that caught only air.

"I can't. I'm an android."

"Are you?" asked Galen an instant before one of the cowboy's friends sank his fist in his stomach. "Ummph!" Galen croaked.

Tentatively, almost shyly, Sam gently poked one of the cowboys in the back with a rigid finger.

"Wha' the hell . . ." The cowboy turned to see who had given him the love tap.

Sam hauled back and launched a right at the man's jaw. The punch connected and lifted the cowboy a meter into the air and sent him flying backwards into an empty table and chairs.

"Hey!" Sam said, looking wonderingly at his hand. "I can fight!"

"Of course you can."

"Shall we clean up this saloon, Tex?" Sam asked.

"That's the idea."

With Sam's enthusiastic participation, the brawl ended with all four cowboys counting stars.

"I thought androids couldn't harm human beings," Sam said to Galen, who was gingerly working his jaw back and forth. "That's what Dr. Bussot told me."

"What makes you think you're an android?" Galen said meaningfully.

"You mean . . . ?" Sam Houston said, tapping the side of his head.

"Yep. Why do you think I wanted you for my partner? Don't you get it yet? You're a human being in an android's body."

Sam turned his hands over and stared at his palms as if seeing them for the first time. He flexed his fingers and then picked up a plasglas mug. Closing his fingers like a vise, he watched the mug shatter.

"So whatta you think?" asked Galen, throwing down a roll of credits to cover the damage.

"I think I'm going to like this!"

2

SAM HOUSTON TURNED OUT TO BE SUCH A FINE ADDITION TO what had previously been a one-man operation that after just twenty months Galen Yeager had difficulty remembering what he did before he teamed up with the human android. Certainly, he reminisced, he would have been in a tight spot on Weald without Sam to back him up.

It was after midnight before Galen Yeager and Sam Houston ventured out. Weald's Kilmer City was a hard-working town and closed up early, so the streets were mostly deserted at this hour, apart from the odd drunk staggering home past the curfew time to sleep it off.

Kilmer City was small enough (really undeserving of the appellation "city") that Yeager and Sam could walk the length of the main street in just under twenty minutes.

Galen and Sam heard the engine whine as the two-man patrol floater eased up behind them. It halted beside them, sending whirlpools of dust dancing about their feet.

"You there, identify yourselves, please," an authoritative voice called from the patrol floater. A harsh light picked out first Yeager's face and then his partner's.

Yeager shaded his eyes. "Hello. It's just me—Galen Yeager, the journalist from Terra." His cover for this trip was as a writer for a prominent scientific publication; since Yeager often contributed articles to the magazine, he was stretching the truth far less than usual. He nodded toward his partner. "And I think you recognize my friend and companion, Sam Houston."

"Yeah, we recognize him," the voice from the shadows of the floater said.

"Are we breaking some law?" Yeager asked. "I mean, I didn't think the curfew took effect until two A.M."

"That's right," the voice replied. "No, you're not breaking any laws, it's just that it's dangerous to be out on the streets of Kilmer at night. There's still a fair amount of predatory native wildlife that gets into the city despite the eradication programs."

"I'm sorry; it's just that I couldn't sleep. Sam and I decided that a walk might be just the thing."

"I understand, Citizen Yeager," said the second shadowy figure in the floater. "But it's not safe to be out and about this late. My advice is for you to go back to your hotel and take a laxer if you can't sleep."

"Yes, I will. Thank you."

"Good night," the first voice said. The light moved off Yeager's face, leaving behind a dull red blotch that jumped before his eyes.

"Good night," Yeager responded dutifully.

"Good night," said Sam Houston.

The patrol moved on, probing the dark streets with questioning shafts of light that penetrated into every doorway and possible hiding place.

"The government building is just ahead," Galen Yeager said to his partner.

Sam Houston nodded. Then, realizing that Galen could not see his head bob up and down in the near-total darkness, he said, "Yes, I remember it from our earlier visit. It was the day we arrived in Kilmer."

"Did you bring our 'key'?" Galen asked. It was strictly a rhetorical question, since Sam was not the type to forget something so important to the night's activities.

In response, Sam slipped the little box out of its hiding place and opened the door of the building quickly and noiselessly—Sussel timelocks were ridiculously easy to manipulate if you had the right equipment. He waited for Galen to step inside and then followed, closing the door behind him.

An earlier survey of the security had reassured the two of them that the interior contained no alarms or other unpleasant surprises. Yeager put on a pair of night glasses and headed for the stairs. Not needing the glasses, Sam Houston trailed behind.

"Stairs," Yeager whispered, shaking his head at the frontier elements of this raw, new planet.

The 1.24 gravity (compared to Terran standard) strained Yeager's leg muscles. A devotee of lift/drop tubes, he was unused to climbing stairs, and he arrived at the third floor with his breath rasping raggedly in and out of his throat.

"You're letting yourself get out of shape," Sam chided him. Unable to disagree, Yeager made a mental note to get in some extra time on the exercise machines on board the starship which would carry him and Sam back to Terra when this job was done.

This job. It wasn't over just yet.

Sam Houston and Galen Yeager walked softly down the hall. They passed several offices, none of which was the one they were looking for. Their weight made the karkka-wood floor creak and groan in protest. It was an alien sound to Yeager and made him marvel at the laws of supply and demand. Elsewhere karkka wood was so scarce and expensive that only the very rich could afford it in *any* form, yet here it was so plentiful and cheap—harvested in vast quantities—that they used it as building material. It was archaic but somehow appropriate. Wooden floors; incredible!

The door they were looking for loomed before them.

ASSISTANT UNDERSECRETARY
FOR INTERNAL AFFAIRS
PUBLIC AND PRIVATE WORKS SECURITY
ARNOLD T. STANKO

the door proclaimed proudly.

Galen just shook his head and raised his left hand. The little box he held emitted a stream of electrons which he hoped would key the door locks. The locks, their internal mechanisms successfully deceived, opened. Yeager and Sam Houston went in.

As an agent of the Principate Secret Police, Galen's assignment was to find out why shipments of karkka wood to Terra and to other priority markets were below projected—and, hence, *expected*—quantities.

Yeager's sanctioned snooping was politically important because highly placed government leaders owned substantial shares of the companies poised to clear-cut Weald's forests for the wealth the karkka wood brought to its harvesters. The senators and consuls who had their snouts in the trough demanded a good return on their investment. Or so Hashem Fedalf, director of the PrinSecPol, and Yeager's boss, had impressed upon him before he and Sam left Terra.

A half-hour after they'd entered the office, an enlightened Galen sighed at the boldness—and stupidity—of what they'd uncovered in the records. Fully thirty percent of the money the logging conglomerates made from selling the karkka timber had been stolen by Stanko and a few confederates.

Graft was an accepted part of any economic empire, with kickbacks and bribes greasing the way for deals which would enrich highly placed officials. Still, Galen mused, one had to play the game by the rules, and one of the rules was that you didn't take more than your position entitled you to. And Stanko was taking more, much more, than a man in his job was allowed.

A little "vigorish" was permitted, of course, Galen conceded. Pilfering was just another cost figured into the normal business expenses, but Stanko was *too* greedy, and the resulting drop in income was what had brought first Hashem Fedalf and then Galen Yeager and Sam Houston into the picture.

"Damn fool," Galen said to Houston. "Did he really believe no one would miss it?"

"Sociopaths believe they can get away with anything," Sam told him. "They talk themselves into believing their invulnerability."

"I guess so."

Without warning, the door swung open. A fat little man, sweating profusely, stepped into the room, followed by four others; they didn't look like choirboys. Galen Yeager's eyes focused on the small automatic slug-thrower the man clutched in his chunky fingers. The others had standard energy pistols.

"Well, well, what have we here?" Arnold T. Stanko asked of Galen, still bent over the file printouts he'd ordered up from the office's obliging computer. Then his eyes swept over Sam Houston dismissively.

"Would you believe we're soliciting contributions for the local chapter of the Star Scouts?" asked Sam conversationally. Galen's lips turned up in a smile at Sam's comment, but his eyes were cold and hard. Sam joked through situations like this; he didn't.

When Galen said nothing, Stanko eyed him and said, "You're a cool one, Wagner . . . no, it's Yeager, isn't it?" The fat man wiped his forehead with the back of his hand. When Galen didn't reply, he continued, "I suppose you and your friend here are from Terra—some kind of spies."

"You must have been expecting us, or someone like us," Galen said evenly, gesturing at the papers on Stanko's desk. "No one can steal from the Principate so openly and not expect someone to start getting suspicious. That was rather foolish of you, Arnold."

Anger flashed in the fat man's eyes. "Don't call me Arnold— and don't patronize me, either! Sure, the 'smart' way is to take a little here, a little there, spending years doing it. Then, if some unexpected audit doesn't spoil things, you take what you've skimmed off and retire. The only catch is that by that time you've burned out your youth on jerkwater planets like this one and the money can't buy back the lost years."

He took a step forward, his voice rising. "Seven years, seven years I've been sweating and vegetating on this hellish planet." His eyes bulged and he shouted, "It doesn't even have *one* decent restaurant! Well, I'm not going to be buried alive while I can still get out and enjoy myself."

"I never thought of it that way, Arnold."

"Don't mock me!" Stanko screamed. "I'll kill you!"

"Won't that upset your plans just as thoroughly as me making my report?"

A look of animal cunning crossed Stanko's face. "The monkey-cats will be blamed—if your body's ever found, that is."

<That's a reasonable assumption,> Galen "said" to Sam Houston. *<Those arboreal predators are as vicious as they come.>*

<What about me?> Sam Houston hated to think he was being overlooked.

<Give Arnold some time. He'll think of something.>

"Hey, Mr. Stanko," one of the fat man's toughs said. "I think these guys are communicating."

"You have a microencephalonic implant?" Stanko asked Galen Yeager.

"Yep," Galen confirmed. "And you know what else?"

"What?" asked Stanko suspiciously.

"Sam is armed."

Sam Houston raised his right arm, pointed his index finger at Stanko, and burned the fat man's hand off at the wrist. Stanko screamed in pain and surprise.

Only one of the other four had his weapon ready; he fired at Sam but missed, the beam passing through Sam's shirt. Ignoring the other's effort to re-aim, Sam coolly burned a small hole through the man's forehead and then did the same for the man beside him.

By now the others had raised their energy pistols, but Galen Yeager had already contracted a muscle in his wrist and caused his needle gun to leap into the palm of his hand. Calmly, with the careful precision of a professional, he shot the remaining two men dead.

Sam Houston picked up the slug-thrower and handed it to Galen Yeager. "This is a beauty," Galen said, turning it over in his hand. Then he looked at the small hole burned through Sam's outer clothing. "You okay, Sam?" he asked.

"I'm fine. Even if he had hit me, it would take a rifle on full power to penetrate my polycarbon skin."

Galen turned his attention to Stanko. The little fat man had propped himself against one of the walls, clutching the stump of his wrist in his other hand. There was no bleeding; Sam's shot had cauterized the arteries and veins. And, in all probability, shock was keeping Stanko from feeling much pain.

"I guess that was pretty stupid, huh?" the fat man asked.

"You'll get no argument from me," replied Galen.

"Say, how much do you make a year?" Stanko asked, small coals of hope still burning in his eyes.

"More than you'd think," Galen said, leveling his gaze on the defeated bureaucrat. "Anyway, your money doesn't interest me."

"What can you get for taking me back? Reassignment to another dungheap like this one? Is that what you want?" Stanko laughed bitterly, adding, "You're trapped just as surely as I am.

So why not let me go? It can't mean that much to take me back."

Stanko gestured broadly. "I don't suppose you really sub-scribe to any 'we always get our man' theory anyway—you look like an intelligent young man." He shrugged, obviously feeling more confident that he could get the situation under control. "Letting me go makes sense—and money for you. Taking me back doesn't do a damn thing for either of us."

Galen Yeager stared at the fat man before him as he might stare at something spit onto the pavement. "Take you back? You don't understand—we're not going to take you back to Terra; Sam is going to kill you."

Silence.

Then, a halfhearted laugh escaped from Stanko. "Jesus and Mohammed, you had me going there for a second, Yeager. You're trying to scare me, to get me to name names, to sign a confession, to admit to kidnapping the Lindbergh baby."

"The Lindbergh baby?" Galen didn't understand the refer-ence.

Sam Houston stood watching, silent and impassive. His stol-idness seemed an affront to Stanko. "Hey, how the hell can this damn 'bot use weapons, how can it kill people?"

"Very professionally," Galen replied.

"Cut the crap," snapped Stanko. "You know what I mean. Constructing artificial beings capable of using weapons, of kill-ing human beings, was outlawed decades ago—after the robot wars."

"Sam isn't a robot."

"All right," Stanko said patiently, but rolling his eyes at Galen Yeager's strict interpretation. "So he's an android, not a robot, and—"

"No," Galen said. "Not exactly." He sighed. "Really, though, this conversation is getting us nowhere. Believe me when I tell you, Sam *can* and *will* kill you."

<*The way you talk! No wonder no one wants to play with me.*>

Looking at Sam and then at the bodies of the men the android had killed, Stanko said, "I guess I have to believe you."

"Good," said Galen Yeager, relieved that his threat to have Sam commit cold-blooded murder had finally succeeded in get-ting Stanko's full attention. "Just put out your hands for the restraints, and before you know it you'll be back on Terra."

"No," said Stanko, shaking his head. "I'm not going back. I don't have many options open to me, but one is to deny you that small triumph." A look of concentration crossed the fat man's face, and wisps of blue smoke poured from his mouth and nostrils.

"Shit!" exclaimed Galen, grabbing Stanko's shoulders and shaking the already dead man as if to wake him up. Resigned to the reality of the situation, the frustrated agent released him.

Stanko slumped over, his eyes wide in recognition of his death. Sam leaned down and gently closed the dead man's eyes. Then he turned at stared at his friend and partner.

"Sonofabitch!" Galen Yeager shouted, kicking the wall. "Fuck this job! I'm supposed to be an agent, not a goddamn executioner!"

II

Hashem Fedalf's office was comfortable but unostentatious. It was difficult for Galen Yeager to believe that from here Fedalf controlled thousands of agents. The room was dominated by a very old wooden desk, scarred and battered but still giving useful service. Some of the younger staff members of the Principate Secret Police joked that the Declaration of Independence of the United States of America could have been signed on that very desk; it was *that* old.

Galen noted the few oils hung on the walls. To his eyes they were well executed but possessed a brooding intensity—all dark colors and bold, savage strokes—that probably served Fedalf's purpose well. A weathered and deteriorating wooden bookcase leaned against one wall, its shelves groaning under the weight of books it had been supporting for many years. The books themselves were antiques, mystery novels in their original cloth bindings.

Galen Yeager was bold enough to be leafing through one of Dorothy Sayers's Lord Peter Whimsey mysteries when Fedalf swept in through the open doorway. "Hello, Galen," he said warmly. Then he noticed that his young operative was holding one of his treasures. "Um, would you mind replacing that copy of *Hangman's Holiday*, Galen? It's very valuable."

"Certainly." Putting the book back into the vacant spot on

the shelf, Galen asked, "What was that little paper rectangle in it?"

"Something called a 'bookmark,' " Fedalf informed him, always willing to discuss his obsession. When he saw the puzzled look on Galen Yeager's face, he added, "You use it to mark the place where you stop reading."

"Oh."

After pouring himself another cup of the sweet, black coffee that he consumed by the liter, Fedalf said, "Come. Let's go down the hall to the conference room."

"As you wish." Galen heaved himself up from his chair. Not the tallest person in the world himself, Galen was always just a bit surprised to see that he was a few centimeters taller than the mustachioed director of the PrinSecPol. *It's his position,* Galen theorized. *You expect a man as powerful as Fedalf to be taller, to be larger than life.* Then he rebuked himself for such naive thinking; he had met many people in positions of power who seemed, if anything, smaller than life.

"May I ask why we're going to the conference room?"

"I'm having an ESPer in to sweep my office for bugs," Fedalf confessed. Candor with his agents was one of his strong points.

"Even you have to worry about things like that?" Galen asked.

"Even me." Fedalf pulled at his moustache. "Especially me." He stopped in front of a door and pressed his palm against the glowing entry patch. "Let's go in, shall we?"

Galen frowned as soon as the sensors turned on the interior lighting. To his way of thinking, the conference room was very modern, perhaps too modern to be comfortable. Its furniture and decor were such that he and Fedalf, built on a far less grand scale, seemed diminished.

Continuing to cast his eyes around the conference room, Galen decided that it could easily represent the present state of the Principate. Both dwarfed the people who had built them. The most able administrators could no longer cope with the dimensions of the empire. *Wrong word,* Galen thought. *The Principate is the accepted term.* "Newspeak," he muttered under his breath and then thought, *Poor Orwell—dead and mostly forgotten these many years.*

"Please," said Fedalf, indicating two easy chairs flanking a small plaswood coffee table. As soon as Galen was seated, Fedalf sat down himself. He placed his small cup of coffee on the table in front of him.

Galen smiled at the action. "I guess it had to get its name from somewhere."

"What? Oh, yes—coffee table."

"Did you bring me down here so I wouldn't touch any more of your antique books?" Galen asked, not entirely facetiously.

"No. I was telling you the truth when I mentioned the debugging going on in my office."

"What *am* I here for?" Galen asked. "I mean, it's not every day I get a face-to-face meeting with the director."

Fedalf took a sip of his coffee before answering. "Rob MacKenzie tells me you've spoken to him about quitting. Is that true?"

Galen made a sour face. "Yes, it's true." He looked down at the floor and, speaking in a low voice, said, "I was not pleased with my last assignment. I was surprised and annoyed at being handed a 'goon's' job. I'm a first-class intelligence operative, not an enforcer. I didn't like having to threaten a man so convincingly that he resorted to taking his own life."

"I see," said Fedalf, continuing to sip his coffee thoughtfully.

Neither man spoke for a while; each seemed content to allow the silence to grow until it filled the room. Finally, Fedalf said quietly, almost inaudibly, "I shall speak to Chang in Operations; it will then be unlikely that you will be asked to perform such distasteful functions again."

Galen looked up, meeting the other's eyes. "Thank you."

Fedalf nodded. "I should not like to lose one of my best operatives." He sipped his coffee and peered evaluatively at Galen over the rim of his cup. "Do you wish a leave of absence, Galen?"

"I . . . ah . . . I don't know." And suddenly he *didn't* know. When he asked for this face-to-face meeting, he had intended to resign or, failing that, to at least get several weeks off. Now he stared at Fedalf with renewed interest. Unless he was reading the signs incorrectly, the director seemed poised to propose something. "What if I say yes?"

"Then I will say be on your way, and may Allah keep you."

"But if I say no?"

"Suppose I offered you an assignment that seems more than likely to turn out to be about nothing, but which would allow you plenty of free time to indulge yourself in whatever activities you wished to pursue? What would you say to such an offer?"

"Are you offering?"

"Yes."

After Galen had considered Fedalf's offer for several seconds, a bitter expression crossed his face. Fedalf guessed correctly what was behind that look of distaste when Galen admitted, "If I stay around here, I may run into Adrianna."

"You may," agreed Fedalf. In fairness, he added, "But it's a big city and an even bigger planet."

Galen had already made up his mind. "My answer is yes," he said. Fedalf closed and opened his eyes as if giving thanks. "So what's the assignment; what's up?"

"Ah, there's the rub, Galen. I'm not sure." He smiled at his young agent's look of confusion and added, "I simply mean that something is bothering me. Something is in the air . . ."

"In the air?"

"Yes. I have the oddest sensation that something is going to happen soon."

"Here?"

"You mean Terra?" asked Fedalf. He shook his head. "No, I don't think so."

"Then where?"

"Patience," counseled Fedalf. "First things first. I did something some would consider odd for a person in my position: I spoke to a wise man—a prophet and a holy man—about my . . . my premonition."

"Then you have the Ability yourself?"

"A little—as do you. It is what makes us both so successful at what we have chosen to do." A faraway look came into his eyes. "The wise man I spoke of, my old teacher, said a storm was coming. Those were his words: 'A storm is coming.' I asked him where this storm would begin and what would be its impact."

Fedalf paused and took another sip of his coffee. Galen tugged on his earlobe. *That cup must be bottomless*, he thought.

"Well?" asked Galen finally. "What did he say?"

"He said the storm would not begin here, on Old Earth. That's what he called Terra: 'Old Earth.' He said little else except that this storm would begin with the 'ancient' and end with the 'young.' ''

Galen, who had been leaning forward, straining to follow Fedalf's words, settled back when he realized that the director was finished speaking.

"But what does that mean? Did he explain himself?"

Fedalf shook his head. "No. Like so many farseers, he often speaks in riddles—but in riddles which truly predict the future."

"What are you going to do?"

"Do?" Fedalf seemed surprised by the question. "Why, I'm sending you and Sam Houston to Luna."

"Luna? Why Luna?"

"I thought about the way he said 'Old Earth.' That made me think of the age of Terra's satellite, the 'Moon.' It's probably just a hunch that will prove to be hollow. If so, there's your vacation. If not . . . Well, let's just say then that you'll be thrown into something worthy of your talents, Galen."

3

"I JUST LOVE ARMSTRONG CITY," SAM SAID, BEAMING.

"It *is* a pleasant place," agreed Galen, staring at a well-endowed Cousteauean female passing them in the terminal, her bared breasts bobbing in the low gravity.

Sam saw what Galen was staring at. "Ah, yes, native customs. Partial nudity is such a localized phenomenon back on Terra."

"My thoughts exactly," Galen said.

"Why do I get the idea my leg is being pulled?" asked Sam.

"Because of the sharp tug on it?" Then, looking askance at Sam, Galen added, "Sometimes I wonder if you really *were* a male in your previous incarnation."

"Oh, I was," replied Sam seriously. "I have one crystal-clear recollection of accidentally entering a single-sex comfort facility and encountering a contingent of outraged young women. Their anger forced me to make a hasty retreat."

"What about memories of . . . ah . . . you know—doing the old 'in-out, in-out'?"

Sam lowered his eyes modestly. "Please—a young lad has special recollections which are his alone to treasure."

Galen's sighing in response to Sam's comment was cut off by the sight of a customs 'bot patiently awaiting them. "Ah, shit," he said softly.

"Good day, gentlemen," the customs 'bot greeted them pleasantly. While humanoid, it was not intended to fool anyone by attempting to pass for human—and it assuredly would not have, excepting perhaps sightless persons. "I am pleased to welcome you to Luna. Is this a first visit for either of you?"

"No, it is not," Galen said as calmly and with as little inflection in his voice as he could muster. He hated officialdom and authority figures like policemen, judges, civil-service bureaucrats—or customs agents. Given his own occupation, this unthinking hostility didn't make much sense, but Galen never stopped to consider the paradoxical nature of his dislike for bureaucracies and their functionaries.

"You are Terran-born?"

"Yes."

Turning to Sam, the 'bot asked, "You are of Terran manufacture?"

"They didn't find me in the pumpkin patch."

"That's a yes," offered Galen. *Sam is such a smartass!* he thought.

The 'bot made a face that was meant to be a smile and pointed to a retinal scanner. "Step up to the scanner, please," it told Galen.

Grudgingly, Galen did as the 'bot requested. A green light glowed and a soft chime sounded. "Thank you, Citizen Yeager," the 'bot said in response to the identity confirmation.

Turning to Sam, the 'bot said, "In accordance with A-Prime-Directive 4862: Are you the android known as Sam Houston?"

"Yes," replied Sam, responding to the formal sequence which compelled androids to speak the truth.

"Are you here on any business which might be construed as illegal or dangerous to human beings in any way whatsoever?"

"No," lied Sam. *<Good thing they can't read our minds, eh?> <Behave yourself. This transmission could be intercepted.>*

"Very good," said the 'bot once it had made certain that Sam's response had been recorded. Responding to an internal flow of information it had received earlier from the customs people on Terra, the 'bot said, "You have two suitcases and two musical instrument carrying cases with you, I am told. May I see them, please?"

"Of course," Sam said, indicating the small null-gee cart that contained their luggage.

The 'bot inspected the suitcases. "All seems satisfactory," it stated when it was finished. It opened the first of the two instrument cases, the smaller one, and examined the instrument it found inside. It removed the fragile violin and stared at it dispassionately. At Galen's intake of breath, the 'bot looked at him and asked, "Is this wooden implement valuable?"

"You could say that," Galen told it. "It's worth about seventy-five thousand credits."

"And the other one, the larger one?"

"The 'cello? It is worth about fifty thousand."

"Interesting," the 'bot said, replacing the violin carefully. "The smaller is worth more than the larger."

"A diamond is worth more than a lump of coal," Galen pointed out.

"Quite so," the 'bot agreed. Then it asked, "You are not planning on selling either implement while you are on Luna?"

"No."

"Then you may both pass," the 'bot said. "Enjoy your stay on Luna."

"Thank you," said Galen, his tone belying his words.

"Goodbye, Mr. Chips," Sam said as they walked over to the baggage retrieval area. Stacking their luggage, Sam said, "There now, that wasn't so bad, was it?" When Galen glared at him, Sam muttered *sotto voce*, "Well, it wasn't."

Galen Yeager tensed as they approached a particularly difficult passage in the string quartet. While both he and Sam were doing well, playing better than they had the last two times they'd attempted this particular piece, there was something missing. Galen decided that the absent element was soul.

Galen and Sam's one rule of playing was that nothing short of an earthquake should stop the music, so they played to the end, Galen shooting furious looks at the two musicians the computer was projecting visually and aurally into their room. The computer-generated surrogates were supposed to emulate the finest players, but to both Galen and Sam, they seemed poor substitutes for their regular VR partners back on Terra.

Raising his chin and removing the Karensky tucked under it, Galen Yeager said, "Damn! I miss our partners." Not being real, the *faux* musicians took no offense at being openly denigrated in this way.

"I know what you mean," agreed Sam, nodding. He caressed the 'cello that was clasped between his legs and then leaned back.

Sam scratched his nose thoughtfully. Although he was no longer sensitive to such things as itching, androids were programmed to emulate humans as completely as possible, and, since Sam emulated a typical android emulating a human, he occasionally performed actions like that. "Maybe you and I should just play by ourselves and forget these two."

Galen nodded glumly. "End program, please," he said.

The phantom second violin and viola players slowly faded away and were replaced by a two-dee image of a debit card floating in the air. "Your account will be billed thirty-seven and one-half credits," a pleasant female voice announced. The debit card evaporated into thin air.

Galen sighed. He was annoyed and disappointed that the music had failed to provide him with his usual feeling of having accomplished something satisfying. "I wanted to continue to practice our quartet pieces, but not with those two stiffs."

"There's always a direct linkup with our house computer back home," Sam suggested.

"Do you have any idea how much that would cost?" Galen asked.

"A lot?"

"A lot," he confirmed. "No, I guess it's you and me." Putting down his violin, he dug out several compositions for two, chose an old favorite, and gave it to Sam. "Ready?"

"Ready, maestro."

Like two long-time lovers who knew each other's rhythms, they began.

II

As they left the sports dome, Sam asked, "Was jai alai invented on Luna or on Terra?"

"Good question," replied Galen. When he didn't add anything else, Sam knew that Galen hadn't a clue to the correct answer.

Sam glanced around at the crowd streaming out around them and boarding the moving sidewalks. "I'll bet lots of these Lunatics are going for a drink," he said pointedly.

"You know me too well," Galen admitted ruefully. He *was* a bit self-conscious that Sam could sense his desire for a drink.

"You should adopt a cheerful outlook on life—like me," argued Sam. "Then you wouldn't need to drink."

"Uh-huh," Galen responded dubiously.

"Anyway, shall we eeny-meeny-miney-moe someone and follow him?"

"Nah, I want to go to a real bar."

"Since when is a sports bar not a 'real' bar?" asked Sam.

"Let's find a spacer's bar, a place where they serve up the real stuff—stiff drinks, dirty jokes, and head-turning gossip." Galen rubbed his chin. "We should find plenty of good places the closer we get to Yomano Spaceport."

"Then after you, Lewis."

"Why, thank you, Clark," said Galen, surprising Sam by playing along with his nonsense.

Galen chuckled to himself. *Charters and Caldicott is more like it*, he thought. He made a face when he realized he had no idea who "Charters and Caldicott" were; it was just something he'd picked up from Hashem Fedalf. Since Fedalf inhaled old mysteries the way fat people devoured potato chips, Galen guessed they must be characters from an old mystery novel series.

Galen and Sam made the transition from their north-south sidewalk to one going east-west without incident. Moving sidewalks were always dicey, but were made even more so when one visited Luna. Moving from belt to belt was a skill you picked up from constant practice; on Terra's satellite, your muscle memory was bollixed by the subtle changes wrought by the lower gravity. More than one tourist overcompensated and ended up kissing the flexible polysteel belt.

Galen glanced upwards, his eyes finding the apogee of the dome far above. The dome was all there was between them and the vacuum of Luna's barren surface. He gulped. To take his mind off the exceedingly remote possibility of being sucked out a breach in the dome, he eavesdropped on tourists and pedestrians around him until the . . . well, *pedestrian* nature of their conversations bored him. Nearly half of the tourists seemed interested in talking about nothing except about when to reserve spacesuits for the almost mandatory visit to the Apollo 11 shrine in the Sea of Tranquility.

"I need a drink," Galen muttered.

"Your wish is my command," said Sam, pointing out a spacer bar just off the beltway called The Black Spot.

"Ah, now this is a real man's drink," Galen gasped, putting down his glass.

"What is it?"

"It's called a Götterdämmerung."

"A Götterdämmerung," repeated Sam. "What's that? And what's in it?"

"It's a German drink. You know, the sort of thing Odin quaffed while preparing to double-cross the other gods in Valhalla. As to what's in it, the bartender said it contained schnapps and other more esoteric ingredients."

"Oh." Sam shrugged and glanced around the bar. *Well, Galen was right about one thing,* he thought. *This place certainly has an interesting clientele. We should be able to pick up* something *from a collection of hard cases as gnarly as this bunch.*

After watching a squat, heavy-gravity-planet spacer trading jokes with a laserbeam-thin man who seemed more two-dimensional than three, Sam whispered to Galen, "Hey, doesn't this remind you of the cantina scene in *Star Wars*?"

Galen's forehead wrinkled in concentration. "What's *Star Wars*?"

"Never mind," sighed Sam. They were two words he used a lot whenever something from his shadowy past bobbed to the surface of his consciousness and he tried sharing it with Galen. Galen didn't have an abiding interest in ancient times, so references pertaining to anything more than fifty years in the past tended to elude him. Not always, Sam conceded, but usually.

"So, we gonna sit here the rest of the afternoon or what?" Sam asked finally.

"Did you see me speaking to the bartender while you found us a table?"

"Sure."

"Well, I was asking him for the name of the local know-it-all, the rummy who'll fill you in on all the dirt for the price of a drink."

"And?"

"And here he comes now," Galen said, standing up.

*   *   *

"You the guy Hans told me was lookin' to buy a little information?" asked a small, scruffy man whose tiny red nose twitched like a rabbit's.

"That's me."

"Sid Magee's the name," the man announced. "And you two gents is . . . ?"

"I'm Galen Yeager and this is Sam Houston."

The small man just nodded, apparently unimpressed at being introduced to an expensive android companion. Neither he nor Galen offered to shake hands. "Glad to meetcha. Can I sit down now?"

"Please."

"Thanks." Sid Magee stared meaningfully at Galen's glass.

"Oh, waiter," Galen said to a passing servibot. When he had the 'bot's attention, he asked Magee what he was drinking.

"The usual," Magee said, and it was sufficient for the 'bot.

"A regular patron of this establishment, I see," said Sam.

"Yeah," grunted Magee.

"Tell me, Citizen Magee . . ." Galen stopped when Magee held up his hand.

"Sorry. I don't say nuthin' 'til I have my first one," Magee explained as the servibot rolled up with two scotches and put them down in front of the grubby man. Galen caught a whiff of Magee's ripe odor and leaned back.

After draining the first scotch in one gulp, Magee said, "That's a helluva lot better. I feel human again."

"I know what you mean," said Sam, causing Magee to gape at him.

"Ain't you a . . ."

"Yes."

"Oh."

"Can we talk now?" asked Galen patiently.

"Sure we can," Magee said. Turning to the servibot, he said, "Bring me another round."

Galen raised his eyebrows and exchanged a look with Sam but said nothing. Sam pinched his nose but also said nothing.

Clasping the thick glass between his hands as if it was the most valuable thing in the universe, Magee leaned forward conspiratorially and asked, "See them Legionnaires over there?"

He nodded his head in the direction of a table surrounded by young, crew-cut men in khaki uniforms.

"Yes."

"Well, them boys is off the *General Woodard.*"

"The *General Woodard*?" asked Galen. The name sounded familiar.

"She's the prettiest damn starship you'd ever want to see." His eyes glittered. "Pretty like a coral snake. The *Woodard* is a battle cruiser, one of the biggest and best in the Principate's fleet. To hear them boys tell it, when they's had too much to drink and start in on braggin', they's headin' out soon for a little visitin'."

"Visitin' . . . er, visiting?" Galen asked as the 'bot returned with Magee's drink.

Magee looked at his drink and shrugged. "You *could* buy me another drink right now," he said. "But I don't want to be like the kid who ate everything in his Easter basket in one sitting. He ate so much so fast that he hugged the crapper all night," the rummy said pointedly.

"Meaning?" asked Sam.

"Meaning if you was to put some credits in my hand, I can still be buyin' my own drinks after you two are long gone. I doan gotta gulp 'em all down at onct."

"Sounds reasonable to me," said Galen. He gave Magee a fifty-credit note.

"Thank you, boy," Magee said gratefully. Pocketing the money, he leaned forward again and said, "They say the *General Woodard* is leaving 'fore the week is out to pay visits to several of the colony worlds that have been kickin' up their heels a little too much lately. They want to drop by and show them who has the power."

"Gunboat diplomacy, eh?" said Sam.

"Huh?" asked Magee. "Doan know nuthin' 'bout that. I *do* know that they is gonna put on their little act for Harriman, Made It, Amazona, Cousteau, Salvation, and Yeltsin, to name a few."

"That's interesting," mused Galen.

"Mean anythin' to ya?" asked Magee.

"Not really," said Sam, instantly regretting his words when Galen shot him a look which said, "Never let others know what you're thinking."

"Information is always useful," allowed Galen.

"Yeah, well—"

The bar was rocked by a massive explosion outside that hurled all the bottles and glasses in shelves and on tables to the floor.

"Jesus!" exclaimed Galen. "What the hell was *that*?"

Someone stumbled into the bar and shouted, "The *General Woodard* is gone! It just blew up!"

III

The twenty-four hours after the *General Woodard*'s destruction were a whirl of activity for both Galen Yeager and Sam Houston. It hadn't taken the local authorities long to ascertain that the *Woodard* was a victim of sabotage. Now it was a matter of finding out who the saboteurs were.

Galen used a secure line to contact Armstrong City's PrinSecPol headquarters to formally inform the commandant of his presence. While both Rob MacKenzie, Fedalf's assistant, and Galen had previously agreed that his mission, such as it was, should be off the books, the blowing up of the *General Woodard* made it impossible for him to remain anonymous. Even with Fedalf's blessing, he would be stepping on too many toes by not playing by the rules.

"Here's the list of departees just before and after the *Woodard* went kerblooey," Sam said, putting a plaspaper printout in front of Galen.

Galen scanned the list with a keen eye. "Christ, I didn't know that many ships came and left in such a short period of time!"

"Armstrong City has one of the busiest spaceports in the home system," Sam said, watching Galen's finger trace down the list.

"One hundred and twenty-three arrivals and departures within two hours," said Galen, shaking his head. "It's a wonder there aren't more accidents."

"The port authority's P-Q-G brain matrix computers are the best money can buy," Sam pointed out. "For what they cost, there shouldn't be *any* accidents."

"Uh-huh," said Galen. Then he stiffened—almost imperceptibly, but it was enough for Sam to pick up on.

"What is it?"

"Look." His finger jabbed the plaspaper in two places. "Didn't the smelly one say—"

"The 'smelly one'?" Sam guffawed. "I like that."

Galen just nodded. "Didn't Magee say the *General Woodard* was going to drop in at Salvation and Cousteau, among others?"

"That he did."

"Well, two privately registered starships, one from Cousteau and one from Salvation, left less than forty-five minutes before the *Woodard* was blown up."

"Could be a coincidence," Sam said, staring at the printout.

"Could be," acknowledged Galen. "As a matter of fact, there's nothing to say that the saboteurs have to be from one of the planets the *Woodard* was scheduled to visit."

"No, there doesn't," Sam agreed. "But you think there *is* a connection, don't you?"

"Yes."

"This is asking for too much," Sam said, "but I just might get lucky." He went to their terminal and accessed the PrinSecPol headquarters computer's files. "The registry of the *Flying Dutchman*, please," he asked the computer.

"The *Flying Dutchman* is registered to Gar Varro, of Cousteau."

"Gar Varro . . . ?" said Sam wonderingly. "Isn't he—"

"Yeah," said Galen. "He's the head of the planet's Liberation Party."

"Have you heard the name Gar Varro before?" Galen asked the holographic image of Hashem Fedalf. He would have been shocked if the director of the PrinSecPol had not.

"You mean the leader of the so-called 'Liberation Party' on Cousteau? Why are you interested in him?"

"It seems a vessel registered to him left Yomano Spaceport just minutes before the *General Woodard* blew up."

"And you think he had something to do with it?"

"If not, it's a very curious coincidence."

"You have a point," conceded Fedalf.

"So Sam and I think we ought to go to Cousteau and do a little sniffing around this guy."

Fedalf nodded. "All right. I'll authorize that."

"Thank you, sir." Galen reached out to break the subspace connection between Luna and Terra.

"Wait a minute," said Fedalf. "Don't be in such a rush."

"Sorry," apologized Galen.

"While I'm agreeing with you that you should place yourself in Varro's immediate orbit, don't limit your investigation by focusing exclusively on Gar Varro and his people."

"Do you know something I don't?" asked Galen. "Something I should know?"

"It's my turn to flash a name at you."

"Go ahead."

"Suo Hann," said Fedalf.

"Suo Hann . . ." repeated Galen softly.

Galen snuggled back in his cuddle chair, pointed a finger at Sam, and said, "So shoot, o informed one."

"Your wish is my command," said Sam, before adopting a more serious demeanor. Having downloaded and assimilated the files that had been tight-beamed to them, Sam began his briefing on Gar Varro.

"Gar Varro was born in the north, on an island the colonists call the Crescent. The strongest sentiments for and against independence from the Principate center on Norland—the whole northsea area." Sam made a face. "I suppose that is because there are very few unaltered Cousteaueans there; almost no 'drys.' "

"Drys?"

"Yes," began Sam, shifting into his lecture mode. "The first settlers on Cousteau had been genetically manipulated in order to develop lungs that could extract oxygen from sea water more readily than from air."

Galen whistled appreciatively. "That must have been some trick."

"It was," confirmed Sam. "But it was made easier by the fact that Cousteau's oceans have a higher concentration of oxygen in them than Terra's."

"And they just whipped up a batch of these water-breathers and dropped into the seas on Cousteau?" Galen knew how deliberately dense his question was, but he loved playing the obnoxious student to Sam's tolerant tutor.

"Of course not." Sam was the very picture of patience as he explained. "They began as embryos. After the genetic engineering, they were returned to their mothers' wombs for natural childbirth. Their lungs do not develop fully until they reach four years of age. At that point they are able to spend almost half the twenty-two-hour day in the water."

"And when they're out of water, they're called drys?" asked Galen innocently.

Sam closed and opened his eyes. "No, those whose lungs did not fully develop were forced to take jobs on land. These physically immature amphibians—in other words, those who are *not* really amphibians at all—often found positions in the Principate bureaucracy and, perhaps because of the almost innate hostility and prejudice against them—"

"Aren't human beings wonderful?" interrupted Galen.

Ignoring Galen's comment, Sam continued. "Because of the very real prejudice against them, these so-called 'drys' were said to form a deeper bond of loyalty to Terra and to the Principate than to Cousteau and their own heritage."

"That's very interesting."

"It gets better."

"How so?"

"This Suo Hann that Fedalf mentioned . . . ?"

"Yeah?"

"There isn't a lot of information on her, but there is one thing. Hann is an unusual name."

"That's right," piped in Galen, snapping his fingers. "It's only four letters, not five."

"There is a reason for that: Her father, it turns out, was a dry."

PART TWO

GAR VARRO

4

GALEN AND SAM WERE ENJOYING THE HOVERCRAFT JOURNEY
from Nemo, where Cousteau's main spaceport was located,
to Midland, the large island that was the seat of the council
government.

The hovercraft smoothed out all but the largest waves and
swells, but even so at least half the passengers were either clos-
eted in their cabins dosing themselves with seasickness remedies
or hanging forlornly over the rail feeding the fish and sea birds
that trailed the craft.

"Look at that," Galen said. "Imagine all those people getting
seasick. I can't understand it. I mean, if you think about it, it's
just a matter of mind over stomach. If you believe you're going
to get sick, then you get sick; if you refuse to allow yourself to
get sick, you don't—it's as simple as that."

Sam gestured toward the rail. "Don't tell me, tell them."

Galen found the salty, crisp air a tonic to spacesickness,
whose claustrophobic embrace had been smothering all but the
hardiest travelers who'd shared the psychologically debilitating
quarters aboard the starship *Truman*. A quick glance about him
revealed many of the same faces he'd grown used to seeing on
board the *Truman*. But that was only natural, since most of the
offplanet visitors were either businessmen or members of the

Principate's massive bureaucracy. Quite logically, such people were drawn to the planet's center of profit and power.

A florid, sweating man beside Sam announced, "You know, from space the distance from Nemo to Midland looks damned short—maybe the width of a thumbnail. But I've traveled that thumbnail's distance many times, and it's always a good six hours by hovercraft."

"That so?" Galen said. "Well, Sam and I are in no particular hurry to get to my destination. I'm just going to continue to enjoy the fresh air."

"Good idea," said their new acquaintance, glancing at Sam. "I think I'll have me a little pick-me-up at the bar, since we've got a long way to go yet. You want to join me?"

"No, thanks," Galen replied. "I have no taste for the indoors right now."

Galen felt the forward surge of the hovercraft lessen a bit and the whine of the engines became less pronounced; they were slowing. (Technology had made possible utterly silent-running engines, but *complete* silence made passengers uneasy.)

Soon the hovercraft was again racing across the water at top speed. Galen looked back at the wake and saw, as well as felt, that they had veered off to the right of the course they had been following. They were no longer headed directly for Midland.

Suddenly the intercom chimed for attention and a woman's authoritative voice announced, "This is the captain speaking. We've altered course to respond to a distress call. For safety's sake, all passengers are advised to return to the interior seating sections and put on their life jackets. Thank you for your cooperation."

<I wonder what that was all about?> Galen said to Sam.

<I imagine we'll be finding out shortly,> Sam replied.

Human nature being what it is, not only did very few passengers retire to the inside, but many of those inside elected to venture out—sans life jackets—to see what all the fuss was about.

Galen was about to ask a passing crewman why he was carrying a powerful-looking energy rifle when he overheard another crew member telling a skeletally thin man, "It's a Berserker attack."

Berserkers! Galen didn't know whether to feel fear or excitement; all accounts of Berserkers stressed their mindless savagery. To see one of these monsters of the deep so soon after landing on Cousteau was a possibility he could not have counted on or hoped for.

<Seems this is your lucky day,> Sam told him dryly.

Galen had just pressure-locked the last flap on his life jacket when someone shouted, "There, look there!"

Eyes smarting from the wind-borne salt spray, Galen made out a small sailboat just a few hundred meters off the starboard bow. Immediately, the hovercraft came to a full stop. The roar of the engines died and, with nothing to replace that purposeful noise, the sounding stillness of the sea fell over them. A few great-winged birds drifted overhead, riding the invisible currents of their own ocean of air.

Its engines stilled, the hovercraft now rose and fell lazily with the unhurried rhythm of the sea. Since the only other immediate point of reference was the tiny sailboat bobbing atop its own pattern of swells and troughs, the feeling of gut-wrenching motion was intensified and soon the silence was broken by those at the rails who'd suddenly remembered their stomachs.

The sailboat lay dead in the water and appeared devoid of activity. Slowly, the hovercraft edged closer. Proximity brought no further signs of life. It was soon evident, however, that the small boat was sinking, the sea rushing into some unseen gash beneath the waterline.

As the sailboat, white and fragile-looking, listed badly to port, its deck rose as if to meet the watchers and Galen suddenly had the uneasy feeling he was watching a living thing gasping out its last minutes of life.

A large bubble surged to the surface and burst in a spray of white foam. The small craft shuddered and slipped quickly beneath the waves, one last sigh of air escaping to mark its passage. The sea swirled and eddied over the spot, then resumed its normal motion as if to deny it had swallowed the human-crafted waterbug that had skipped and raced across its surface.

"Goddamn Berserkers!" a red-haired crewman murmured, his rough features hardening into a grimace of hatred. Galen looked more closely at the sailor and saw a large tear form in one eye and run down the man's face to drop anonymously into the cruel sea.

The hovercraft, unable to do more, moved off.

II

The streets of Bandar, Cousteau's capital city, teemed with the electricity of a city full of life. Bandar's population of ninety thousand souls made it one of Midland's larger cities, second only to Krow.

Galen and Sam, unescorted, wandered about freely; Galen found walking the streets of a city the best way to get a handle on its mood, its "feel." So far, Bandar's feel was one of exhilaration tinged with suppressed anger. While most people smiled or paid no attention at all to Galen and his human-appearing partner, a few somehow sensed their offworld status and radiated ill-disguised hostility.

"Was it like this in the American colonies, I wonder?" Galen said to Sam. "Did the Americans resent the British so openly before their revolution—despite paying far less onerous taxes than any Londoner of equal means?"

"Taxes you place on yourself are one thing," Sam replied. "Taxes imposed on you by someone else are another matter."

"I guess so."

Galen shrugged off the bad feelings that were directed at the two of them and allowed his gaze to sweep the streets they wandered down. People walked briskly, though some occasionally paused to gulp air to reduce the oxygen debt their surface exertions induced.

Here and there street venders sold their goods with loud cries imploring the shopper to stop and examine what treasures were available for so little money. "Hey—gelfish, gelfish, here. So fresh they're still wrigglin'. Who'll buy? Just a credit a kilo. Hey, gelfish!"

Another vender called out, "Sea roses. Lovely sea roses for your girl. You mister, sea roses for your wife?" The man the old woman had singled out shook his head no. She shrugged and continued her calling, "I got 'em . . . sea roses."

"It's certainly far different from getting on the shoppers' walkway on any street on Terra," Galen observed.

"You're right," agreed Sam. "Midland seems to have only recently gotten moving sidewalks and walkways."

"Hmmm," Galen said. "I rather like this way of seeing the

stores and pushcarts. It's quaint, but then some might say that about what I'm used to."

Galen discovered that a pedestrian could set his own pace, and this was an inducement for stopping more often. Against his better judgment, Galen bought a ring. The man selling it wanted seven hundred credits.

"That's not a bad price," Sam said, taking the ring from Galen and examining it closely. Galen rolled his eyes in disgust. Like all tourists in Bandar, he wanted to bargain like a local, aware that it was expected. But he didn't need Sam's "help."

"I'll give you three hundred and fifty credits for it," he told the peddler.

"Sure you will—and who wouldn't? This ring is worth at least a thousand credits; I'm only selling it because I need the money," the peddler countered.

"It *is* pretty," Galen admitted. "Let's say four hundred and fifty credits."

"Six hundred credits."

"Hmmm . . . I don't know," said Galen. "Tell you what; I'll go to five hundred and fifty credits, and not a centicred higher."

"Done and done," said the street peddler. "I'm sure your sweetheart will like it very much, sir."

"I'm sure she will," agreed Galen.

"Just who *are* you going to give it to?" Sam asked him as they walked away with their prize. "It's too small for my fingers."

"It's perfect for Fedalf," Galen retorted. *Who* will *I give it to?* he wondered.

Walking on, they covered a great deal of distance before they realized it. Pausing to lean against a building, Galen confessed to Sam, "Lordy, I'm unused to walking so much, especially after being confined on the *Truman* and then the hovercraft."

Sam looked around. "How about stopping over there?" he suggested, pointing to an outdoor cafe. "We can take a rest and you can order a pick-me-up."

"Looks perfect," Galen agreed. Soon he was sipping a tall, cool drink called a Sailor's Delite.

"What's in that?" asked Sam.

"I have no idea," Galen admitted. "I could ask."

"Maybe it's better not to know," Sam told him.

"Maybe you're right."

Watching the parade of amphibious Cousteaueans walking

past their table, a metal-and-plaswood concoction shaped to resemble an octopus supporting a circular serving surface, Galen said, "I'll bet some of these folks are 'drys.' "

"That's a safe bet, I'm sure," Sam said.

Galen knew from his external that, save for an autopsy, there was no definitive way of telling the water-and-air breathers from those who breathed only air. And yet . . .

<What is it?> Galen asked Sam privately. *<The way they walk—their bearing?>*

<Yes,> agreed Sam. *<I think that must be it.>*

While many Terrans thought all Cousteaueans looked alike, both Galen and Sam were learning to spot minor differences in build and coloring among the passersby.

Galen sipped his mystery drink. Whatever it was, it *was* quite good.

After receiving a nudge from Sam, Galen glanced at a young woman, taking in her long legs and generously proportioned bust. For some reason she made him think of the holos he'd seen of Tey Varro, although she didn't resemble Gar Varro's daughter at all.

The girl was with a nonaltered male—Galen could see no throat markings—and for the first time he appraised her sexually. She looked up and caught him staring at her. Her gaze kindled something within him and he blushed, turning away.

<Now what made me do that?> he asked Sam. *<There's no barrier to sex between a Terran and a Fib . . . Fib?>* A pained expression crossed Galen's face and he put down his drink so hard that the people seated at the next table gave him a peculiar look.

"Fib?" he said softly. "Jesus, why not kike, rolly, nigger, wop, hopper, horseface, or sod?"

"C'mon," Sam said, putting his hand on Galen's arm. "It just slipped out, for Pete's sake. You're no racist."

"Maybe not, but I think I've been in the goddamn spy business for too long. I'm starting to think like a lifer." His eyes widened. "Like a Legionnaire."

"Bullshit!" said Sam. He hated it when Galen started stuff like this. Galen was all too eager to give himself a hard time for imagined faults.

Galen finished the drink, threw down a tip, and said, "Let's go."

"Don't you want to wait for your hair shirt?" Sam muttered in a low voice. If Galen heard him, he gave no sign of it.

III

Galen Yeager and Sam Houston entered Gar Varro's home in Bandar trailing one of Varro's ubiquitous assistants. Galen suspected the man was really more a bodyguard than a political assistant, after observing the professional way in which the muscular young man had looked him over and had casually brushed against his clothing to check for concealed weapons. Since everyone knew that androids were bound by internal restraints against using weapons, the bodyguard didn't waste time on Sam.

<See how much more trustworthy I am than you are?> Sam told Galen.

<If they only knew.>

Because of the dampness and the fishy air, Galen found the house a bit depressing and stifling. Still, the brightly glowing walls and the art were effective in cheering up the overall atmosphere.

Varro's house was spacious and airy for the home of a citizen of Cousteau. It was awash in bright colors, the walls dazzlingly painted to offset the inevitable sense of pervading dampness and sea rot.

Such a rainbow of colors was not in itself unusual, but Varro's walls seemed to glow with extra brightness—perhaps drawing energy from their owner's physical presence when he was home.

The bright colors of the walls were complemented by strips between the wall panels which pulsed with the phosphorescent light of domesticated algae. The algae's continuous soft light mimicked the diffuse lighting of the sea, and Galen thought it did much to make the room feel comfortable. *For a Cousteauean, that is,* he amended.

All the nonliving furniture was sturdy and utilitarian as well as being waterproof and noncorroding. The living furniture was imaginatively chosen: from sparkle-shelled giant conches to semianimate pillow plants. Bubble fish, captive in a transparent discarded stomachfish sac, continuously emitted pearl necklaces of bubbles.

Galen noted that each house was an unlikely combination of unfettered open spaces shoved up against claustrophobically tiny personal retreats for meditation and for the regaining of a sense of closeness. The pervasive feeling of things pressing in further catered to the mental well-being of the average Cousteauean, Galen supposed. *Prison must be no real hardship for them,* he mused.

Someone with excellent taste had juxtaposed ocean artifacts—bones, spines, and manmade objects which had become art by becoming encrusted and distorted by growth—and holomontages of sea scenes.

Galen was about to make a comment when a muscular young man strode purposefully into the room, looked both Galen and Sam over, and announced, "Gar Varro."

A tall man wearing a flowing, loose-fitting robe tied at the waist glided lithely into the room. *<He obviously keeps himself in good condition,>* Galen said to Sam.

<Yeah, well, maybe you two can arm wrestle later.>

Varro's forehead glistened and his dark eyes bore straight into Galen. "Allow me to welcome you to my home. I am Gar Varro."

<What a surprise,> joked Sam. *<If he hadn't cleared that up, I might have taken him for the Creature from the Black Lagoon.>*

<Who?> asked Galen.

<Never mind.>

Galen shrugged, which puzzled Varro, and said, "Thank you, Citizen Varro. I am Galen Yeager, and this is my friend and partner, Sam Houston." Sam nodded, smiling blandly.

Galen also smiled and held out a small package. "Coffee," he replied to Varro's look of inquiry. "I understand it takes a great deal of protein to purchase a kilo on Cousteau."

"Thank you," said Varro seriously. "I'm pleased you took the trouble to learn one of our customs. I hope I can repay you during your stay."

They shook hands—Varro noting the Terran's strong grip, and Galen feeling the webbing between the Cousteauean's fingers.

"Forgive me if this is a thoughtless question," asked Varro, "but do I shake Citizen Houston's hand as well? I have met very few artificial humans in my life."

<Look in the mirror, Flipper.>

<Be nice,> Galen admonished Sam. Even though Varro

couldn't hear Sam, Galen was discomforted by his partner's shameless habit of making fun of everything.

"While many people feel it is proper to do so, it's not necessary," Sam told the Cousteauean leader. <*How's that, Miss Manners?*>

<*Better.*> Had Galen given his annoyance more thought, he would have been forced to admit that he was more than a little jealous of Sam's unabashed cheek and relentless wisecracking. He might even have remembered something he overheard Sam say to Dr. Bussot: "When they handed out a sense of humor, Galen thought they said 'a sensitive tumor' and turned it down flat."

"I see," said Varro in response to Sam's reply. After a moment's hesitation, he put out his hand. Still smiling, Sam took it and shook it. Varro seemed surprised that Sam's hand felt no different from anyone else's.

The niceties of introduction out of the way, Galen now sensed Varro's direct gaze on him. What Varro saw was a youngish man in his early thirties, with tightly curled auburn hair framing a face seemingly devoid of guile or duplicity. His blue-gray eyes were clear and deep.

Varro ran his eyes over Yeager's slender frame, judging that it made him appear taller than he really was—one hundred and eighty centimeters, perhaps. His hands, however, ended in short, strong fingers that belied his unimpressive build. Varro could still feel a tingling in his own fingers from Galen's grip.

As for the android, Sam Houston looked too much like a holvee star for Varro's tastes; more like the impossibly handsome men one saw in advertisements than the person next door. Varro wondered if that was why so many people seemed uncomfortable around the artificial humans.

His inspection over, he said to Galen and Sam, "Please have a seat, gentlemen," pointing to a comfortable-looking sponge couch, and seating himself on a large pillow plant.

"Is that thing alive?" asked a startled Galen.

"Oh, yes—as are many of the pieces of furniture you see here about you, including that couch you're sitting on. We Cousteaueans are never far from the sea, even in our decor and our art."

"I see I've got a lot to learn," Galen said with a smile that suggested he'd known Varro for years.

Varro smiled too. "That's certainly true." Then his eyes narrowed almost imperceptibly. "Of course, one needn't travel all this way to learn about our way of life. I understand many Terran universities possess an enormous amount of Cousteauean studies and lore. What has brought you and your companion here in person?"

Galen studied the older man in the diffuse lighting the algae emitted. Unlike many of the other genetically engineered humans, the amphibious Cousteaueans differed little in outward appearance from nonaltered humans. The face Galen examined was essentially a human face: the eyes slightly larger and the ears less apparent. Varro breathed through flaring and broad nostrils, and it was only when he turned his head that Galen could see the closed exhalatory slits on his thick neck. The clothing hid any body differences, although Galen knew there were few.

After some consideration, he finally said: "What brought Sam and me? That's easy." He waved his hand at the room. "This brought me. One can read about life on any of the colonies . . ." Galen noted that Varro stiffened slightly when he said colonies, so he quickly amended that to "council worlds," and continued, "Or one can insert the appropriate external for a 'virtual' tour, but there's no substitute for the real thing." Grinning boyishly, he added, "I can certainly afford to indulge my whims."

Inwardly, Galen smiled. Talking about his inherited wealth almost always made others drop their guard—the "poor little rich boy" stereotype carried with it a useful cliche: that those born to wealth are usually self-indulgent fools.

"Yes, you have the means to satisfy your whims," Varro conceded. "And the connections, too."

"Actually," Galen said, his voice crisper now, "I have better connections than you can imagine." He'd decided to quit toying with Varro and tell him the truth—sort of.

"Eh? I don't understand. . . ." Varro wet his lips.

<Of course he doesn't,> Galen told Sam. <He's not the right man to front a revolution.>

<He could be,> disagreed Sam.

<Maybe,> allowed Galen. <But I doubt it.>

"Perhaps we ought to go into your office," Galen said to the Cousteauean leader, glancing at the disinterested bodyguard in the corner who was trying to dig something out of his nose. "What I have to tell you is confidential."

5

THE INFORMATION THAT GALEN HAD FOR VARRO WAS MORE than "confidential"; it was explosive. Galen had decided the best way to win Varro's confidence was to betray the network of Legion operatives Nevin Feller, the director, had infiltrated on Cousteau. What better way to demonstrate his bona fides than to "confess" that he was a Legion agent who was willing to betray his fellows to Varro?

Still, Galen knew he was taking a deadly chance—as did his chief. Hashem Fedalf had agreed to allow Galen to expose his rival intelligence director's personnel with great reluctance, saying morosely, "If Feller should hear of this damned stunt, I'm cooked."

"This is incredible!" blurted Gar Varro. He looked across his desk in disbelief. "I know the Magistracy is opposed to our requests for a more autonomous government, but for the Legion to infiltrate our industry, our institutions, our entire planet, as thoroughly as you describe is outrageous."

Galen Yeager just shrugged. "It's standard procedure. When the Legion discovered that I had asked for leave from the university to come here, they recalled me."

<*I cannot believe how easily the lies roll off your tongue, meat boy,*> marveled Sam.

<Practice.>

"To spy on Cousteau!" fumed Varro.

"Well, it wasn't put to me quite as dramatically as that," said Galen, grinning self-consciously. "I was simply told to keep my eyes and ears open and to report anything I discovered about separatist movements and leaders—such as you and this Suo Hann, whose name has just come to my attention."

Varro reddened. "Ours is not a 'separatist' movement, and it is not even really a revolutionary movement."

Sam found that disingenuous at best. "Oh. Then why is your party called the 'Liberation Party'?" he asked coyly.

"*I* did not choose our party's name," Varro said pointedly. "As for our eventual goal, we seek nothing more than to govern ourselves while remaining a full and equal member of the Terran Principate."

"You pretty much have self-government now."

"Please don't patronize me," sighed Varro. "The drys govern us, and they do what their masters in the Council Office tell them to do. Our natural resources are not developed, they're ravaged. Food production is expected to go up and up—no excuses. And all the time, the drys are selling us cheap!"

Regaining his composure, Varro asked, "Do you know where 'Principate' was derived from?" When Galen shrugged, Varro explained, "It comes from the Roman Empire, from the Latin *princeps.*"

"Princeps?"

"It means first among equals. The Principate is theoretically—note my use of the word 'theoretically'—a government which vests its power in the Council of Planets. As a full member of the Council of Planets, Cousteau is supposed to have a certain percentage of the power. But like all the other Council members, we are impotent. Instead, all meaningful power resides in Terra's three-member Magistracy responsible for executing the Council's orders. *All* of it."

"And you hope to change that?"

"I do."

"Peacefully?"

"I once thought it the only way. Now I don't know." With a sigh, Varro added, "But this is no time to discuss politics with you. You have admitted being a member of the Legion; why?"

"That's not easy to say," murmured Galen. He allowed his

eyes to meet Varro's for a moment before looking away. "The fact is, I am not really a member of the Legion in the truest sense."

"I am not sure what you're getting at, but I was about to say that you do not strike me as a member of the Principate's armed forces."

"I'm not. It is too expensive for even the Principate to keep a really large standing army in times of peace, so an organization called the Shadow Legion was developed to supplement the regulars. Promising young men and women"—and here Galen attempted to look sufficiently modest—"are given scholarships to the Legion's Academy. Each recruit is trained to be a skilled professional in a business or scientific discipline of his or her choosing.

"As for me, I was one of the rare ones: I attended my own university and was recruited just prior to graduation. After graduation and one year's service with a Legion outpost, the new agent is either placed on the 'inactive' list or goes to 'sleep' until his skills are needed."

Varro wrinkled his brow quizzically. "Sleep?"

"Yes. As a member of the Shadow Legion I was a deep-cover agent, a sleeper."

"Me, too," said Sam.

When Galen laughed despite himself, Varro asked, "What is so funny?"

"It's a private joke," Galen said. "Maybe someday I can explain it to you."

"I hope you do," said Varro, who had no idea what Galen and Sam were talking about.

"Anyway," Galen continued, "the Shadow Legion serves the Principate as a reserve and highly trained military force to provide for the rapid expansion of the regular Legion and other armed forces in a time of emergency."

"Very impressive," Varro fumed. "You still haven't told me why you're revealing all this to me."

Galen clasped his hands behind his neck. "As you might imagine, a deep-cover agent like myself occasionally finds it difficult to resume active status. I've been doing field work and pursuing the academic interests I was trained for the last ten years," he lied, "and I've seen a lot of ways of living"—<*That's true*,> Galen said to Sam—"and I've lost whatever 'secret agent' mentality I might have had"—*<and that's becoming true.>*.

"To put it bluntly, I don't much give a damn which side wins out in this issue, but I think you deserve to know what you're up against."

"That seems frank enough," Varro said, seeming to accept Galen's confession at face value.

<See?> Galen ragged Sam. *<He's easy. It's like shooting fish in a barrel.>*

"Yes," continued Varro. "Too frank to be believable."

<Ha! See yourself!> retorted Sam. *<He's sharper than you're giving him credit for.>*

"You don't have to bet your farm on my word," Galen told Varro. "Just listen to what I have to say."

Varro crossed his arms. "I'm listening."

"I'll give you the names of as many Shadow Legion intelligence actives and sleepers as I can. That should prove that what I'm telling you is the truth. In return, I want to hear nothing of your plans, of your organization, or of what you plan to do with the information I'm giving you. I'm no double agent." Very little of that was true, but Galen knew he had to feign disinterest.

"Such generosity," said Varro skeptically. "What *do* you want?"

" 'There ain't no such thing as a free lunch,' eh? Well, you're right. I do want something. I want to work with your people studying the Berserkers."

II

"Something's coming in from Terra on the subspace communicator," Sam told Galen. "It is an immediate-reply, authority prime-A signal."

"What the hell can that be?" Galen wondered.

"Hush," cautioned Sam, "no static, please."

Galen fumed slightly as Sam patiently recorded the message and then decoded it for him. "Well?" he asked finally.

"As you wish," responded Sam, starting the 'player.

"Hello," said the holographic image of Hashem Fedalf. "If I do not refer to you by name in this message, there is less chance of anyone learning your identity if it is intercepted.

"I have reason to believe that the order to blow up the *General Woodard* did indeed originate with the extremists on

Cousteau." Fedalf smiled and added, "Just as you suspected. This is clearly an attempt to weaken the will of the Principate. But knowing the Magistracy as I do, I cannot believe that this foolish act will accomplish anything other than causing a brutal retaliation."

Fedalf paused. "Then again, that may be *precisely* what the terrorists are hoping for. You are to intensify your efforts to ingratiate yourself with your target."

Again Fedalf paused; he stared intently out at Galen, his dark brown eyes burning. "I suspect that this is the work of Suo Hann and her people, or possibly even the Liberation Party."

"Hmmph," said Galen, shaking his head at that idea.

Fedalf's image continued. "It is imperative, then, that your inquiries go forward; you *must* stay as close to Ahab as possible," Fedalf said, using Varro's code name. "Guilty or innocent, he's now the epicenter of controversy—the 'independence' leaders of every Council planet will be under intense suspicion until those responsible for the bombing either reveal themselves or are caught."

Fedalf's features softened. "Be careful."

The image collapsed in on itself and faded to nothingness.

"Sam," Galen said happily, "that was one message I was glad I received. Now we can really go to work."

Summoned into Varro's presence, Galen wasted no time: "Yes, I know," he told Varro before the other could speak.

"You know?"

"About the *General Woodard*. That *is* why you wanted to see me, isn't it?" asked Galen. "Your intelligence operatives have learned that the Magistracy has discovered a connection between Cousteau and the sabotage of their warship."

"It's about time I stopped being surprised by anything you have to say," Varro said with a tight smile.

"I have impeccable connections."

"As good as mine, apparently," said Varro. "If I had any doubts concerning your status as a Shadow Legion agent, they've been eradicated by your confirmation of these events." Furrowing his brow, he asked, "I suppose you even know what I'm going to do next?"

"Not for sure, no, but I'd guess you're planning to call a meeting with your people," said Galen.

"A good guess, Yeager. Yes, as head of my party, I must consult with members of my party. Many of them have positions in the local government. I must ask for their thinking even though the real power resides in the Governor and the Council."

"And then what?"

"I don't know, really." Cocking his head quizzically, Varro asked, "Do *you* have any ideas?"

"As a matter of fact, I do," Galen said, "and I'll tell you all about them on our way to your party headquarters."

Varro snorted. "Pretty sure of yourself, aren't you?"

"What have you got to lose by taking me and Sam along?"

"Everything," Varro said dryly. "But come along, we must prepare for our journey—I am important, but not so important the floater will wait for me."

III

"So, how did the meeting with your party officials go?" Galen asked Varro as he and Sam walked through the streets of Bandar with the Cousteauean leader and his bodyguards.

"Not well."

"That's too bad," sympathized Galen. "What was the problem?"

Varro shook his head. "We go over the same ground again and again. We are too indecisive to reach any kind of consensus as to what must be done."

"I see," said Galen.

Galen noticed Varro stiffen a few seconds before Sam nudged him. <*What?*>

<*Look for yourself.*>

Galen then saw the political graffiti that had caught the attention of both Sam and Varro. There were several messages scrawled on a wall: "Down with the Principate!" "Suo Hann and Freedom!!" Finally, and most ominously: "Death to the Magistracy!!"

<*It says 'Suo Hann,' not Gar Varro,*> Sam pointed out to Galen.

<*It doesn't take a genius to figure out who has the confidence of the Cousteauean people, does it?*>

<*No, it sure doesn't,*> Sam replied.

"Suo Hann!" hissed one of Varro's bodyguard/aides. "Why is it always Suo Hann?"

"Come, let's move along," Varro said. "We cannot help what people think."

When they stopped to peruse the wares at an open-air market that spread out like a colorful tablecloth across a broad plaza in the heart of Bandar, Varro turned to Galen and said, "You seem to be enjoying yourself."

"He likes these places," Sam Houston said.

"You enjoy shopping and bargaining, eh?" Varro asked.

Galen nodded reluctantly. "Up to a point. I enjoy looking at goods, but when I find something suitable I stop looking and buy it."

"And the bargaining?"

"I must admit that I enjoy that more."

Galen seemed embarrassed by this revelation, and Varro wondered if it was because of the Terran's privileged background. He speculated that the young spy might have subconsciously convinced himself that to bargain, to get something at less than its asking price, was somehow unworthy of a person wealthy enough to afford to pay full price without a second thought.

The market was awash in bright, vivid colors—reds, greens, blues, and yellows. The vegetables, from tomatoes and corn to onions and carrots, were obviously fresh—looking for all the world as if they had been hand-harvested with loving care that very morning. They probably had, Galen realized.

"This is a wonderful place," Sam said, responding to the panoply of sensory delights the market provided.

After Varro shot him a strange look, Sam felt compelled to explain: "I may not be human, but I have first-rate intelligence and olfactory circuits—and I *am* made in my creators' image." When Varro still stared, Sam added, "So don't look so fucking surprised!"

<Sam,> Galen told his partner, *<you're incorrigible.>*

"In my defense, I can only reiterate that we do not have many artificials on Cousteau," Varro hastened to say.

"Apology accepted."

Galen kept the smile that turned up the corners of his mouth to himself by turning away to examine an impossibly crimson tomato. As he stared admiringly at it, a spray of pulp and seeds burst from the tomato and his smile faded to a puzzled frown.

"Hey! What—"

While Sam shoved both Galen and Varro to the ground in the blink of an eye, one of the bodyguards gurgled and toppled over backwards, already dead from a needle gun shard which had caught him flush in the throat. Flexing a muscle in his wrist caused a similar weapon to leap into Galen's hand.

Galen spotted the attackers immediately—three men and a woman less than ten meters away. His heart pounding, he rested his arm on top of the fruit stand and pumped out three ceramic shards that, as far as he could tell, missed their targets completely.

"My God!" exclaimed Varro, only now realizing that he was the target of people who meant to kill him. Seeing a needle gun in Sam's hand, Varro was puzzled for a moment, then wrongly assumed that the weapon was for show, since an attacker couldn't see the android's giveaway golden eyes beyond a few meters.

The bystanders near them were slow to react to what was happening. Only a few had seen the bodyguard collapse, bright arterial blood sluicing from his throat.

With their element of surprise now vanished, the attackers opened fire with noisier and heavier weapons—energy pistols and a small, lightweight automatic slug-thrower. It was the slug-thrower's distinct chatter that finally alerted everyone in the crowded plaza to what was going on.

With plasteel slugs whizzing past his ear like angry hornets, Sam nonchalantly reached across the open space separating him from the surviving bodyguard crouching behind a plaswood crate, seized the man's tunic, and pulled him to his side. When the bodyguard cursed at him, Sam said, "It worked, didn't it? You didn't get hit. Now forget about spouting colorful adjectives concerning my ancestry and stay with your leader."

Catching Sam's eye, Galen made an "I'll-go-this-way" gesture immediately followed by an "and-you'll-go-that-way" one. Sam nodded.

Sam scurried across the rough plascrete on his hands and knees. Impervious to "pain"—or at least the equivalent sensory input—Sam was able to scoot along at an amazing speed.

Popping up from behind a flower stand, Sam directed a stream of ceramic shards at one of the three male attackers. After a shard passed through the man's wrist—which he looked at in surprise—he turned to stare open-mouthed in the direction it had come from. Sam's next shard passed between his lips and struck the roof of the man's mouth. Blood gushing from his mouth, he fell dead across a flower stand.

<One down,> Sam told Galen.

Galen's own volley, fired from a prone position, struck another of the attackers in the ankle. The bone snapped with a loud crunch and the man tumbled to the ground, where he was an easy target for a more lethal shard.

<Correction,> said Galen *<That's two down.>*

<It's two to two now? That's no fun anymore.>

<You're right,> agreed Galen. *<Anyone can beat those odds.>*

<I guess it's time for the Golem to do his thing, eh?> asked Sam.

<Yep.>

Picking up a one-meter-by-one-meter slab of plaswood and holding it in front of himself like a shield, Sam unleased an unnerving yell and rushed at the two surviving would-be assassins. Stunned into inaction just long enough for Sam to cross the space separating them, the two held their fire until it was too late.

Sam smashed the plaswood slab into the duo and knocked them backwards. Throwing down the superfluous slab, Sam swept the weapons from their hands.

"Way to go, José," Galen cheered, leveling his gun at the demoralized terrorists.

Against the vehement protests of his bodyguard, Varro also approached the assassins. "Who are you?" he demanded. "Why do you wish to kill me?"

The two exchanged a glance fraught with meaning. "Hey!" shouted Galen.

Too late.

With smoke coming from their mouths and the exhalatory slits in their throats, the two assassins' eyes rolled back in their heads and they collapsed like rag dolls.

"Mother of God!" exclaimed Varro.

"Not again!" Galen moaned.

IV

The aircraft that carried Gar Varro and his Terran visitors was a regularly scheduled commuter which hopped and skipped across the seas from major island to major island before reaching the Crescent, the large island which was their destination. The plane was a strange combination of anti-grav rotors, multiposition wings, and flying boat.

As Varro explained to Galen before take-off, "Everything on Cousteau must take into account the sea. Since we have many offworld and unaltered visitors and business people who frequent our airlines, our aircraft must float as well as fly. It does not happen often, but occasionally an aircraft is forced to land at sea. When that happens, it must become a boat."

"Yeah," agreed Galen. "Cousteaueans can breathe underwater, but the rest of us can't."

Varro and Galen had the opportunity to talk on the flight, since there was no one seated beside them. Sam had again made himself scarce at a look from Galen.

"I hope I'm doing the right thing," said Varro, "returning home while things in Bandar are so unsettled."

"I doubt you really had a choice," said Galen. He knit his brow and continued. "Even if we assumed that you would not be the target of another assassination attempt—a large assumption, I might add—I think you'd have been arrested before too long had you lingered in Bandar."

"Arrested?"

"Yes. The Council—the colonial government—can't allow a rallying point, a strong leader, a center to any possible protest, to exist. You and your followers would start to take on a dangerous mass."

"I suppose you're right," Varro admitted grudgingly. Then he brightened. "It'll be good to see Tey again."

"Sam and I are looking forward to meeting her."

Varro gave Galen a look of appraisal. "Sam," he said. "Sam Houston . . ."

"Yes?"

"He *is* an android, is he not?"

"Of course," replied Galen. He didn't need a map cube to see where this was heading.

"Then how is it he was able to participate in my defense?"

Galen smiled, grateful for the way Varro had phrased his question; it allowed him an easy out.

"That's the whole point, Citizen Varro. Sam is capable of defensive activity. While it's true that Sam appears to have weapons which he fires, they are simply mock devices which mimic the flashes and sounds of the real thing."

"But I saw him take a human life with my own eyes."

Galen shook his head. "Sam just pointed his *faux* weapon at the assassins. It was fire from *my* weapons that killed them."

"I see," said Varro. Galen thought he still sounded a little dubious.

"Come," said Varro, when the aircraft touched down in the small city of New Baltimore. "My people will be waiting for us at the docks."

They had little luggage with them, and what there was was mostly Galen's. It had pained Galen enormously, but while still on Luna he'd sent their musical instruments back to Terra. He shuddered at the thought of what Cousteau's heat and humidity could do to their exquisite veneers.

Sam gathered up what they had brought, saying, "Work, work, work. Tote that barge, lift that bale."

At the harbor front, Varro searched for docking berth number 107. "There it is," said Varro with a nod of his head. "There's 107—and my sailboat, the *Bec II*."

Varro picked up the pace and Galen followed as best he could. Sam, of course, had no difficulty keeping up with the Cousteauean leader. Soon, the boat loomed large and Varro was shouting greetings to the crew.

"It's good to see you again, Gar," said one of the older members of the crew, whose close-cropped black hair was streaked with gray. From the broad smile that creased the man's face and the way he eagerly took Varro's hand, Galen guessed he was a long-time friend.

"Dio, you old rascal," said Varro, confirming Galen's supposition. "You look well." He glanced about at the others. "You *all* look well." They pushed in around him, hugging him.

Sam and Galen stood off awkwardly to one side until the others deigned to acknowledge their presence. "And who are these outsiders you've brought us, Gar?"

"Galen Yeager, a young friend from Terra itself, and his companion, Sam Houston. Mr. Houston is an artificial," he added unnecessarily.

A younger man was impolite enough to permit a look of distaste to cross his face, but Dio and the others just guffawed and said, "Ho, an air-sucker and an artificial to see your farm, Gar! You *have* been too long among the sophistos of Bandar."

Galen's eyes met Sam's. *<Calling me an air-sucker is probably their way of letting me know that while they'll accept me as Gar's friend, they won't allow me to see them with their defenses down.>*

<Uh-huh,> replied Sam. *<And slipping a fish gutter between your ribs would probably be their subtle way of letting you know they don't like you.>*

"This 'air-sucker' and artificial, as you so bluntly phrased it, saved my life on Bandar."

"Saved your life?" someone said. "How?"

"I was the target of an assassination attempt. If it were not for these two, I doubt I would be standing here today."

They looked at Galen and Sam with newly acquired respect in their eyes. "Sorry, Gar, we didn't know."

<Looks like a case of news not *traveling fast,>* Sam said.

The gear Sam had carried with him was seized by strong hands and quickly and efficiently stowed in the sailboat. Galen gulped slightly at the thing's size. It was larger than the one the Berserker had attacked on their voyage to Bandar, but not by much. The thought of facing the open sea in such a tiny craft, if only for sixty or seventy kilometers, caused him to swallow hard.

With the wind filling the semirigid sails, they were soon at sea once more and making for the scattered archipelagoes that provided the anchoring point for Varro's sea farm. Galen had not had a chance to exchange more than a word or two with Varro since they'd come on board, but it was clear to him that the Gar Varro he'd first met, the politician, was slowly shedding his official life and slipping gracefully back into one he'd been forced to abandon when he went to Bandar.

6

"WE MUST SAIL AROUND SHARD ISLAND," VARRO SHOUTED TO Galen, raising his voice to combat the ever-present wind, "and then the small land masses that comprise the surface portions of my farm will be but a few minutes away."

Just as Varro said, his sea farm loomed on the horizon in minutes. The water was becoming shallower as the sailboat made for the island that was the core of the farm. Galen noticed several shapes sluicing through the water toward them. Since no one else seemed alarmed, Galen quickly guessed that they were boka, the genetically altered dolphins that served as watchdogs for the herds of sea cows.

Soon the streamlined, silver boka were circling the sailboat, leaping high out of the water to call out Gar Varro's name: "Gar, Gar, Gar."

"Hello, Herman. Hello, Dutchy. Hello, Melville," Varro shouted to the frolicking boka.

"How can you tell them apart at this distance?" wondered Galen, since the "fish" all looked the same to him.

"How does a Terran farmer distinguish between the individual sheep of his flock or each cow in his herd?" Varro asked. Answering his own question, he said, "I just know them."

With their finny escort, they sailed up to the docks and made fast to the moorings. Galen took in the sights around him, filing away his first impressions. There were several other sailboats tied up at the dock and at least four engine-powered vessels with several hovercraft and two-man boats in among them. Galen saw that one of the older, less fully equipped sailboats was named the *Bec I*. Cousteaueans of all sizes, shapes, and body markings swarmed over the busy docks.

A fishy, somewhat decaying smell hung over the docks in a miasma of humid air, and while Galen noted it, he knew he'd soon become accustomed to the rank odor. *Forget the odor*, he thought. *Everything else is gorgeous.*

A small crowd of people had gathered at the slip the *Bec II* was slicing toward, and a tall, striking-looking young woman shouted greetings, then rushed up to Varro and hugged and kissed him as soon as the sailboat docked.

So that's Tey Varro, Galen told himself. *Speaking of gorgeous . . . Her holos sure don't do her justice.*

The thirty-year-old Tey Varro was both muscular and voluptuous; her firm body was clearly womanly, yet just as clearly fit. Topless, as was the custom of the young women of Cousteau, Tey enveloped her father in her arms, her breasts flattening against his chest. The sight aroused something in Galen. Blushing, he looked away.

As Galen was averting his gaze, Tey Varro glanced over her father's shoulder at the brown-haired young visitor from Terra. He was certainly attractive to her—in ways in which the young men of the sea farm were not. He looked strong and in good shape beneath his short-sleeved tunic—she could see the bulges of his biceps—but he lacked the sun-blistered, full-bodied muscular definition and ample chest that amphibians quickly developed as a consequence of a life spent in the water.

Staring at her, Galen discovered Tey Varro's eyes on him. Their gazes locked for a moment; then she looked away first. *That's interesting,* Galen thought. *Either she's shy, or she's learned a few universal female devices, even out here in the middle of nowhere.*

Galen studied her closely cropped hair. What was the style called again? Oh, yes—a brush cut. She was darker than her father and reminded Galen of the black African strain in his own ancestry.

Varro felt his daughter tense slightly and immediately understood why. He took hold of her shoulders and stepped back to look at her before running his hand through her hair and saying, "I want you to meet someone, Tey."

"The young man who saved your life?" Galen remembered that she had been informed about the assassination attempt against her father, and the fact that she had not told anyone else impressed him.

"Yes, the very same."

Galen smiled as Varro nodded in his direction and said, "Tey, this is Galen Yeager. Galen, my daughter Tey."

"I'm pleased to meet you," said Galen as he took her hand and held it briefly, feeling an electric tingle.

"And I you, Galen Yeager," said Tey Varro. "I've never met a Terran spy before." There was a twinkle in her emerald eyes.

"You've hardly met a *Terran* before," said Varro.

Galen looked pained. It was not just what Tey Varro had said about his being a spy, but how loudly she'd said it in a semipublic place. "I'm not sure what your father told you about me, but it almost certainly is an exaggeration. I'm just a scientist who happens to work for the Legion now and then."

"I see," said Tey, giving every indication she believed his story about as much as she believed in the godwhale. "And your successful defense of my father was simply the good fortune and timing of a talented amateur? Uh-huh."

<Gotcha!> Sam told him. Putting down the luggage he'd carried ashore, Sam said to Tey and her father, "Yes, we artificials have no feelings. Everyone please feel free to ignore me."

"Forgive me, Mr. Houston," said Varro, genuinely distressed at his lapse. "Tey, this is Citizen Yeager's partner, Mr. Sam Houston." Again unable to prevent himself from stating the obvious, he added, "He is a most advanced artificial being."

"I'm pleased to meet you, Mr. Houston," Tey said, taking his hand.

"The pleasure is mine," said Sam, bending over her hand in the old manner. The action flattered Tey Varro more than she would have thought. She enjoyed the attention being paid her by both man and machine.

Varro, for some reason Galen could not fathom, was looking very pleased. "Come," he said when the introductions were over, "let's go to the house and both Galen and I can refresh ourselves and get cleaned up."

"Sounds good to me," said Galen.

"Maybe I can take an oil bath," Sam said brightly.

Galen decided that Gar Varro's Northsea home was more than the equal of the one the Cousteauean leader maintained on Midland. Varro's first home had somewhat surprised Galen, but the shock of seeing the living furniture and domesticated algae in real life, not as holo images, had abated and Galen was better able to appreciate how the two halves of Varro's life—the wet and the dry—were effortlessly linked by his homes.

Both Varro and his daughter had gone off on a private underwater swim, leaving Galen and Sam alone in the house. "I guess they trust us with the silverware, huh?" asked Sam.

"That seems to be the case."

As water lapped at the steps leading from the underwater entrance to the deep pool that dominated the house's main living room, Galen and Sam meandered about. Despite Sam's crack about the silverware, Galen did feel unworthy when it came to Varro's apparent trust in the two of them. Being an intelligence operative made him feel unclean sometimes.

"Look at that," said Sam, pointing.

"Yeah, I see."

Sam had called his attention to a wall which did double duty by also being a glass-enclosed aquarium housing a remarkable assortment of sea life. As Galen pressed his face up against the glass, electric darters—shooting off tiny sparks of electricity—ricocheted around the interior. A strange octopuslike thing with nine arms pulled itself over to the glass to return Galen's stare with its large, cyclopean eye.

"Hello," the nonplused Terran addressed it.

"It likes you," Sam said, joining Galen in peering closely at the multilimbed sea creature.

When it pulled back in fright, Galen said, "But not you, apparently."

"Sure, trust the one who's likely to have you prepared in a butter sauce," said Sam, tapping the plasglas with a fingernail.

Having followed Varro's advice to change into swim trunks, Galen walked across the smooth floor toward a wall decoration and felt his toes sink into the "carpet" in front of the brightly colored wall.

"Hey, Lone Star. What do they call this stuff we're stand-ing on?"

"A rug."

"Could I get a straight answer out of you just once?"

Sam relented. "All I know is it's some sort of sea moss that creeps about the living room, keeping the floor free of unwanted growth. Without it the floor would soon be slick and slimy because of the damp air."

"Slick and slimy?"

"Yeah, like your tongue in the mornings."

From across the room the wall decoration that had caught Galen's eye was clearly a portrait of Tey Varro. But, up close, the portrait resolved into individual bits of coral—each piece a part of a living mosaic.

The house was mostly on one floor, and Galen and Sam completed their tour by examining one of the meditation rooms. Apart from a single seat, a stool, the meditation room was with-out furnishings or decorations.

"That room can't be bigger than two meters by two meters," observed Sam.

"I know. Just looking inside makes me feel claustrophobic."

"Uh-oh," Sam said. "I know what your usual cure for that is."

"You got it, professor."

Sam made Galen a drink in the kitchen/dining complex and they discussed the rest of Varro's home, the underwater portion.

It was there, Galen knew, that Cousteaueans had their sleeping quarters—gently floating inside a confining mesh while they slept. "I wonder what sort of dreams a person has when he sleeps in water?" Galen mused.

"Wet dreams?" asked Sam so swiftly that Galen blew almost half his drink out his nostrils.

II

Trailing water, Gar and Tey Varro returned, making their way up the plascrete steps into the living room. Running strong-looking fingers through her closely cropped hair from front to back to squeeze out the excess water, Tey Varro saw Galen seated on the sofa and said, "I see you've found the omo."

"Would you like another?" Gar Varro asked.

Galen shook his head. "No, it's tasty but it's also kind of potent. It puts hair on your chest, if you know what I mean." When Tey laughed at that, Galen added, "I take it that's a Terran expression you've never heard before."

"No, I haven't," agreed Tey. Looking down at her chest, she said, "I hope it's just a figure of speech."

Galen found himself staring at her breasts. "Ah, yeah. I don't think you have anything to worry about." To change the subject, he asked, "Did your swim go well?"

"It did," said Varro. "Tey wanted to show me a few things before the four of us go for a formal tour." His eyes crinkled and he added, "I'm almost as much a tourist here as you. Tey's been running the place for me while I've been off in Bandar for the past several years."

"It's not difficult," Tey said. "I had a good teacher who left me a pretty good working setup."

"When do Sam and I get the grand tour?"

"Tomorrow will be soon enough," Varro told him. Almost as an afterthought, Varro added, "That's when you'll breathe water for the first time, too."

The exchanger that Gar Varro held in his hand looked like a sheath of mucus trailing long streamers. "Tourists, since their diving is limited to shallow areas, and since they *are* just that—tourists—get mechanical versions which work almost as well," Varro explained.

"What do you mean, 'since they are tourists'?" Galen asked.

Varro sighed. "Once the exchanger is in place, these two appendages go into your nostrils and down your throat into your lungs."

"And then I can breathe water?" Galen asked, staring at the limp mass of translucent flesh dubiously.

"Well, sort of," Varro told him. "Since you have lungs meant for breathing air only, your exchanger will extract the oxygen from the sea water and convey it into your lungs, where it exchanges it for carbon dioxide."

Sam gave Galen a poke in the ribs and said, "Hence, the term 'exchanger.' Get it, boy?"

"I get it." Seeing the look on Sam's face, Galen added, "Um-m-m . . . I'm *really* going to get it, aren't I?"

"Yes." Feeling merciful, Sam did not elaborate.

"It . . . ah . . . it is a somewhat unpleasant feeling, I'm told," admitted Gar Varro, "but one soon becomes used to it."

"Uh-huh. Like a sonic disrupter shoved inside your ear canal, I suppose."

"You don't *have* to see the whole farm," Varro told Galen. "Or you could use a mechanical exchanger."

"Like a tourist?" Now it was Galen's turn to sigh. "I don't want to be a typical air-sucker. If wearing that lump of phlegm is what it takes, then by God that's what it takes."

"Good man!" said Varro, clapping him on the arm.

"How . . . how, ah . . . ?"

"When Tey gets here with the numbing agent," said Varro, "we'll slip your exchanger on. It'll cover your nose and mouth, but you'll have to wear goggles to see."

"Hey, Galen qualifies as a 'numbing agent,' " volunteered Sam. "When he plays the piano, that is."

"Again, I must confess to having met few artificials such as yourself," Varro said to Sam. "But even to my unqualified eyes, you seem remarkably human."

"Everyone has his faults."

Tey showed up within a few minutes and saw Galen looking dismally at the exchanger. "So, father's told you about wearing the exchanger, I see," she said.

"Yes," said Galen. "The things I do for Hash . . . ah, Nevin Feller."

<Almost blew it, keed.>

<Tell me something I don't know.>

"Anticipation is the worst part; I'll numb your nostrils and throat and we can start," Tey suggested.

"Yes, let's get the hell on with it," Galen replied.

Tey opened a jar of cream and told Galen to coat the inside of his nostrils and then to open his mouth wide while she sprayed the back of his throat. "That should work in about twenty seconds," she told him, putting away the spray.

The two amphibians helped Galen to lie down on his back and got the exchanger ready. "Try to get into the water as soon as we put the exchanger on," directed Varro. "Are you ready?"

"As ready as I'll ever be."

"Oh-h-h, I can't look," said Sam, turning away in mock distress.

"Remind me to disassemble you first chance I get!"

"Here we go," Varro warned him.

Reflecting later on that moment, Galen realized that he remembered very little about it; it was as if he had blocked the unpleasant experience from his mind.

And it *was* unpleasant: Galen felt the wet, clammy mass of the exchanger settling on his face as Tey expertly guided the slender tendrils into his nostrils. "Relax," she told him. "I know it's hard to do, but just close your eyes and relax."

Galen tried to think about other things, but he couldn't fool his conscious mind into looking the other way: He felt the tendrils touch the back of his throat and he almost gagged. Then, mercifully, they reached their destination. The exchanger settled over his nose and mouth, slits on its back opening and closing.

"Okay, into the water," commanded Varro. "C'mon, Galen."

They helped him to his feet, and before he knew it the sea was rushing over his head. Uncertain what to do, he nerved himself to take a breath, drawing in air through his nostrils.

To Galen's surprise, his lungs filled with oxygen-rich air which tasted okay. Well, actually, the air tasted like socks washed in warthog sweat.

<*It could be worse,*> Galen told Sam when he joined them in the sea. <*I don't know* how, *but it* could *be worse.*>

Galen became aware of Varro and Tey hovering near him anxiously. "How are you doing?" Varro asked. Galen made a thumbs-up gesture to indicate all was fine.

"Good," Tey said. "Now, you may find this hard to believe, but since the exchanger is only *covering* your mouth, while the tendrils are in your nostrils, you can speak if you're careful not to move your mouth in such a way that you break the seal around it." When Galen looked dubious, Tey said, "No, really. Go ahead, try it."

"Ohtay, but ah doan thinn itz gonn worg," said Galen, his voice muffled but certainly audible. "Hey, thass not bad," he admitted.

<*You sound like Linda Lovelace,*> Sam chided him.

<*Who?*>

<*Forget it. Way before your time. Way before my time, actually.*>

"You'll get better with practice," Varro said about Galen's attempt at speech. "Now, shall we begin the grand tour?"

*   *   *

To his surprise, Galen soon found himself growing accustomed to the exchanger hugging his face. And, with their flippers on, he discovered that he and Sam could actually swim faster than either Varro or his daughter, despite the amphibians' slightly webbed toes. Since Varro was using a sea sled to tow them through the water, however, Galen had little chance to show off his unexpected underwater proficiency.

Gar Varro and Tey seemed surprised that Sam could join them in the sea. "Are you . . . ah . . . *waterproof*?" was how Tey indelicately put the question to the android.

"Waterproof, shockproof, and I tell the day, month, and Luna's phases, from new moon to full," Sam told them proudly.

Tey colored slightly. "I guess we must seem like such . . ." She paused to search for the right word. "Like such provincials."

Galen shrugged. "You said it yourself—you don't get many artificials out this way."

"Certainly none this good-looking," Sam said, making his two hosts smile.

"C'mon," said Galen. "Let's go 'see the elephant.' "

Galen admired the efficiency of the changes both Tey and her father had undergone to return to mankind's primal home, the sea. As he remembered Sam telling him at one point, the greatest obstacle the genetic engineers had to conquer in redesigning the human lungs to extract oxygen from sea water was how to eliminate carbon dioxide.

The carbon dioxide difficulty was finally overcome, only to leave the scientists facing another problem: deep diving so compressed the chest—and, hence, the lungs—that it was difficult for the first human amphibians to breathe at depth. Eventually, the designers had further modified the lungs as well as simply strengthening the ribs to withstand more pressure.

The sea farm was not at all like Galen had been led to believe it would be; as a working farm, it little resembled the artificially tidy farms presented on holos.

The sled pulled them out into the vastness of Varro's holdings, and Galen felt a reassuring calmness under the penetratingly blue sky that dominated from horizon to horizon, visible through the remarkably clear sea water. Galen watched as several of the friendly boka rejoined them, happily circling around them and chattering away. "They act as our 'sheep dogs,' " Varro explained. "They herd the sea cows and watch for unwanted intruders."

"Gar, Gar, Gar," one of the boka kept calling in a high, squeaky voice.

"Will they fetch a stick?" said Galen, surprising himself by how clearly the words came out despite the exchanger.

Tey laughed, causing a stream of bubbles to flow from her mouth and the small exhalatory slits at the sides of her throat. "They're very much like dogs in their loyalty and friendliness. And, since they don't know about titles, my father is always just 'Gar' to them, as I am 'Tey.' "

"I see," said Galen.

"New mans," said a boka.

"Yes, Nelson," said Tey. "Galen. Galen and Sam."

"Gay-len," mimicked the boka Tey had called Nelson. "Gay-len an' Sam."

Tey faced Galen as he held onto the sled beside her. "Now they'll all know your names in a few hours," she told him.

"Gay-len, Gay-len," several of the other boka called out experimentally. "Gay-len an' Sam."

Gar Varro's farm was divided into several fair-sized sections. He told his Terran visitors that the one they were in now was devoted to the sea cows and their calves, while the more rambunctious bulls were kept in a separate enclosure. Galen shook his head at that; the "enclosure" was fully ten kilometers in every direction, allowing the sea cows plenty of area to roam around in as they sought out the microscopic animals they fed on.

"How many cows are there in this section?" Galen asked Tey, blinking behind his goggles.

"At least fifty or so," Tey replied, her jade eyes looking dull and clouded. That bothered Galen until he realized that they were protected by nictitating eyelids. That also explained why she rarely needed to blink.

"Don't the cows 'overgraze' the area, then, so to speak?"

"Not really," Tey explained. "The barriers which keep out orns and Berserkers are still porous enough for the krill the sea cows depend upon to be swept through the grazing areas. Look," she added, "there's a cow now."

Through the marvelously clear azure water Galen could see two large shapes looming in the distance. "And the other?"

"Her calf. The calf is nearly two-thirds grown; that's why he's almost as large as his mother."

"Come, we'll get closer," said Varro.

"There's no danger, is there?" asked Galen.

"Not really," answered Tey. "The real problem is with the adult bulls, not the cows or their calves."

As the sled drew them close to the feeding mother and offspring, Galen began to appreciate their size. "How big is that beast?"

"Maybe forty or fifty meters," said Tey. "The bulls run to sixty meters or longer."

"Jesus!"

Galen noticed a large, grouperlike fish swimming by. He'd have thought the fish enormous before he'd seen the sea cow. But now . . .

Gar Varro stilled the forward motion of the sled and allowed it to drift slowly toward the sea floor. The sea was only twenty or thirty meters deep at this point, and they would retrieve the sled readily enough when they were through.

Sam watched benevolently as Tey took Galen by the arm and led him off. The two swam underneath the sea cow. "Look at her teats," Tey suggested. "She can produce upwards of forty liters of milk a day to feed her calf."

Gaping at the living milk machine hovering above him, Galen noticed that the calf was swimming slowly alongside his mother, filtering out the plankton in the water. "I take it he's off the bottle now, so to speak?"

"Yes, but we've bred the cows to produce milk for a year after each birth. She's about to be impregnated again and will produce another calf in about a year," Tey said. "Her milk-producing capacity will return at that time."

As they watched the sea cows, the mother's surprisingly tiny eye on that side of her head swiveled toward Galen and Sam. "Hi, there," said Sam pleasantly.

The cow swished her tremendous tail several times and swam away, her calf in pursuit. The water roiled, and Sam and Galen felt themselves being tossed around like guppies in a washing machine. Tey swam over to Galen and stilled his motion.

"Was it something I said?" asked Sam.

Tey smiled. "They tolerate us and are harmless, but they like their privacy, too."

"I'll retrieve the sled," said Varro. "There's much more for you to see."

Although Tey had said the protective barriers were "porous," she wasn't entirely accurate. What surrounded the sea farm was a vast force field designed to keep large animals in—and out—and to allow smaller fish and sea creatures unimpeded entrance or exit. Approximately every hundred meters or so, massive plasteel poles were driven deep into the sea floor. The poles maintained the invisible force field, amplifying the signal and linking it to the next pole.

While the force field was generally effective, it couldn't keep out a really determined intruder if it was large enough and belligerent enough to smash its way in—like a Berserker. That's how Varro's son Bec Varro had died, Galen had learned.

Gar Varro slowed the sled and pointed out the shimmering water ahead to Galen. "That's the force field," he told the young Terran. "See how the water is distorted and blurs what is behind the curtain of energy?"

"Fascinating," said Sam. "Can we get through here?"

"Oh, yes," replied Tey Varro. "Father will set the sled's controls to automatic and it will pass through; the field is only sensitive to lifeforms."

"What about us?" Galen questioned. "We're lifeforms."

"Most of us, that is," Sam said, shooting a look at Galen.

"Yes, but we're too small to be sea cows or bulls—or orns or Berserkers. The field will allow us to pass through unharmed if we move slowly and deliberately." She looked at Galen's face, creased with concern, and added, "Please don't do that. You'll break the seal your exchanger has established. Besides, all you'll feel passing through is a slight tingling in your fingers and toes."

"Here we go," said Varro, sending the sled through by itself. The three humans and Sam followed slowly, and Galen felt the strange tingling sensation Tey had mentioned.

"There, that wasn't so bad, was it?" asked Tey.

"Bad? Let's do it again!" exclaimed Galen. Tey smiled, bubbles flowing from her throat. She had to admit that this Terran spy was no ordinary air-sucker.

"We are now in the bulls' enclosure," cautioned Varro. "Ordinarily they will not harm us, but breeding season is fast approaching, so take care."

The bulls were solitary creatures, so it was a while until they came across one. Plunging from its feeding near the surface, the massive bull cut off an immense arc of light from the sun as it effortlessly dove toward the sea floor.

"Whew!" said Galen. "And I thought the cows were big."

"As much as this bull dwarfs a cow, so does a Berserker dwarf a bull," said Tey. She looked hard at Galen. "Father says you would like to see one close up; is that so?"

Watching the tremendous bull swim out of sight, Galen finally answered, "Yes, but let me add a coda to that: I'd like to see one close up *and* live to tell about it."

Several boka rejoined them at that point and Tey Varro said, "There's not much more to see here once you've seen a bull. Let's continue our grand tour by going to the section of the farm where we raise our crops."

"Lead on, MacDuff," said Sam.

7

THE SLED HIT A PATCH OF TURBULENT WATER AND GALEN bumped into Varro beside him. "Sorry," said Galen.

"Don't worry about it," said Varro. "This sled wasn't meant to haul around four people."

<Instead of Gar Varro, I'd much rather be bumping into Tey,> Galen told Sam.

<Be careful you don't get too excited—that swimsuit doesn't conceal much,> cautioned Sam.

"We're almost at the shelf farms," Tey announced.

The shelf farms, Galen recalled, were areas of the sea floor just a few meters under the surface of the water. There sunlight warmed the sea, and nutrients were deposited after being washed into the ocean, and plants and well-adapted shellfish flourished.

Surrounded by boka sing-songing the names "Gar," "Tey," "Sam," and "Gay-len," the three humans and the android again abandoned the sled to the sea floor and proceeded under their own power.

As schools of silver-colored fish zigzagged past him in perfect unison, Galen marveled at the color erupting from the shelf farm beds. In addition to the fish, purple-shelled mussels contrasted with the vibrant reds, greens, and shocking pink of the rows of algae.

Galen noticed long underwater grasses waving in the gentle currents and asked Tey what they were. "Kyrro—sea wheat," she replied. "Some of our other farms, where the nutrients and ocean floor are different, host underwater fields of quadro-rice, 'oyster' beans, and soyyba."

"What's that?" Galen asked, pointing to a waxy-looking plant covered by fingerlike appendages.

"That? That's just a weed, an intruder," Tey replied.

"Oh." As Galen watched, a large fish, seemingly all jaw and teeth, began biting off the plant's twenty-centimeter-long protuberances.

Staring first at the fish and then at the bulge in Galen's swim trunks, Sam said, "I'll bet seeing stuff like that kinda dampens one's enthusiasm for going skinny-dipping."

"I should think so," Galen replied seriously. Then he turned to Tey and said, "This all looks impressive. You must do quite well financially."

"It's a living," was all Tey would admit to.

Ah, the universal social faux pas—*asking someone how much money he or she earns,* Galen mused.

"Come," said Varro, "let's go back for the sled. There's one last thing I want you to see today."

"And what's that?"

"The slaughterhouse."

"Don't worry," said Tey when she saw Galen make a face. "It's above water. If the smells get to you, you won't be wearing an exchanger over your mouth."

Gar Varro's slaughtering operation was confined to a small building on one of the more isolated outlying islands. As he explained to Galen, "The bulls and sea cows become upset and unmanageable once they smell blood in the water. Therefore, we've established our meat-processing plant as far away from the rest of the farm as possible."

Varro, Galen, Sam, and Tey Varro bobbed on the surface of the water, just inside the sea entrance to the series of fences that guided the sea cows toward their final destination.

"When our meat animals and our older breeders are ready to be processed," Tey explained, "the boka herd them into this section. When the plant is ready to receive them, the cows are herded into a series of 'runs.' The entrance of the first run is rather like the mouth of a funnel. Soon, though, the run narrows and a series of chutes ensure that the cows can only go forward; before they know it, they're lined up and ready to be killed and processed."

"Sounds a bit gruesome," said Galen through his exchanger.

"Let me take that off," said Varro, reaching for the white mass hugging Galen's face.

"It *is* gruesome—and bloody and unpleasant," replied Tey. "But people must eat, and the output of this one farm sustains several thousand people a year. Cousteau feeds itself and other planets, too." She made a face and added, "People turn up their noses at what goes on at a facility like this, but very few of them mind the result—a prime sea cow steak cooked just the way they like it."

"Well, *I'm* a vegetarian," Sam said with mock seriousness.

While Tey stared speechlessly at Sam, Gar Varro tugged gently on Galen's exchanger and it reluctantly released its grip. The Terran grimaced but remained silent as the tendrils were pulled up his throat and out of his nostrils. Varro and Tey admired his fortitude—as did Sam, although he'd never admit it to Galen in a million years.

They had left the sled at the entrance of this section, and now they abandoned the water itself. Ahead of them lay only the maze of gates and fences that guided the sea cows to their fate. They would have to travel the rest of the way on foot.

When they climbed out of the water, the first thing Galen noticed was the awful smell. As they approached the slaughter-house and rendering plants, the vile odor increased in intensity. "Whew," said Galen, his eyes stinging. "I've never smelled anything this bad before."

"What about your lucky tennis shoes?" asked Sam.

"Oh yeah, I forgot about them," allowed Galen.

The quartet entered a three-story white building that was about two city blocks long. Varro's employees, all around them now, paid them no mind as they went about the business at hand, although Varro occasionally said hello to long-time friends.

Again Galen noted the Cousteaueans' distinctive individual coloring. It suddenly occurred to Galen why their pigmentation leapt out at him: On Terra, humans were becoming ever more homogeneous. This was the result of a centuries-long attempt to obliterate racism by mixing once-primary skin colors into a generic human flesh tone. Oddly enough, Galen reflected, it had happened coincidentally with the rise of genetically induced variations in the human form.

"Follow me, please," said Tey as they penetrated deeper into the building's interior.

Tey led Sam, Galen, and her father to a small holding pool a dozen meters inside the building. "Here is where the sea cows enter and are tranquilized," she explained, pointing to the water lapping lazily at the edge of the pool.

As she spoke, a cow was herded into the holding area. An employee of the farm raised an air rifle and fired a large dart into the side of an uneasy cow; within minutes the animal ceased its agitated movements. The walls and the floor of the pen moved up and in to support the great beast's bulk, and the dazed creature was propelled forward—rather like a vehicle in an old-fashioned assembly line, Galen thought.

"The next step," said Tey matter-of-factly. As they watched, a worker approached the cow and, after lowering a massive copper plate onto its head, sent a fatal charge of electricity through the unconscious animal's brain. Immediately, two smells competed with each other for the distinction of being the most stomach-churning: the odor of burned flesh and of a massive amount of fecal matter.

"What . . . ?" began Galen, putting his hand over his nose.

"They lose control of their sphincters when they're zapped," explained Tey. "It's not a very pleasant smell."

"Hm-m-m," observed Sam. "On Terra, we lose control of our 'sphincters' once we elect them to office."

"Will you stop already!" implored Galen.

" . . . Elect them to office?" Tey repeated slowly, mulling over what Sam had said. Then her eyes widened and she giggled—catching Galen off guard. He scratched his head slowly; maybe there was something to Sam's wiseacre act after all.

"There is still much to see," said Varro, thrown off balance by his guests' odd conversational exchanges. "Come, let's follow the process all the way through."

Squat and powerful nonhumanoid androids attached cables to the electrocuted sea cow and the carcass was pulled forward. Robotic arms with laser cutters on the end expertly sliced away first the outer skin and then great slabs of the blubber underneath. Again, the smell was sinus-draining.

"We use every centimeter and every kilogram from each cow," said Tey. "The skin and bones will be processed into fertilizer for agricultural use on prairie planets. Since the cows give their lives and bodies for us, we take pains to waste nothing."

They followed the carcass down the assembly line and Galen watched in amazement as the once massive sea cow was reduced to bones, the rib cage looking for all the world like white barrel staves. Then the bones themselves were cut apart and hauled away, leaving nothing behind.

"I've never seen anything like that before," confessed Galen.

"Very few offworlders have," Tey told him.

"It's great to be a VIP," Sam observed.

Tey cocked her head at her father and asked, "Think we should show them the bulls and cows breeding, father?"

"I thought breeding season hadn't started yet," Galen interjected before Varro could respond.

"Any time now," Tey said, "there are always a few early bloomers who are ahead of the rest of the herd."

"To answer your question, Tey," Varro said, "I don't see why not. Sam and Galen will enjoy the sight."

After the slaughterhouse, Sam had asked Galen, "Think you'll ever eat again?"

Galen's immediate answer had been a firm "No!"

But that fanciful response to the sights and odors he'd encountered disappeared the moment his stomach growled. When it came time for Varro's wizened household organizer to supervise the serving of the dinner the barrel-shaped domestic 'bots had prepared, Galen was hungry enough to eat an orn.

As famished as he was, Galen could not help but notice how incredibly old-looking the wrinkled prune-faced woman who commanded the 'bots appeared. The tattoos on the sides of her face and on her neck were distorted by the sagging of her flesh. A bit ashamed of his feelings of disgust caused by the ravages of time on Varro's housekeeper, Galen glanced appreciatively at Tey. There were no tattoos on her firm young flesh . . . well, none that he could see.

"I take it your household supervisor has been with you a long time?" Galen asked Varro.

"Dya?" Varro said as the old woman waddled away, satisfied that the meal was to everyone's liking. "She has been with my family for nearly eighty years. She was my nanny first, and then Bec's and Tey's. Now, since I have no wife and Tey is kept busy running the farms, she is my housekeeper."

Galen shook his head in amazement and then turned his attention to the food the little 'bots had placed on the table.

"This looks good . . . mostly," Galen said. "What is it?"

Tey pointed to the dish which had been placed in front of each of them and which was obviously the main course. "Well, this is bass on a bed of algae and quatro-rice; those green and pink squares are tube flowers; this is cheese made from sea cow milk; we have raw Cousteauean oysters and clams on the half shell; and, finally, a special wine."

"Special?"

"Yes," said Tey. "Try some. I think you'll like it."

"Okay," said Galen, picking up his wine glass. "Here goes." He swallowed a generous portion and pondered it a moment. "It's good." Then, as if surprised, he repeated, "It's really good."

Tey beamed, pleased not only because Galen had not hesitated to try the wine but also that he genuinely seemed to like it. "It's my own vintage," she told him. "I make it with sea grapes."

Galen tasted everything and found it all to be quite pleasing. The textures and colors were not what he was used to, but then he'd tasted the food of many worlds and found that most of it was good; Cousteau was no exception.

"I imagine I must make a terrible dinner guest," Sam said after Dya had served coffee and seaweed cakes to everyone except him and had left after directing black looks in his direction. "No matter how good the meal may be, I rudely decline to eat." Sighing, he said, "I *can* eat for show if I have to."

"You're a wonderful dinner guest," Tey objected, placing her hand on his arm. "You are witty and knowledgeable—and you never talk with your mouth full."

"Thank you," replied Sam, touched by her sincere reassurance.

Annoyed at the attention Tey was paying Sam, Galen turned to Gar Varro and asked, "I understand you have a little something planned for tonight?"

"Yes, I thought you and Sam might like to meet some of the local people. Many of them are my employees. In addition, Tey grew up with most of them."

"They are her friends, eh?" asked Galen.

"Yes," replied Varro.

"Good. I can't wait to meet them."

II

It was the wine that made him do it, Galen realized later.

"How are you doing with your exchanger, air-sucker?" asked a sullen-looking young man named Oli Foore. Staring into the muscular Cousteauean's eyes, Galen guessed that he was one of Tey's rebuffed suitors.

"This is a *party*," rejoined Tey before Galen could think of a proper response. "We are here to honor my father's guests, not insult them, Oli."

Galen cringed. Having Tey come to his defense was the last thing he needed. "To answer your question—pretty good," Galen finally said. He took another sip of Tey's wine.

"Pretty good?" said Foore dubiously. "What the hell does that mean?"

Galen's look told Tey not to "help" him anymore. "It means just what I said. Not terrible, not wonderful—pretty good," Galen said more mildly than he felt. He took another sip of wine; actually, it was more a gulp than a sip.

"To me, 'pretty good' means swimming out on your own to kill an orn," sneered Oli Foore. "Not going sightseeing with female guides or other hand-holders like all the rest of the air-sucking tourists."

"Kill an orn?" said Galen. He glanced at Tey, cocking an eyebrow.

"Killing an orn with nothing but a spear gun is an archaic ritual for the young men," Tey explained haltingly. "It is a barbaric and old-fashioned custom rapidly falling out of favor."

"That's right," agreed Foore. "We're becoming as spineless and helpless in the water as air-suckers and drys." He thumbed his own chest. "*I've* killed an orn that way. No one but a coward shrinks from such a challenge. Cowards and air-suckers from Terra, that is."

Having overheard most of the conversation, Sam beamed, <*Don't be foolish, Galen. Taking him up on his challenge is precisely what fishboy here wants you to do. Don't fall into his trap. You aborted the assassination attempt on Varro; you don't have to prove yourself to anyone.*>

<*That was playing a game I'm used to,*> Galen responded. <*I need to play one of their games and win.*>
<*Please don't do this, Galen.*>

The sea, always moving, always alive, pulled and pushed at Galen Yeager's body. He hung suspended in the clear blue water, just another particle of solid matter serenely floating a few meters below the agitated surface. He felt strangely at home in Cousteau's oceans, felt his inner being attuned to the restless movement of the currents. But amid the motion he was still. He waited.

Galen waited in a place where the blinking rhythm of day and night rarely intruded. He waited in a timeless place, the beat of his heart measuring the movement of the tiny ocean within him.

Great and small fishes swam past him. Here and there the somber tones of gray and blue were riven by flashes of bright color as garishly hued fish stuttered through the water in staccato bursts. Living fireworks, exploding silently, fish rushed by him, ignoring the languid strokes of his arms and legs which kept him in place. Life was abundant here, as was death.

Plankton clouded the water like dust swirling in a shaft of sunlight, each mote precious for its link in the food chain. Tiny swimmers ate the plankton, and were eaten by larger fish, who in turn were eaten by still larger fish. It all happened silently. Life seemed serene, without fear—perhaps because death came so quickly and without resistance.

Suddenly the calm sea roiled with color and motion. Schools of fish, twisting and turning as one, flashed past in frantic retreat.

Galen sensed the taste of danger in the water that had alerted the smaller fish. He sensed it as clearly as he did the various currents tugging at him. He resisted the currents unconsciously, paddling slowly with his flippers and hands to stay motionless. He unslung his spear gun and checked its charge.

Again he waited, peering through the goggles that protected his eyes from the salt of the sea. The silence was smothering; he both felt and heard the blood pounding in his ears.

The thing he had come to challenge appeared.

A great monster of the sea, unchanged for millions of years, glided silently and effortlessly through the water at a right angle to his position. Its rows and rows of teeth, always growing, always pushing forward and upward, were a testament to its role as one of the eating machines of the sea. It was an orn.

Unused to judging distances and sizes underwater, Galen nonetheless estimated the creature's length to be approximately ten meters; not a record if he remembered correctly, but close enough. *Jesus! Look at the size of that thing! Who is going to be the hunted now?*

Galen watched the orn's head turn this way and that as it tasted the sea water for anything edible. Like a king and his court, the orn was accompanied by a few scavenger fish awaiting any scraps that might drift their way.

When the orn became aware of his presence, it changed direction to begin a sweeping turn that would eventually bring it around to him. He had hoped it might already be gorged or, failing that, find his lack of movement uninteresting. From its movements, Galen assumed the orn was hunting—and it seemed to find him very interesting indeed.

Galen knew his puny spear gun would be little defense against a creature the size of the orn. He cursed the pride which had led him to undertake this hunt. Still, he had to act; the hungry and determined orn would not break off contact without something to show for its troubles.

It swam a bit faster, turning slightly on its side to better seize him with its teeth as it passed. Galen took aim and fired his spear gun before the great predator completed its turn. Outracing an accompanying stream of bubbles, the spear caught the orn just behind the midpoint of its body, punching into the horny skin with a solid *thunk*. Several scarlet ribbons streamed from the orn's pierced side, but it paid them no attention.

Moving with more rapidity and economy of motion than he was capable of under normal situations, Galen reloaded the spear gun and fired again. The second spear struck the orn with as little effect as the first. Completing its turn, the orn flicked its powerful tail and sliced through the water to attack Galen. His cool demeanor gone, Galen fumbled with his third and final spear; horrified, he watched it slip from his suddenly fat and clumsy fingers.

Galen thought that he could detect a look of resolute malevolence on the monster's "face." He realized he was attributing human feelings to a primordial beast that killed out of hunger and instinct rather than cruelty and villainy. Such emotions were the province of humankind. Probably the orn was simply hungry—too hungry to give up easily on such a large hunk of meat.

Determined to put up a fight, no matter how futile it might prove, Galen swung the heavy, blunt end of the spear gun at the approaching orn, striking the massive fish sharply on its nose. The great predator shook its head in puzzled anger as it passed by.

Pushing off from the orn's attack, Galen's hands beat the water and he barely avoided those deadly teeth as the monster circled back and tried to scoop him into its mouth.

Again it bore in on him, and his hastily drawn knife rasped futilely along the orn's side, never even breaking the skin. He was not especially surprised by his failure, since he knew from his external that the orn's skin was as tough as it was flexible. It was probably all but impossible to slash the monster's hide with a common underwater hunting knife.

The orn turned and Galen calculated his chances—regretting the decision immediately, since they appeared to be "slim" and "none." He could not get away; neither could he hope to avoid the orn's jaws indefinitely. *Shit! I always wanted to die in bed. Maybe not my own, but somebody's.*

Then it happened. It was so sudden and unexpected that Galen had little time to comprehend what had occurred before his startled eyes. The orn, leaking blood from its damaged side, was there one second and gone the next.

An even larger monster had smelled the blood quickly carried by the incessant motion of the water and had risen from its hunting deep below to seek out its source. The gigantic creature simply closed its mouth on the much smaller orn—as the orn had intended to do to Galen—and carried it, still thrashing, back down into the depths.

A wall of water smashed into Galen like a shock wave. The attack had roiled the sea, and tons of water quickly radiated outward. The slap of the water knocked the air out of his lungs, and the slits on the exchanger's back opened and closed as it hungrily ingested more of the oxygen-rich sea water.

The sea stilled. All that remained to attest to what Galen had seen was a curtain of blood hanging in the water. Slowly, it began to dissipate. He decided not to wait around to see what it might attract. He swam back to where he'd left his one-man sled. Wide-eyed fish gulped in curious amazement at him as he passed by. Life was returning, as it must, to this area of the sea again.

Galen was somber. He'd gotten his wish at last. He'd seen his first Berserker.

Gar Varro, Sam Houston, Tey, and Galen watched the recording made by the tiny camera in Galen's goggles over and over again, as if they couldn't believe what they were seeing.

"So that's a Berserker," said Sam, more as a statement than a question.

"That's a Berserker, all right," confirmed Gar Varro. "And our young friend here is very lucky to be alive."

"Ah, I had that orn right where I wanted him," said Galen. "If that damned Berserker hadn't come along to—"

"To save your Terran behind, you'd have been the orn's supper!" snapped Tey. She softened enough to say, "Father is right, Galen Yeager. You could easily have been killed. Why must men always be hostages to their damned male pride? You allowed Oli Foore to goad you into a stupid act!"

"It wasn't that," Galen protested. "I . . . ah . . ." He couldn't find the right words; neither could he deny the truth of what she'd said. He *had* hoped to impress Tey Varro with his willingness to accept her ex-suitor's challenge. *I've impressed her all right,* he realized. *I've impressed her with my stupidity!*

Although he despaired of getting a chance to undo the damage he'd done, one came sooner than he could have anticipated or hoped for.

8

GODDAMN EXCHANGERS! THOUGHT GALEN.

"You okay? The exchanger's working?" asked Tey Varro.

"Yeah, it's working."

Amused by Galen's tone, Tey told him a series of "simple" medical procedures would make the fleshy facehugger unnecessary.

"No, thanks," he replied. "I think I'll stay an air-sucker for now."

Their swim represented work for Tey, but it was pure pleasure for Galen. Tey asked him to accompany her as she swam out near the processing plant to check on an old cow destined for a one-way trip to the slaughterhouse.

"I think she's fine," Tey explained, "but she's been acting a little sluggish; I've got to give her a close-up inspection before I can allow her to be turned into food for the masses."

"You do your own inspecting?"

"Yes," replied Tey. "Anyone caught selling bad meat goes to prison for a very long time, so we do a pretty good job of policing ourselves."

Ten minutes later, Tey impressed a symbol on the old cow's side that confirmed the beast's fitness for human consumption. "Nothing wrong with her," Tey told Galen. "She's just a little older than most. She's slow moving 'cause she's tired. The slaughterhouse will be a blessing."

Just then there was a commotion: The water grew agitated, and Galen could hear boka screeching at each other in their peculiar, high-pitched voices. "What is it?" he shouted to Tey.

"It's a bull," Tey told him. "He's coming this way. He breached the barrier between the bulls' section and this one."

"What should we do?" asked Galen, impressed by her business-like manner.

"Quick, let's swim into the chutes. Maybe the smell of death in the water will deter him; it's the mating season that's got him crazed."

As they swam into the series of fences and chutes, Galen asked, "What can he do? He's big, but he hasn't really got the teeth of a predator, has he?"

"No," agreed Tey, "but he'll get you between himself and the sea floor or another object and crush you to death."

"Oh."

"Swim faster," Tey said.

Suddenly they were joined by a frightened-sounding boka. "Tey," it squeaked, "hurry. Bull coming."

"Thank you, Rachel," Tey said. "We'll grab onto you, okay?"

Without waiting for the boka's response, Tey and Galen grasped her dorsal fin from either side and held on; it was like being pulled by a flesh-and-blood sled.

The massive bull, crazed beyond sensory stimulation, ignored the smell of blood in the water and propelled itself into the chutes with powerful swishes of its massive tail. Soon it was just meters behind Rachel, and the two humans could hear it making a curious, grunting sound.

Fearing they would not escape with their lives, Tey stole a glance at Galen. His face was set and determined-looking, not frightened. She thought of his encounter with the orn and how confident he'd been that he would find a way out of the situation. Suddenly, she knew they had a chance to survive.

"Bloody, bloody, bloody," sing-songed Rachel nervously as the water turned pink.

The bull caught them just outside the killing chamber, butting into them with his wide forehead and sending all three of them swirling away like bits of paper trapped in a whirlpool. Slammed up against the wall of the chute, Galen went "OOMPH!" as the force of the impact knocked the air out of his lungs.

Having done her part, the terrified boka managed to get under and behind the bull and swam out the way they'd come. "Tey!" Galen shouted as best he could with the exchanger hugging his face. "Tey, are you all right?"

Then he saw her: The enraged bull was trying to pin her to the wall with his head. Tey was barely able to keep herself from being trapped, and her success so far only served to further enrage the bull. Galen broke the surface of the water and swam above the frenzied conflict below him. He got a handhold on the uneven surface of the wall, reached down to grab hold of Tey's arm and yanked, successfully pulling Tey to the surface and away from the bull.

"Thanks," she said, shaken.

Again they swam for the interior of the killing room and again the bull followed, bellowing and grunting in rage. The two humans, pushed by the water being punched ahead by the bull's bulk, preceded the enraged beast into the holding pool.

The bull thrashed its massive head and Galen tried to get out of its path. But the enraged creature caught him and almost pinned him to the wall. As Galen scrambled atop the bull's head, the beast whipped it upwards, throwing him completely out of the water. He landed beside a startled worker. "By the savior!" the man shouted, more in wonderment than fear.

"Bull attack," gasped Galen, struggling to his feet.

For the moment, Galen could see, Tey was safe. She had managed to get above the bull; it couldn't see her just yet, but it was only a matter of seconds before it found her again.

"Those controls," Galen asked the worker. "Do they raise the cage?"

"Why, yes."

"Do it!"

The man pressed a stud, and the walls and the floor of the holding pen began closing in on the bull and on Tey, lifting them from the water. Tey grabbed hold of the bull's dorsal fin as the enraged beast thrashed back and forth. She looked like a Terran cowboy atop a rodeo bull. Galen could see that if Tey lost her grip, she might fall between the bull and the walls and be crushed to death.

"The copper plate," said the worker.

"NO, goddamnit!" rasped Galen. "You'll electrocute Tey." He looked around frantically and saw a long plastic pole. Quickly, he picked it up and swung it against a piece of heavy machinery, shattering it. A bone-numbing shock radiated up his arms.

The three-meter-long piece of the pole that stayed in his hands was tipped by a jagged point. "Hang on, Tey," he called out through his exchanger. "I'm coming."

"Hurry," she said, feeling her grip loosening as beneath her the bull slammed back and forth.

Holding the pole as tightly as possible, Galen ran to the edge of the platform and leapt headlong at the bull's head. The creature's tiny eye was rolling about as the jagged tip of the pole punched into it and into its brain, causing a tremendous gout of blood to burst from the shattered socket and drench Galen.

The creature writhed and thrashed for a minute or so, then was still. Her strength gone, Tey let go of the enormous appendage she was clinging to and, totally exhausted, slowly slid to the floor of the cage.

"Are you all right?" Galen asked, the concern obvious in his voice.

"Yes, I think so," said Tey. Then she got her first good look at Galen. "My God, you're covered in blood; are *you* hurt?"

"I seem to be all here," Galen said. Then he looked up to see a worried-looking Sam approaching.

Since his keen hearing had recorded Tey's question, Sam chose to hide his concern for Galen by assuring Tey that "Galen will never ride a bicycle again, but he looks okay otherwise." Then he glanced down at the pole sticking out of the unmoving bull and said, "Bullseye."

"Please, father—I am perfectly okay," Tey protested when Gar Varro and the stooped Dya accompanied Doctor Willo into her room.

"Of course you are, my dear," agreed the doctor, setting down his heavy black bag and opening it. "But your father has asked me to give you a brief examination nonetheless." As ancient as Dya, Doctor Willo would have been an anomaly on most planets in the Principate. With the growing sophistication of robot medicos, human physicians were almost unheard of. They were anachronisms everywhere but the more backward planets.

"You have such a terrible bruise on your stomach," Dya remonstrated, jabbing the air with a gnarled finger. "You must allow the doctor to examine you."

"Indulge an old man, Tey," Varro said. "You are my only child now."

Tey knew when she was outnumbered. "Oh, all right." Reluctantly, Tey allowed herself to be poked and prodded and her internal organs scanned. At least the doctor had been truthful—the examination took only a few minutes, despite its thoroughness.

"There, that wasn't so bad, was it?" asked Doctor Willo as he put away the tools of his trade.

"No, it wasn't," Tey admitted.

"Thank you, Sar," Varro said to the white-haired physician. The old man nodded, said goodbye to Dya, and then tottered out of the room.

When Tey caught her father staring curiously at her, he quickly dropped his gaze and pretended to study the lines in the palm of his hand.

Tey had seen his act before. "What is it now, father?" she asked, putting one hand on her hip and shooting him an inquisitive look.

"Tey—have respect for your father!" warned Dya.

Tey stared closely at the smug expression on her father's face. *The sly old dog!* she marveled to herself. *He's brought Dya along because he knows she won't allow me to "talk back" to him.* The twinkle in her father's eyes was all the proof Tey needed to be sure she'd guessed correctly. He even nodded almost imperceptibly.

That was too much for Tey, Dya or no Dya. "Come on, father," Tey told him sternly. "You're burning up with desire to talk to me about something. What is it?"

Varro raised a hand to silence the ready-to-hector Dya. The old woman set her jaw but said nothing. "You are so much like your mother, Tey," Varro said, touching her hair gently. "You have her looks and her ability to see right through me."

"Is that what you wanted to talk to me about?" asked Tey, knowing full well it wasn't.

"I simply wish to speak to you about our guest."

"About Sam Houston?" Tey said innocently.

"No, not Sam Houston. You know who I'm speaking about."

"Oh, Galen."

"Yes, Galen," Varro said. "Dya, tell me what you observed earlier today."

"I saw this little one and the air-sucker kissing. Kissing—on the lips. He has not even petitioned her father for the privilege of calling upon her and he is kissing her!"

"Is this so?" Gar Varro asked.

Tey colored and looked down, unable to meet the gaze of either of the other two. "I . . . I wanted to thank him for saving my life at the slaughterhouse."

"There are other ways to show one's gratitude."

Tey nodded, seemed about to say something, then paused. After a moment's hesitation, she said to her father, "Galen is . . . well, *different*. He is not like all the others."

"That's to be expected," Varro countered. "He's from Terra, and . . ."

"And he's an air-sucker," Tey finished for him. "Just like Dya said—a Terran air-sucker. Yes, I know all that. It's just that there is something noble and brave about him. He was foolish to confront the orn the way he did, but I can't help thinking he did it for me. And then . . . at the slaughterhouse, he would have sacrificed himself for me."

"There are many here who would do the same!" insisted Dya.

"You sound like a teenager with your first crush," Varro chided Tey, the words coming out a little more reprovingly than he might have wished them to.

"I am a grown woman, father!" Tey snapped back.

Varro backed off a bit. "Forgive me, Tey." He waved a hand, not wanting to win the battle but lose the war. "It's just that I am a father who wants the best for his daughter. If what you feel for this Terran is just a passing infatuation, then I see no harm in your taking him as your lover." He paused, hearing Dya's sharp intake of breath. "But"—and here his expression changed—"if it becomes something more serious, then I fear for your future happiness. You are my only daughter, but you are Cousteauean before all else."

Tey nodded. "I understand, father." She took his hand in hers. Speaking as much for her own benefit as for his, she said sincerely, "I cannot say for sure that I love Galen. Not yet."

After dinner, Varro excused himself and Tey, Sam, and Galen found themselves alone. "Shall we go for a walk?" Tey questioned.

"Sure," agreed Sam enthusiastically, now as smitten with Tey as Galen was.

Galen glared sharply at Sam. Sam pretended to clear his throat. "Uh, I think, actually, that I'll catch up to your father," he told Tey.

"Oh, stay with us," Galen begged, his plea surprising Tey. She had no way of hearing what he said privately to Sam: <*Do and I'll kill you!*>

"No, really," Sam said, making a show of waving him off. "There are several questions I wish to put to Citizen Varro about local politics." He hurried off. Tey watched him go with feelings of relief and expectation.

Galen and Tey followed a path from the house toward the docks. Galen was all too aware of the warm, gloriously female presence beside him.

"Did you really wish Sam to accompany us?" Tey asked.

"No, not really."

Tey nodded thoughtfully and then asked, "Do you mind if I take your hand, Galen?"

"No."

He felt a tingle of electricity as her fingers entwined his. Galen was amazed at how readily he'd come to want Tey Varro, to sweep her into his arms and kiss her long and hard. He had not really done so yet—it was she who had kissed him after he'd saved her life. Further, it was a kiss of gratitude, not passion. At least that was what he'd thought.

As if she was reading his mind, Tey stopped suddenly and turned to face him. Her serious green eyes bored into his blue-gray ones. "I like you, Galen Yeager. You . . . you are not like the others, the ones we call air-suckers."

"Thank you . . . I think."

Tey smiled. "I also like your modesty. You attract me very much." Her gaze dropped and she said, "I can see the feeling is mutual."

"Are all the women of Cousteau as bold as you?" he asked.

"I don't know. I'm not all the women of Cousteau." Then she smiled slyly. "With you I think they would be."

"Be quiet," said Galen, opening his arms. She stepped in close to him and put her arms about him, her mouth finding and covering his. As her tongue sought his, he clutched her tighter to him, feeling her nipples harden against her chest.

Suddenly, she pulled back and looked him in the eye. "I do not love you, Galen Yeager," she admitted, "but I want you to make love to me."

"Come," he said, taking her hand again. He led her down to the beach, the grains of sand almost luminescent under the benign gaze of the moon hanging overhead like a massive silver sphere.

They began.

II

"Good morning!" said Galen so cheerfully that Varro couldn't help smiling.

"My, you're in a good mood today, Galen," Varro said, putting down his fork and indicating that the young Terran should join him at the breakfast table.

"Yes, I took a walk along the beach last night and then slept like the proverbial baby."

"Yeah," grinned Sam. "He tossed and turned and fussed all night. He finally cried himself to sleep."

"Don't listen to Sam," Galen said. "He wasn't there."

"Who was?"

"Paddington Bear," Galen shot back quickly. "I never go anywhere without him."

"Did P.B. bite you on the neck?" Sam asked maliciously.

Galen's hand was halfway to his throat before he realized Sam had laid a trap for him, one that he'd obligingly sprung. "Heh, heh," he laughed uneasily.

Just then Tey came out of her room, and the look she and Galen exchanged spoke volumes to Varro, as if he needed any more evidence after Galen and Sam's routine.

Varro coughed politely and said, "I've had word from Bandar. It seems the Magistracy is acerbating an already serious and tense situation by stationing more troops on Cousteau—Legion shock troops, no less."

Galen sat down and said, "That's stupid. That's sure to piss everyone off even more."

When Galen remembered what happened next, he always laughed at how cliched their reaction was: as soon as he'd spoken, he and Varro looked at each other with recognition dawning slowly in their eyes.

"Sonofabitch!" said Galen. "That's what the saboteurs are hoping for!"

"I think you're right, Galen," said Varro.

"What are you two talking about?" asked Tey, joining them at the table.

Varro turned excitedly to Tey and said, "That's it, don't you see, dear? That's why the *General Woodard* was blown up—to cause Consul Zajicek and the rest of the Magistracy to act rashly and crack down hard on us."

Sam folded his arms and looked like the cat who swallowed the canary. "Took you two geniuses long enough to put two and two together."

Ignoring Sam, Tey turned to Galen and asked, "Does this mean you think you know who sabotaged the Legion ship?"

Galen looked at Varro, who nodded. "Suo Hann and her followers," Galen said.

Exhausted by their lovemaking, Galen reluctantly told himself, *I'm no teenager anymore, that's for sure.* He raised himself up on one elbow and extracted a Mellow Yellow from the pack beside the bed. "Like a happy stick?" he asked Tey.

"No, thanks," she said dreamily as she ran her fingers along his side, from his thigh to his shoulder. Galen lit his cigarette, drew a deep breath, and lay back down beside Tey.

She snuggled her head against his comforting presence and announced, "That was fantastic. I guess it *is* better when you love the person." Then she raised herself up and regarded him with her solemn jade eyes. "I said I love you," she murmured wonderingly. "I hardly know you, yet I'm feeling something I've never felt before." She smiled and repeated, "I love you."

Smoke hanging about his head, Galen looked at her for a long time and she found it hard to read what was in his eyes. Then he put his cigarette down and, drawing her to him, kissed her and said softly, "I . . . I love you, too." Galen seemed as surprised by that admission as Tey had been by her own. Things weren't supposed to happen this quickly, were they?

Aware of the enormity of what they'd both said, of what they both had committed themselves to, they held each other in mutual respect and apprehension.

"What should we do about it?" asked Galen. "Do air-suckers ever marry fibs?" he asked, deliberately using the vulgar appellations.

"It's happened before," Tey explained, "but it's not a frequent occurrence." She considered before saying, "Love does not necessarily imply marriage."

"I know that," Galen said. "But if I ask you and you say yes, what will your father say or do?"

"What I want him to," Tey said firmly, and Galen had no difficulty believing *that*. She played with the sparse but curly hair on his chest. "He respects you, and after what you did at the holding pen to save my life . . . well, I think he would be proud to accept you into our family." She looked sad for a moment and said, "I think my father sees a lot of himself—and Bec, too—in you."

When Galen winced, Tey asked what was the matter. "I haven't been exactly truthful—completely honest—with your father."

"Oh, is that all," said Tey with a wave of her hand. "He knows that; he knows you haven't told him everything. Do you think he is that stupid?"

"Before I met him, perhaps I did. But now, no." Galen looked into her eyes, feeling that he could fall into them and be lost forever, and said haltingly, "There are other things you need to be told about me, terrible things."

Tey put a finger to his lips. "Hush. Tell me some other time; it's not important."

III

Gar Varro and Dio Saggi, one of Varro's foremen and perhaps his oldest friend, swam out to inspect the place where the crazed bull had smashed into the cows' pen.

Varro was feeling good. He had many reservations about Galen Yeager, yet the young Terran was clearly a man of superior talents and abilities; that Tey seemed to have fallen in love with him was not what he'd normally have wished for his daughter, but then she so far had shown little interest in the young men of his sea farm. And, quite frankly, Varro knew few of them could offer her much in terms of money or a prestigious family name. Even on Cousteau, people knew the names of Orin Yeager and Piet Voorhees, Galen's deceased father and grandfather.

Varro sighed. An air-sucker; a dry. That would go over great with his comrades and political allies, he thought ruefully. Still, Tey *did* seem to love him and he *had* saved her life. His, too, he reminded himself.

A fair man, Gar Varro grudgingly admitted to himself that his own dear wife's father had not exactly been impressed with his future son-in-law. The young Gar Varro had not seemed much of a prospect to Jac Pomma. Pomma was a wealthy man, and he was worried that Gar was interested in his daughter primarily for her inheritance. Varro shook his head. *Fathers and daughters!* he marveled to himself.

"We're almost there, Gar," said Dio, breaking into Varro's reverie.

"What? Oh, yes, good."

As a concession to the bulls' rambunctious character during the mating season, each man carried a spear gun. "Just like the old days, eh, Gar?" said Saggi. "Just like the times we would play hooky and chase woolly lobsters."

"Yes, Dio, just like the old days."

Dio Saggi laughed and said, "But we're men now, Gar. We don't have to ask our mothers' permissions to swim out past the barriers or to stay out as long as we want."

"That's right," agreed Varro. "But you know what, Dio? Once you don't have to ask, once you can do it anytime you want to, it isn't the same anymore."

"No, it isn't," Saggi said. "Nothing's the same anymore."

"We're the same, Dio."

"No, not even we are the same, Gar," Saggi said sadly.

"We're older and wiser, is that it?" asked Varro, grinning.

"No, that's not what I meant." Saggi shook his head as if in pain. "You've changed, Gar, you've changed a lot. Did you know that?" Saggi asked, his close-cropped, gray-streaked black hair waving minutely in the current.

The look on his old friend's face puzzled Varro; it seemed an odd mixture of affection and hatred. What had he done to anger Dio? he wondered. "What's the matter, Dio?"

His face hiding nothing now, Saggi unshouldered his weapon and pointed it at Gar Varro. "Please put down your spear gun, Gar."

Varro felt he had been slapped hard across the face. "Dio, what is this, a joke?"

"It's no joke, Gar." Saggi frowned and shook his head. "You are the brother I never had, the friend who knows me best. But you are also leading Cousteau to disaster. Suo Hann and others like her have the right idea."

"And what is that?"

"Revolution. It is the only answer. We must drive the Principate from Cousteau and take control of our destiny."

"You're mad!"

"No, my old friend; I'm not mad, I'm a patriot."

Varro snorted. "The father of his country—a murderer. A man who would stoop so low as to kill his oldest friend."

"For freedom. For the future of our planet."

"Orn shit!" spat Varro, slowly turning in the water and presenting his back to Saggi. "Go ahead, patriot, shoot me in the back."

"When it was decided to kill you," said Saggi, ignoring Varro's proffered back, "I accepted the task. I could not allow a stranger to kill someone I grew up with; it is my duty—that is why I volunteered."

While Saggi was preoccupied with justifying himself to his intended victim, Varro eased his knife out of its sheath on his utility belt. He knew he had little chance against a spear gun, especially one in the hands of so skilled a marksman as Dio, but he was unwilling to die without a struggle.

"Gar. Dee-yo." The shrill voice of Horatio, one of the boka, startled both men. Already in the process of turning back to face his would-be assassin, Varro kicked with his webbed feet and closed the distance between them.

Saggi had half-turned toward Horatio at the sound of the boka's voice before he realized his error. He had no time to aim, so he just pointed the spear gun in Varro's direction and fired.

Gar Varro felt a sharp, stinging pain as the spear passed partly through his left forearm. Undeterred, he lunged with his knife and drove the blade home in his former friend's throat. Saggi's eyes widened and he gasped out, "Hunngh!" as blood was pumped out his exhalatory slits.

Horatio, upset and disoriented, swam in circles sing-songing, "Bad, bad, bad, bad."

His arms outstretched and slowly rising and falling with the current in the water, Saggi, his dead eyes open as if in wonderment at what they were seeing, drifted backwards and away.

Varro looked at his wounded arm; the spear had penetrated through it and was trapped, half in and half out. Little blood was flowing from the wound, but Varro knew that he could easily bleed to death in a few minutes if he did not get medical help; he could fall into shock even faster.

"Horatio, come here," he ordered.

"Blood. Bad, bad," the boka said nervously.

"Yes, blood. Yes, bad," agreed Gar Varro. "Bad man. Bad Dio."

"Bad Dee-yo?" repeated Horatio dubiously.

"Tried to hurt me—tried to hurt Gar."

"Hurt Gar."

"But Horatio was a good boka; Horatio helped Gar. And Gar needs Horatio's help again."

"Horatio help Gar," the boka said proudly.

"Yes, Horatio help Gar back to the others. Gar needs help."

The boka swam over and allowed Varro to grasp his dorsal fin and hang on. "Horatio help Gar."

9

"I DIDN'T REALIZE THE SERIOUSNESS OF WHAT MY FATHER IS involved in before," Tey was saying. "Dio was his oldest friend. For him to attempt to assassinate my father is . . . is—"

"Yes, I know," said Galen soothingly. "I know."

Tey bit her lip and said, "And I thought I had to grow up when I took over running my father's farms!"

"You did," Galen said. "Now you've got to grow up politically."

Tey hugged him and kissed him, then looked him square in the eye and asked, "Are you going to divorce your wife?"

Caught by surprise by her abrupt shifting to a subject Galen was stunned to realize she knew anything about, he asked, "What do you think?"

"Don't get cute. Are you or aren't you?"

"Why . . . uh . . . of course."

Galen was chagrined to admit to himself that he *hadn't* thought about Adrianna and their empty marriage. Their families had engaged teams of lawyers expert in contract marriages before the documents were finalized and signed. A divorce would be neither easy nor inexpensive.

Tey nodded solemnly. "Then tell me who you are and why you're here. All of it. I want to know what sort of man I'm marrying."

"It's not a pretty story."

"I can take it."

"I guess you can," he said with admiration in his voice. "I want a nice stiff shot of omo and then I'll tell you the whole gruesome tale." His tone had been light and almost joking, but now it was as if a cloud had passed over his face: He looked grim and reluctant. "I'm going to tell you everything," he said as Tey brought him his drink.

"I don't need to know *everything*, do I?" she said, suddenly abandoning her earlier insistence on hearing it all.

"Maybe not," he admitted, "but I *need* to tell it—to perform an act of self-exorcism." He took her chin in his hand, turned her face toward his, and looked deep into her eyes. "If you change your mind about me after this, I'll understand. I haven't exactly been one of the good guys all my life."

He left nothing out. He told her about his early years first. Having never been off Cousteau, Tey's eyes opened in wonder at his recounting of his education at the University of Boswash, one of the great hive schools where one hundred and twenty thousand students attend classes in kilometer-high buildings. He told her about his studies in xenology and his field work on Faroom, Cleopatra, and Snow Mass.

Galen recalled his recruitment into the PrinSecPol by a wily old veteran named Harry Shadling, the one and only agent on Cleopatra. He told Tey that the first man he'd killed, three years later, was an arms dealer who double-crossed and murdered Harry.

"I was so overwhelmed by murderous rage," he explained haltingly, "that I just kept firing; I stood over him and emptied my full charge into his body, cutting him in half." He looked down for a moment, then up at Tey—who stared at him with a sad smile of understanding.

"It was both harder and easier to kill the next time," he continued. "Harder because it wasn't personally motivated, it wasn't revenge; easier because it's always easier to do something a second time, even taking a human life."

Explaining the scar her fingers had found, Galen told Tey about Martha Bellers, the woman who sank eight centimeters of knife blade into his back before he blew her head off. He told her about all the others, ending with the last—Arnold Stanko.

"There's one thing more," he began hesitantly. He dropped his gaze to the floor, unable to meet her eyes. "It's about Stanko and my threat to resign my position."

"Yes?"

"What made me so angry at Fedalf was really the disgust and loathing I felt for myself." He looked lost. "You see, the reason this minor bureaucrat's death affected me so much was my reaction after I got used to the idea that he had killed himself.

"I liked it," he said in a small voice. "It touched something unspeakable inside me. I was glad he was dead. Even worse, a part of me felt cheated—the part of me that wanted to kill him."

Finally done, Galen Yeager looked at Tey and said, "Not a very pretty story, huh? I won't blame you if you say you want nothing more to do with me."

Tey was silent for a moment; then she wrapped him up in a tender hug of understanding, forgiveness, and love.

"Tey, I—"

"Sh-h-h. Hush now. You've said enough. You aren't the monster you think you are."

With Tey holding him, Galen was surprised to feel his eyes filling up. Several tears rolled down his cheeks. "Some tough Terran assassin, huh?" he managed to get out. "Does this mean that you still—"

"Yes, you moron. It means I still love you and want you to be my husband."

"There's an old Terran custom that calls for the man to give his intended a token of his affection." Galen reached over to the stand beside the couch and picked up the small box he'd placed there earlier for just this moment. "This is for you, dearest Tey."

"What is it?"

"Open it and find out."

Gingerly, as if she were handling a razor fish, Tey lifted the small box's lid and peered inside. She gasped when she saw the ring's brilliantly colored stone. "It's beautiful," she said, hugging and kissing Galen.

"It is nothing compared to you," he laughed through her kisses. "Go ahead, try it on."

Tey slipped it on her finger and held her hand out, admiring the stone. "It fits," she said.

Remembering how and when he purchased it, Galen said, "It's destiny; you and this ring were meant for each other."

"Just like the two of us," she said, adding, "We've got to plan for your divorce, but that can wait until after."

"After? After what?"

"Guess," she said, snuggling in closer to him—if that was possible.

II

"What is it, Sam?" Galen asked.

"Another transmission from Fedalf."

"Good. It appears that we both have news for each other."

When the hookup had been completed and the descramblers activated, Fedalf wasted no time in getting to the point. "I've learned that Feller is going to ask his people to place Gar Varro under arrest. You should be able to intercept the transmission with the codes I've given you. The idiot thinks throwing Varro in prison will make him a can-do hero to the Magistracy." His eyes glittered. "Maybe it will."

When Fedalf looked at him expectantly, Galen said, "My turn?" and launched into an account of Dio Saggi's attempt to assassinate Varro. Then he waited for the message to warp across the galaxy and for Fedalf's reply.

"It's imperative, then, for you to convince Varro to accept the inevitability of Feller's orders; Varro will be safer in prison than walking around with a target painted on his back. Do you think you can sell him on the merits of allowing himself to be taken into custody?"

"I think so," Galen said. Then he was silent for a moment before adding, "I owe it to you to tell you the truth, Hashem. I'm going to tell Gar Varro everything." Having gotten his big announcement off his chest, Galen now fidgeted while the minutes passed as he waited for Fedalf's response.

"Everything?" Fedalf asked finally. "It would pain me enormously to sign an order for your liquidation, Galen. I've come to take a paternal interest in your accomplishments."

Ignoring Fedalf's hyperbole, Galen amended his statement. "No, not everything, Hashem. But enough."

Again minutes passed as the words and image were warped across the vast distance separating the two men via subspace.

Finally Fedalf asked, "Are you turning native, Galen? I can't have that. Not now, not when I need you to counter Feller's moves on Cousteau."

"Going native?" Galen's face wrinkled as he pondered that thought. "Yeah, I guess you could say that; I'm going to divorce Adrianna and marry Tey Varro."

"Mohammed's wives!"

"Don't mention *wives*," Galen said, forcing a smile. It faded and he said, "I'm tired of my fucking job." He stared earnestly into the 'sender. "Don't worry, though—I'm going to do what I can here first. I won't jump ship between ports."

"I suppose I should give thanks for my blessings, no matter how small they might be," Fedalf said, recovering his equilibrium.

"You're taking this all rather calmly," Galen observed.

"You are my best agent," Fedalf told him. When Galen shrugged, he insisted, "Well, you are. And you would not be so good at what you do if you did not like it so much." He sipped from his omnipresent cup of coffee. "Much can happen before you sign the marriage contract."

"Don't hold your breath," said Galen, reaching out to break the connection.

When Fedalf's image had dissolved into nothingness, Galen shivered. Why did his superior's skepticism get to him? The answer, which he did not wish to admit to himself, was that he also wondered if his new relationship could survive the stresses of the next few months, weeks, or even days.

Sam Houston swam effortlessly through the pristine water. He could not summon up any memories of swimming in his old life, but that was nothing unusual; there was much he did not remember. Actually, he had gradually recalled more and more about the old days, the days before his death and long, dreamless sleep.

Just like Han Solo, he thought. Then: *Who the hell's Han Solo?* His recollections were just ragged fragments, shards of images, sounds, tastes, smells, tactile sensations, faces without names, and names without faces—like "Han Solo." *Maybe he was a hol-vee star,* Sam mused.

His old self, his lost identity, was a translucent Peeping Tom hiding in the shadows of his mind. Like a cartoon character trying to catch a glimpse of a gremlin, a ghost, or a shadow by suddenly whirling and trapping it in his hungry gaze, he attempted fruitlessly to see any part of this mysterious watcher from afar.

If what Dr. Bussot and Galen had told him was true, and he had no reason to doubt their veracity, he would never recall his previous life. There was a good chance, however, that more and more of his old personality would assert itself; he was already more than the sum of his limited memory and his more recent imprinting by the Foundation. He was a person.

Of course I am, he told himself. *I'm Sam Houston.*

III

The subspace communicator was chiming.

Galen wiped the film of sweat from his face and wondered, "What's the humidity today, a hundred and twenty percent?" The compact communications console, which unfolded out of a small case, continued its persistent and annoying clamor for attention. Since Galen had begun to rely more and more on Sam and his special circuitry to receive and decode encrypted subspace messages, he was a bit rusty operating the equipment.

"Yeah, yeah, I'm getting there," Galen said, fumbling with the settings and switches. He glanced at the sender identification number, automatically entering it for the machine's accept/reject procedure.

As the console hummed reassuringly and relays deep in space began opening, Galen gasped and stared at the caller I.D. Although he had assumed the call was from Fedalf, he suddenly realized that it was *not* Fedalf's number. It was a number he'd never seen before.

"Well, whoever it is, he or she sure as hell has *my* number," he said, coding in the final digits that would accept the transmission.

The startlingly realistic holographic image that materialized before Galen's astonished eyes was the interior of a room that had been designed to impress and intimidate.

For a moment Galen ignored the man behind the calculatedly large desk and took in the decor. On the walls behind and to the left of the desk were holographic scenes of various Legion triumphs: the landing field where the revolt on

Alpha C was finally crushed, the attack against the strikers at Armstrong City on Luna, and a view of the death camp at Zelmka.

Besides these successes and horrors, the motif of power was further stressed by a communications console that was, Galen thought, too elaborate-looking for the functions it fulfilled—unless you considered its main function was to impress.

The Torgon wool carpet that covered what little of the floor that Galen could see was itself meant to demonstrate the ruthlessness of its owner: All other such remnants of the Legion's subjugation of the Torgon humanoids had been destroyed so as to erase from the conscience of the Principate its occasional barbarism. Galen mused to himself that if he were a ten-year-old boy he would certainly be impressed. As it was, he found it difficult not to laugh.

The man who pointedly ignored Galen, sitting behind his magnificently appointed desk and straight-backed chair while he attended to something on top of the desk, was the Director of the Terran Legion, Nevin Feller.

Feller was a big man with a keen mind behind a dull face. His nose, slightly bulbous and cratered by large pores like the surface of Cousteau's moon, gave him a homey, comfortable look.

Looking at Feller's visage, Galen decided it was a face which could cover any sort of personality if you did not believe the nose. It was the face of a kindly uncle, a jolly yet drab man who might sell shoes or insurance. But Galen knew that the man who wore his ugly face as a mask was not a Kindly Uncle but a Big Brother.

Galen was aware what the galactic *Who's Who* said about Feller, and also knew that most of it was bullshit. The truth was that Feller had joined the Cadre twenty-seven years ago from the regular army, after General Selmon A. Hatch was convicted of treason for plotting to kill his commanding officer in a localized coup attempt. Feller had been on Hatch's staff, but he and two fellow officers were exonerated of any complicity in the plot. Those who sat in judgment of them could find no real evidence to tie the three career officers to the attempt; it had helped that Hatch was certifiably insane.

The stain ran deep, however, and Feller knew that a dark cloud would linger over him for as long as he remained in the regular army. The Legion, Galen was certain, was probably delighted to acquire his services; Feller's personality traits meshed nicely with their requirements.

As director of the Legion, Feller wore the triple-crown insignia on his uniform indicating allegiance to the ruling Magistracy. In reality, Galen knew, whatever allegiance Feller felt was strictly for himself.

Galen found himself staring at the director's uniform. Galen found most uniforms, with their star clusters, rainbow-hued battle ribbons, and eruptions of aiguillettes, more comic than impressive. Feller's was no exception. *Why don't these guys realize how ridiculous they look?* he asked himself with a shake of his head.

Finally, the director, putting aside whatever it was he had been pretending to be busy with, looked up and said, "You are Galen Yeager, I presume."

"Yes, I am . . . er, *sir.*" Galen waited out the short transmission time.

"Good. Can you can give me one good reason I should not have you killed?"

"I beg your pardon, Director Feller?" Galen was all bewildered innocence.

"Don't play dumb with me, Yeager," barked Feller. "Someone fingered my people on Cousteau. A couple of them have been politely shown the door after spending months or even years infiltrating sensitive jobs or organizations. Others have been watched, followed, and otherwise put under surveillance."

"And you think I had something to do with it?"

"I *know* it was you, Yeager. It had to be you. There's no one else." He put a finger to one side of his bulbous nose and rubbed it thoughtfully. "Though how you got the names of all my operatives on Cousteau, I don't know yet," he conceded.

"Believe me, sir," began Galen earnestly, "I haven't a clue who your people here might be. If their names were handed over to someone, I wasn't the one who did it."

Galen was growing more confident by the minute. Feller suspected him, of course—he *was* the obvious suspect. But from the way the director was talking, Galen knew he hadn't a shred of evidence that tied Galen to the disclosures.

The cocky sonofabitch thinks all he has to do is pop up in my room with his trophies behind him and I'll be so scared that

I'll drop a load in my pants and confess everything. Well, think again, Torquemada!

"Humph," snorted Feller. Then his eyes narrowed and seemed to bore through Galen. "Why do you look so familiar to me, Yeager?"

"Well, apart from my holo in the filecube you have in front of you"—when Feller blinked, Galen knew he'd rung the bell at least once—"your people tried to recruit me as a double agent a few years back."

"A double agent?"

Now it was Galen's turn to get a don't-try-to-kid-a-kidder look on his face. "Yes, to continue as an agent of the PrinSecPol while secretly passing along everything to the Legion."

"Too bad you didn't accept. You might have a brighter future ahead of you, Yeager."

Galen just shrugged.

Just then Feller's assistant, a smooth character named Harrison Ye, entered the holo and whispered something into the director's ear. Galen didn't know why exactly, but Ye's sudden materialization within the image unnerved him.

Feller nodded as Ye withdrew. "You may still have a bright future, Yeager—or may I call you Galen?" Without waiting for Galen's permission to use his first name, Feller said, "Citizen Ye has convinced me to repeat my original offer."

"Sorry. The answer's still the same."

"Pity," said Feller with feigned sadness. "I rarely make such an offer twice; I never make it a third time. So be it."

"Is that everything?" asked Galen.

"Everything?" Feller seemed surprised by Galen's question. "Yes, that is everything. I doubt I shall ever see you again, Galen Yeager. Alive, that is." He reached out and broke the connection.

"Bouncing baby Jesus!" exclaimed Galen as Sam entered the room, having caught the tail end of the conversation.

Without saying a word, Sam poured Galen a generous bourbon and water over ice. Holding the glass delicately, he carried it over and placed it in front of Galen and then sat down opposite him.

"Thanks, partner," Galen said as he picked up the glass and took a sip. "Ah, real Kentucky rocket fuel."

"So how did your meeting with Gilbert O'Sullivan go?"

Galen was puzzled at first, then realized that Sam meant the director. "Feller *does* look remarkably like a comic operetta major domo, doesn't he?"

"That or a doorman."

His smile slowly fading away, Galen stared into the glass and then set it down on the surface of the coffee table. "To answer your question: the same as always."

Sam threw back his head and laughed a big, hearty laugh. "That poorly, eh?"

Galen moved to the edge of the sofa, put his hands on either side of his glass in front of him, rotated it back and forth, and finally picked it up and took another sip. "I have a feeling things are about to get hot enough on Cousteau to bring the oceans to the boiling point."

"Who do you think is going to light the fire under the pot?"

"Feller's dropping hints it's going to be him," said Galen. "But I don't know."

"You're putting your money on Suo Hann, then, I take it?"

Galen peered at Sam over the rim of his glass. "And how did you come up with that?"

"I'm not just a pretty face."

"You know," mused Galen, "Feller never even mentioned you during our little talk."

"Good," said Sam. He frowned. "That is, I think so."

Galen Yeager sat on the end of a pier, staring thoughtfully out to sea and watching as the disk of the dying sun began to disappear as if the sea were swallowing it bit by bit, extinguishing the light. As the sun dipped below the horizon, a last flash of yellow-white light visible, Galen took out a happy stick and lit it, drawing the smoke deep into his lungs and sighing. He knew he should be talking with Sam, making plans, but he wanted to be alone with his thoughts.

Startled by a splash in the sea, Galen peered downward. He recognized the silver torpedo shape as one of the sea farm's boka. The boka was quickly joined by several others, all chorusing, "Gay-len, Gay-len."

"Hi, guys," he said, surprised at how much their appearance had amused him despite his resolute desire to be serious and reflective. "What's up?"

"Swim, swim," they said in unison.

"Swim?" he asked dubiously. "Now? It's almost dark and besides, I have no exchanger."

"Exchanger here, Gay-len," said one of the boka he recognized as Rachel.

"Exchanger *where*?" he asked before seeing the small pail held by its handle in the mouth of the boka called Nelson. "What's in the pail?"

"Exchanger, Gay-len," Rachel said with a hint of impatience in her voice. "Gay-len put on, follow."

"Gay-len put on, follow," the other boka chorused.

"All right, all right," Galen said as he tossed his happy stick into the sea. He reached down, grabbed the handle of the pail, and peered at the translucent shape of the exchanger inside. Reaching into the pail, he withdrew the exchanger with all the enthusiasm of someone picking up a mass of phlegm.

"Gay-len put on."

"Let's not rush this," Galen said. He manipulated the tentacles and the slimy body of the exchanger and then lay down on his back. He took a deep breath, announcing, "No matter how many times I do this, I'm *never* going to get used to it." The boka laughed—a chittering, high-pitched squeal of pleasure he'd heard before when something struck them as funny.

Guiding the tendrils into and down his nostrils, he seated the rubbery exchanger, sat up, and pushed himself off the end of the pier. The sea closed around him. Another boka had flippers for him, which he put on. "Okay, 'Galen follow'—now lead on."

After perhaps ten minutes of serious swimming, the boka led Galen toward a distant glow. As he got closer, he could see that the light was coming from a dozen glowfish, confined by exquisitely fine netting. The glowfish were positioned within an underwater garden full of multicolored plants and rocks, some slightly luminescent. In the garden's center, a figure floated, waiting.

The figure resolved itself into Tey. As she beckoned to him to come closer, he could see that she was totally nude. "Hello, my love," she said with a grin. "Like to have a little underwater fun?"

Galen's mouth would have dropped open if the exchanger hadn't been across it. He heard the tinkling laughter of the boka as, their job successfully over, they turned and swam away. "Well?" Tey persisted.

"I . . . ah . . . ah—"

"You can't really say you've made love on Cousteau until you've made love underwater," she told him, swimming up to him and shocking him even more by thrusting her tongue into his ear.

"Ah . . . I . . . ah . . ."

"I like a man who knows when to shut up," she said, taking his hand and drawing him down to a bed of sea moss.

Galen Yeager stopped weighing the fate of Cousteau, and no more that night did he think about anything other than the lusty young woman who gave him her love and her body.

10

LOOKING AROUND THE SMALL, SANDY SPIT OF LAND THAT BARE-
ly measured eight by five meters, Varro decided it was a pretty
poor excuse for an island. "But it'll do for my purposes," he
murmured. Actually, had Varro given it any thought, he would
have realized that there were many such islands in his holdings.
To normal humans, they'd have been infuriatingly inefficient.
For Cousteaueans, at home in the sea, the islands' size was of
no real consequence; they could swim from island to island.

With his back against the trunk of the single facci tree that
sprang from the sorry soil, Varro shaded his eyes against the
sun and stared across the water, looking for Rho's tiny personal
sailboat. Remembering its diminutive size, he assumed it would
be difficult to see with all the glare off the water. He glanced
at his watch and sighed patiently.

Finally, when he was beginning to doubt that Rho would
appear, he spotted the sleek little craft cutting across the sea
toward him.

When Rho reached the tiny island, he jumped out of the
sailboat and pulled it up onto the sandy soil of the shore. With
an unreadable expression on his face, he approached Varro's
resting spot and stuck out his hand. Varro rose and they shook
hands; neither man imbued the act with any enthusiasm.

"It was good of you to come, Rho. Good of you to agree to see me," Varro said.

"I thought of Dio as my best friend—just as you thought of him as yours. He would have wished me to have this conversation with you."

Varro nodded. "I did not want to kill him, Rho. He . . . It was something the circumstances dictated."

"If what you said happened is the truth"—he put up his hand to show that he was not questioning Varro's account of the incident—"then you had no choice if you wished to live."

Again Varro nodded. "You are good to say that."

"Let's sit down," Rho said, indicating the meager patch of shade provided by the tree. When both had settled in, crossing their legs, Rho searched Varro's face and asked, "What is it you want of me, Gar?"

"We have both professed to be Dio's friend," he began diffidently. "Something happened to that friendship, *my* friendship with Dio. Without the necessary maintenance even the best of relationships require, it withered." Varro looked at Rho's fixed expression as if expecting to see a frown or other sign of disagreement. When none was forthcoming, he continued.

"We grew apart. I became a politician and he the friend I left behind." Varro paused, seemingly at a loss for how to proceed. "What I want to know, Rho, what I *need* to know, is how and why Dio came to choose the path he followed. Why did he decide to follow Suo Hann and not me? Why did he choose violence?"

"Is it such a mystery to you?"

"Yes, it is, Rho! It *is* a mystery to me!"

Rho pulled a small flask from his utility belt, unscrewed the top, and offered it to his companion. Varro declined it with a shake of his head. Shrugging, Rho took a long pull himself, wiped his lips, recapped the flask, and put it away.

"You ask too much, Gar. Dio did not wake up one day and say, 'I think that Gar and his party are no longer capable of negotiating with the Principate; no longer capable of working toward our eventual independence.' No, it wasn't as simple as that."

Rho looked out across the sea. "It was a thousand little things." He pointed at a water-carved rock jutting out into the surf. "See that rock, Gar? That one that the power of the sea has worn away?"

"Yes, of course."

"It was like that. It was the day-in, day-out humiliations of being under the thumb of the Magistracy. It was the knowledge of our second-class citizenship, of our benighted position within the Principate; it was the insulting and draining tax burden. It was no *one* thing, Gar. It was *everything*."

Varro put his hands to his chest. "Am I not a Cousteauean? Do you think I am a stranger to these things? Did Dio think that?"

"At the end, yes," said Rho. "He did not think that you were evil, just that you had unwittingly sold us out in the name of moderation. In the name of gradual change. Evolution, not revolution."

"Things *were* changing," insisted Varro. "I could see it, almost taste it. Then . . . Then Suo Hann came along."

"If not her, someone else," Rho said.

Rho leaned toward Varro and said, "Look, Gar, you must understand one thing: To the slave pulling on the oar, 'some day' is too far away. 'Some day' is not a realistic goal. The truth is, the seasons come and go, our planet revolves around the sun, and one grows old. Before you know it you are a hundred years old and you die. That is 'some day'!"

"That's what Dio thought?"

"Yes."

"And the others?"

"I can't speak for everyone."

"But . . .?"

"Many, if not all, of the people I have spoken to lately feel the same way. The time for going to the Magistracy with our heads bowed and asking politely for our independence is long past."

"We have no weapons!" Varro shouted. "Cousteau has no starships, no armies! We are a water world and we do not even possess a navy!"

"What need have we of starships when we have our bodies?" Rho asked rhetorically. There was a look of quiet resolve on his face. "There are almost a million of us. Each one of us is a potential time bomb. I mean that literally."

"My God!"

"Suo Hann has said that we will be free. If the Magistracy and the Principate refuse, we shall destroy their ships, their centers of government, and their hive cities until they understand our terrible resolve." His eyes glittered. "We will crack Armstrong City's dome if we must."

Varro sensed the thick, hot air, the rough bark of the facci tree against his back, and the sand between his toes. He sensed all these very real things at the same time he felt as if he were inside a nightmare. Everything he had worked for was crashing down around him.

After Galen intercepted Feller's coded orders ordering Gar Varro's arrest, he asked Tey and her father to join him in the living room.

"Where's Sam?" Varro asked, looking around the room.

"He went for a swim."

"Oh."

"What happens now?" asked Tey. Galen told her and Varro about Feller's orders.

"My God!" Tey exclaimed.

"Yes, I know," Galen explained, "but I think it's for the best. After what Dio tried to do, I can't vouch for Gar's safety. As odd as it may sound, I think your father will be better off in custody."

He took Tey's hand. "And, according to Feller, Legion regulars were placed on Norland, Midland, and Gasir this week. I fear that a contingent of soldiers will be arriving here at the sea farm any time now to execute Feller's order."

"Don't say 'execute'—it makes me nervous," Varro said, forcing a smile. Then, more seriously: "I'm willing to go along with all this, but I'd like to know what it's supposed to accomplish."

"Fair enough," said Galen. "First, as I've said, it gets you out of the way. Feller won't dare to exec—ah . . . liquidate you because too many people already know or suspect that Suo Hann's organization is behind the assassinations and terrorist attacks.

"Second, you'll become a martyr and a rallying point. Dead, you're a martyr but not a figure people can immediately get behind." Galen smiled and added, "Also, I don't want to begin my new life with the death of my father-in-law on my conscience."

Varro got up, walked to a cabinet, withdrew an energy rifle, and plopped it down on his desk in front of Galen and Tey.

"It seems to me that getting into a prison is much easier than getting out. Wouldn't it be better for everyone, not just me, if I refuse to allow myself to be arrested in the first place?"

"It might be," Galen allowed.

"But you think I should go through with it?"

"Yes."

"Why?"

"If you should flee and go into hiding, simply drop out of sight, Nevin Feller is probably prepared to arrest anyone and everyone who ever had anything to do with you. Once he has them in his clutches, I'd expect him to torture them until someone breaks and reveals your hiding place."

"What if they didn't know my hiding place?"

"They're dead anyway."

Varro pulled open a desk drawer and withdrew a bottle of omo and three glasses. He filled the glasses and gave Galen and Tey one each. "Here's to prison memoirs."

I'm getting to be a regular fishboy myself, Sam thought as he went for his second swim in as many days. This time he chose a more adventurous direction, swimming away from the reefs and barrier islands toward the open sea.

"Sam!" several excited boka voices called to him.

He stopped swimming and turned around, his weight causing him to slowly sink toward the ocean floor. "Who's that calling Sam I am?" he asked gruffly, waiting for the playful boka to catch up to and surround him.

"It's us," one of the boka told him seriously.

"Oh, yes—the fishfaces," he said, continuing to sink slowly toward the sea floor. Something that had been hiding nearby burst from the sand and disappeared in a murky cloud.

"Fishfaces . . . tee-hee-hee," one of them laughed, bubbles streaming from his air hole. "You funny!"

For some reason Sam hadn't yet figured out, the boka found him endlessly interesting. He couldn't get within five meters of the sea without one of them poking his head up out of the water to encourage him to come on in and join them.

"Who do we have here today?" he asked. He was beginning to see subtle differences in their coloring, their size, even their voices, but he still could not tell one from another without prompting.

"We here today is Nemo, Rachel, Ariel, and Jacques," answered one of them in her high-pitched voice. Sam knew the boka was a she because of her slightly smaller size.

"You are Rachel?"

"Ariel."

"I was close," Sam said. Then he asked, "So, my finny friends, what's up?" When the four boka gazed upwards, toward the surface of the sea, he quickly amended that to, "I mean, what's going on? Or did you swim out to meet me just so you could keep me company?"

"Yes," squeaked Ariel. "To keep Sam cump-knee."

"I'm touched," Sam said, "as you can see from the tear in my eye."

The boka didn't know what Sam was talking about, but already they knew him well enough to guess that he was joking. They trilled in appreciation of Sam's jape, and then two of them darted up to the surface for a quick breath of air.

Just as the Cousteaueans were altered humans, the boka were altered dolphins. Besides speech, they too had been given highly efficient lungs. Unlike the Terran dolphins they were descended from, the boka could extract the oxygen they needed from the water; but when they worked and played near the surface, they took advantage of the opportunity to get the oxygen directly. It was only at depth that they breathed water and their blowholes became exhalatory and vocal orifices alone.

"You guys are too easy," Sam said, smiling.

"Sam swim with us?" one of the returnees asked, while the other two now filled their lungs. Sam knew that a boka could make a lungful of oxygen-rich surface air last a long time.

"Sure," Sam said. "Just try to keep up with me."

"We keep up with Sam. We follow Sam," said Jacques, his bright eyes regarding the android cheerfully.

"Why?"

" 'Cause we like Sam," explained Ariel.

"Yes-s-s," agreed Nemo.

"Just how much do you like Sam?" the human android asked.

"Lots," replied Jacques, watching Sam's feet touch bottom.

Ignoring the distraction, Sam asked, "Enough to show me around?"

" 'Course!" exclaimed Ariel.

"Yeah!" seconded Nemo and the others.

"Let's go, then," said Sam. He touched a canister attached to his belt and a series of small bags filled with air, providing him with much-needed buoyancy.

The boka took up positions on either side of Sam and the quintet propelled themselves through the water with powerful strokes of their flukes and flippers.

"Sam swim good for hue-man," Rachel observed as a huge ray glided by, its long streamer of a tail passing right in front of them.

"Would it amaze you, or even scare you, if I confessed to you guys that I'm a machine, not a man?"

"Tee-hee-hee!" they laughed, tickled by Sam's obvious joke.

With Rachel leading the way, Sam and the talkative boka swam farther and farther from the island. Sam's webbed gloves and large flippers did not make him the equal of the boka, but he was again made aware of how much such aids helped him adapt to this new environment.

Engrossed with the act of swimming, Sam paid scant attention to the rapid dropoff of the shelf that encircled the island. Before he knew it, the bottom was too far below to be seen.

"It's getting deep," Sam observed.

"Yeah," agreed Jacques. "Deep."

"Do you guys like deep water?"

"We like deep water," Nemo answered affirmatively.

"Lots of different fish live there, I suppose."

"Lots of fish," Ariel confirmed.

Sam just grinned. *You guys sure aren't sparkling conversationalists, are you?* Sam realized he wasn't being fair. The boka did have fairly large brains; they *were* intelligent—as intelligent as humans, in their own way. But that was the catch: in their own way. Boka were more sensual, more attuned to the physical world, than human beings. Sam vowed to take into account their "differentness" whenever he found himself becoming patronizing about them. As early as the twentieth century, experiments with dolphins had confirmed not only their intelligence but also their otherness—their "alien" mindsets.

Just then Rachel nudged Sam with her blunt nose. "Hey, look at them two bass."

Sam looked to his right and saw two enormous sea bass languidly stroking through the water. They weren't really sea bass, of course, but whenever a native fish had closely enough

resembled a Terran breed, it got stuck with the original's name.
Must make taxonomy a bitch, Sam decided.

When the bass had disappeared, Sam followed the talkative
boka deeper and deeper into the darkening sea. Sam switched
visual inputs when the light from above grew too feeble to
provide adequate illumination.

Sam had thought the sea bass to be large fish, but the creatures
that roamed this nether plane between the surface area and the
truly deep portions of the sea were discomfortingly huge.

"Sam having fun?" asked Nemo.

"It's better than a sharp stick in the eye."

"Tee-hee-hee."

Ariel seemed to hyperventilate—*Is that possible underwater?*
Sam wondered—and then plunged down into the murky water,
quickly disappearing from sight.

Sam wondered what was going on even as his sensitive ears
picked up faint echoes of her range-finding chirps. "Where did
Ariel go?" he asked the others.

"You see soon," replied Jacques.

They dove into an abyss. Sam sensed the pressure increasing
the deeper down they ventured. If Sam knew his Cousteauean
geography, they were swimming down into one of the great
globe-girdling trenches. As rapid and dramatic as the ocean
floor's dropoff seemed to him, Sam knew that this particular trench, the Hobart Trench, was more V- than U-shaped.
Instead of plunging straight down at a ninety-degree angle for
kilometers, the trench's walls were a more reasonable fifty or
sixty degrees.

As they left the sun behind, one of the boka asked Sam, "Sam
can still see?"

"Yes, Nemo."

The boka was pleased Sam had learned to recognize him and
the others. "Good, Sam can see."

"Can *you* still see?"

"Yes-s-s," replied Rachel, "but not with our eyes."

That's right—their sonar. When he listened for it, Sam's
superior hearing could pick up the chirps and squeaks they
emitted and the faint echoes that returned.

"Hey," said Jacques, his sonar picking up several familiar
shapes.

"Yes," agreed Rachel. "You an' Ariel get them."

"Get what?" Sam asked Rachel as Jacques and Ariel disappeared into the gloom.

"You see," Nemo said.

I'm sure glad I don't have a thing about snakes, Sam thought as something long and sinuous wiggled past them in the cool dark water.

Sam quickly saw what the boka were talking about. Several globes of light materialized below them, heading in their direction. "What the . . . ?"

"They glowfish," Nemo explained. "You give food an' they follow you."

Sam conjured up an image of the two boka regurgitating a sardine or two for the hungry glowfish and then put the unpleasant picture out of his mind. *That'd put me right off my feed—if I ate, that is.*

As the balls of light came closer, Sam could see Jacques and Ariel's sleek torsos in the light provided by the six glowfish. *They must be host to colonies of light-emitting algae. That, or—*

"C'mon," insisted Rachel. "We go. We see more better now."

"We go," agreed Sam.

Sam's finely tuned senses noted the change in temperature as they continued their slow downward spiral; it was gradually growing colder and colder. It was nothing to him, but he wondered about the boka.

"Hey, guys, isn't it getting a little cool?"

"Yeah." Rachel nodded her head, the bubbles that produced her voice slipping out of her air hole. As if they reminded her to breathe, she gulped water.

Sam assumed that there was less and less oxygen to extract as the pressure of the water increased. Combined with the cold, that made him a little worried about the physical well-being of the boka.

"We 'bout where we coming," Jacques said.

"Going," corrected Ariel.

The question on Sam's lips was never voiced as he was silenced by the eerie, greenish glow that had appeared far below them.

"What's that light?" he asked.

Jacques, his sharp, collielike snout opened in a grin that looked vaguely sinister in the faint illumination provided by the glowfish, bobbed his head and said, "The thing." Sam could hear the quotation marks.

As they continued their cautious descent, Sam saw that the object was still many, many meters beneath them, perhaps even at an unattainable depth. After that first glance, Sam realized that it had initially appeared closer than it actually was. Its size fostered the illusion it was nearer to them. *It must be immense,* Sam thought.

Since the bottom of the trench was still many kilometers below them, Sam supposed that whatever it was, the object must be resting on a rock ledge jutting out from one of the trench's walls.

"The thing," Sam said. *Now* I'm *doing it!* he thought.

Actually, Sam knew, in years long past, back on Old Earth, people wouldn't have called it a thing, they'd have called it something else.

They'd have called it a flying saucer.

Galen found the trip out to the outer islands to be exhilarating: the *Bec II* slicing through the blue-green water, the endless blue sky, and the cooling ocean breezes acting as an antidote to the blazing sun. The outer, or rim, islands were home to several dozen families headed by tenants or retired ex-employees of Gar Varro's farming operation; it was Varro's wish to speak to as many of his people as he could before surrendering himself to the authorities on Bandar.

"You have all this," Galen said to Varro above the whistling of the wind across the sails. "Why did you become a politician?"

"So that Tey might have it one day," Varro replied. "It is all too easy to despoil a paradise in the name of commerce and progress. I want my people to have the best life possible while keeping the treasures they already possess." After a pause, he asked, "Does that answer your question?"

Galen nodded. His eyes stinging from the salt spray, he leaned closer to Varro and said, "I will do what I can to make your job a little easier."

It was Varro's turn to nod. "Thank you, Galen. If only we could get the Magistracy to share your sentiments."

"Maybe if we got them out here on the *Bec II*," said Galen, grinning.

"Maybe."

*   *   *

By Terran standards, Galen thought, the people of the outer islands lived a rude, basic existence. His view of some of the ramshackle houses, half above and half in the water, reminded him of the Terran slums of St. Petersburg, Osaka, New Delhi, and Greater Los Angeles, the megalopolis that sprawled along the NorAm coast from the baja to Victoria Island.

But first appearances were deceiving. On closer inspection, Galen could see that while they were old and weatherbeaten, the homes were tidy and well cared for. The small circular windows gleamed from recent scrubbings, and the walkways were bordered by bright flowers and carefully manicured shrubbery. The people who lived here may have lacked money, but not self-respect.

As they approached a row of houses, separated from each other by thirty or forty meters for privacy, children peeked out shyly.

"That's odd," said Varro. "Usually they're all over me, begging for sweets and the little gifts I bring them."

"Maybe they're afraid of the bogeyman you brought with you," Galen observed.

"Oh, yes. I forgot about the terrible Terran monster I have loosed among the people."

Galen grinned and made a little bow. Then he cursed, saying, "Damn it! I hate that."

"Hate what?" asked Varro.

"I hate it when a big drop of sweat runs into my eye."

One of Varro's tenants came out of a rude house precariously perched on plasteel pilings, half above water and half below, and greeted his benefactor with a hearty "Gar, my old friend."

"Edo, how are you?" Varro called out to his former employee. "You look well."

The ancient amphibian stepped down onto the crumbling plascrete walkway that connected his home to the shore and limped slowly toward Varro and his party. "I am too old and tired to believe your well-intentioned lies, Gar," he said. "My aches and pains multiply by the day." He stopped halfway across the walkway and pointed a gnarled finger in their direction and intoned, "Take my advice, Gar: When your body begins to betray you, swim out into the Great Trench and call for the godwhale to come and take you. Getting old is an abomination!"

"Edo, that is no way to speak to Master Varro!" scolded an old woman from the doorway. "He has not come all this way to listen to a decrepit old man complain about his lost youth."

"Yes, dear," the old man said wearily. He made a face at Varro. Despite himself, Galen laughed.

"Ho, Gar," the old man said, shuffling toward them again. "You have brought an air-sucker with you, eh?" He cocked his head at Galen. "Are you a Principate septopus, young man, reaching out with your tentacles to take what little remains to us? Have you come to raise our tariffs and snatch the food from the mouths of our children?"

"Tell your friend he's free to say what's on his mind," Galen said. His admiration for Cousteaueans and their in-your-face attitudes continued to grow.

"Edo, you haven't changed a bit," laughed Varro, crossing the last few meters separating them and wrapping the oldster up in a hug.

"Nor you, Gar," Edo said. "You and Dio are still the same rapscallions you were when you two were children, mewling and puking like seal pups." He pulled back from Varro's embrace and looked around. "So where is Dio? Did he not accompany you? I'm still man enough to give him a good thrashing with my stick if he thinks he's too much of a big shot to come visit an old friend."

Varro swallowed and said, "Dio is dead, Edo."

"Dead?" The old man's face registered confusion.

"Yes." Varro licked his lips nervously. "He tried to kill me, Edo."

Edo's rheumy brown eyes widened in disbelief and shock. "Tell me this is not true, Gar. Tell me you are joking."

"I would if I could, Edo. I'm afraid it's no joke."

"But why . . . ?"

"Suo Hann," said Varro simply.

"Ah, yes: Suo Hann," said the old man with a knowing nod of his head.

Galen saw a troubled look on Varro's face. *That's not the response you expected, is it, Gar?*

"What?" one of Varro's guards said.

Galen turned to see the young bodyguard put his hand to the side of his head in a gesture Galen had often seen those with internal comlinks use.

"What is it?" Gar Varro asked his man.

"There are several large floaters coming this way."

"Floaters? Who can they be?" asked Varro, exchanging a look with Galen.

"They are transmitting Legion recognition signals."

"Damn it!" said Varro. "Already."

"Which way are they coming?" Galen queried.

"Huh?" The bodyguard didn't understand the question.

"Are they coming from the farm's main harbor and docking area or from somewhere else?"

The guard spoke into his comlink and quickly received a reply. "They're coming across the open sea."

"Hmmm. Isn't that interesting?"

"What difference does it make which way they're coming?" wondered Varro.

"I would've thought they'd land at the farm proper," explained Galen, "not come directly here. The fact that they did so means they know your whereabouts to the centimeter."

"How could they know that?" asked the guard.

Galen's shoulders rose, then fell.

"Someone is keeping track of my movements for them," Varro told the guard.

"Shall I prepare a defense?" the bodyguard asked.

"Don't be stupid," snapped Galen. "They're Legion regulars."

"The air-sucker is right," agreed another bodyguard. "Besides," he added, putting his hand to the side of his head, "they're almost here."

PART THREE

ADVANCES AND RETREATS

11

FEELING ITCHY AND DRY, TEY TOLD HERSELF, *I'VE GOT TO GET back into the water soon.*

She stepped out onto the veranda that fanned out from the front of the house, shaded her eyes with her hand, and looked out across the flat, waveless sea.

"Where is everyone?" Tey asked Wye Hassa, one of her father's new bodyguards. Like several other young men, Hassa had stepped forward, volunteering to help swell Varro's security forces in the wake of the assassination attempt. Had Tey thought about it, she might have wondered why so few young males had answered the call for assistance. That Suo Hann was proving more attractive never occurred to her.

Having just finished applying a cool and slippery oil to his skin, Hassa was now doing something similar to a wicked-looking slug-thrower. Both the young volunteer and his plasteel weapon glistened menacingly.

"Have you forgotten already?" Hassa asked sternly. "Your father is on the rim islands, fulfilling his role as the economic and moral leader of his people."

Tey didn't know what to make of such a pompous statement. Hassa took his new assignment very seriously. "I'm not sure I like that. You make him sound like Moses. He's just a farmer paying a visit to his tenants."

Hassa wiped the excess oil from the slug-thrower with a cloth. "He is no Moses," he admitted finally. "But he *is* more than a gentleman farmer relying on the hard work and initiative of his tenants."

"Why aren't you with him?"

"Because he asked me to keep an eye on you," Hassa said, holding the barrel of the disassembled gun up to his eye and peering through it at the sky. Apparently satisfied with what he saw, he put the barrel down and picked up the shell chambers and a long, thin brush which he thrust through the seven openings, pushing and pulling vigorously.

"My father is the one who needs a bodyguard, not me." Tey met Hassa's eyes, challenging him to respond.

"I agree," he said, obliging her. "I would much rather be by your father's side than sitting here playing the role of a babysitter."

"I am not a baby!" Tey responded hotly.

"No. You're more like a spoiled teenaged brat."

Her anger disappearing as quickly as it had appeared, Tey almost smiled in response to his words. She understood the source of Wye's annoyance and frustration. With the exception of her father, it seemed that all of the young males were angry about her alliance with an air-sucker. It was more than just the fact of the situation, it was also her open flaunting of her emotions.

"Where is . . . ah, where are our two visitors from Terra?"

"The air-sucker is with your father," Hassa grudgingly told her. "As for the artificial . . ." He gestured broadly at the sea. "He's somewhere out there."

"Alone?"

"Why not?"

"I suppose you're right." Tey ran her hand up and down one of her arms, absently noting how dry and scaly her skin felt.

Hassa held out the tube of unguent he'd used on himself. "I can take care of that for you," he volunteered.

"Thanks. But I think all I need is a swim."

"Suit yourself," shrugged Hassa, still holding the tube out for a moment. Then he put it down and picked up the rag again, returning to his routine.

Tey took several steps toward the beckoning sea and then stopped. Hassa, who was alternately applying fresh oil to the slug-thrower and then wiping away the excess, looked up and asked, "What is it?"

Tey shaded her eyes with her left hand and pointed toward the sea with her right. "Someone's out there," she said. "See them?"

"Them?" queried Hassa, following her outstretched arm. "Who is it?"

"I don't know. They look like specks. But they're getting larger."

Hassa picked up a pair of self-focusing binoculars, peered through them, and abruptly put them down. "Go into the house, Tey. Find Kar and tell him to arm himself and join me out here. Then trip the alarm system."

"What is it?"

"Go!" Hassa shouted.

Tey did as he ordered, but did pause in the doorway long enough to see Hassa pick up a comlink and say into it, "Leader One, this is Home Base. Leader One, this is Home Base. We are under attack!"

"My God!" Sam said. "I don't believe my eyes—and they're the best money can buy."

"Tee-hee-hee," laughed the boka in unison, delighted that their new friend was so impressed by their revelation.

"Can we go down there?" Sam asked.

"Too deep," Ariel said, shaking her head.

"Too deep?" said Sam dubiously. He reached out with his hand, and the perfectly circular thing seemed just beyond his grasp. It was an optical illusion, he realized, but its proximity seemed so real nonetheless.

"Where did it come from?" he asked, unable to take his eyes off the faintly glowing object.

"Dunno," replied Nemo.

"Who else knows about this thing?"

"Nobody else knows about this thing," Jacques chirped merrily.

"What about Gar and Tey?"

"Nobody else knows about this thing," reiterated Nemo, parrotlike. Then he changed his mind. "Now Sam knows about this thing."

"Sam promise not to tell other hue-mans," Jacques told him.
"Huh?"

"Is boka secret. Sam promise: no tell."

"No tell, huh? Okay, I promise." As soon as the words left his mouth, Sam wished he could have them back. How could he make such a promise and hope to keep it?

"Is very deep. Is too cold," said Rachel. "We go now."

Sam wanted to see more. While the cold and pressure might prevent the boka from going any deeper, it had no effect on him. "But can't we . . . I mean, isn't there some way we could—"

"We go now," Jacques said firmly.

"We go now," agreed Sam reluctantly, feeling like Indiana Jones turning his back on some lost treasure. *Now who the heck's Indiana Jones?*

The attackers came in fast and low. The one- and two-man waterbugs they clung to skipped and skated across the placid surface of the water like their Terran namesakes. The bugs' guns spewed out a deadly fusillade that threw up bits of sand and dirt as the plasteel-jacketed slugs tracked inland from the beach.

Small groups of bathers, mostly women and children, shrieked in fear and panic, scattering like antelope with a lioness in their midst. One terrified woman turned first this way and then that. Her confusion and indecision cost her her life as she ran back into the path of the gunfire and was cut down.

"Bastards!" shouted Wye Hassa. He'd thrown down his oily rag and was quickly reloading the slug-thrower. He had no sooner started returning the attackers' fire than he was joined by Kar Brunn.

Brunn hurried from the house, bringing an energy rifle with him, and the two neophyte bodyguards initiated a spirited resistance. If either man was aware that the odds against them most likely spelled their doom, he didn't show it.

Praying that all the noncombatants had vacated the beach, Hassa activated the sea-facing automatic sentry weapons, cursing whoever had made the decision to leave them on inactive status.

Had he not been preoccupied, Hassa might have considered the matter more thoroughly and acknowledged the murderous havoc they could have wrought on unsuspecting beachcombers. As it was, he had no time to understand the reasoning that denied him valuable seconds in incorporating the weapons into the fray.

Taking cover behind several huge rocks whose twisted and distorted shapes were the result of the unceasing sculpting power of the sea, Hassa, Brunn, and the sentry guns made the attackers pay a high price for their brazen assault.

"I got another one!" exalted Hassa.

"Don't get cocky," Brunn told him. "That's only three so far that we've gotten," he said, not bothering to include the toll exacted by the sentry guns. He fired several times and added with grim satisfaction, "Make that five."

The waterbugs leapt onto the beach, their hydrofoils and Kessel anti-magnetic repulse motors enabling them to skim across the sand as easily as the water. The sentry guns kept up a steady stream of deadly fire. But because they were old and had never been used in an actual combat situation before, the guns had difficulty tracking the elusive waterbugs. Even worse, those guns which weren't knocked out of commission by grenades or mortar fire soon overheated or jammed on their own.

The rocks providing the two young Cousteaueans with cover were pounded by streams of high-velocity slugs as the attackers were able to ignore the now-toothless sentry weapons and focus on the human defenders. Despite their disadvantages, Brunn and Hassa managed to continue to get off return fire that wounded or killed foolhardy attackers who squandered their advantages.

Several of the waterbugs and their riders spurted past Hassa and Brunn, flanking the defenders. Before the two could turn and redirect their fire at this new challenge, they were cut down by savage volleys.

One of the attackers climbed off his one-man waterbug and walked over to the two mutilated bodies. After studying them for a moment he kicked both corpses in the head. "That's for costing me too many of my people."

"Shouldn't we get the woman, Lyl?" one of the others asked.

"Yeah, you're right," Lyl Saare said, glancing toward the house. He pointed at one of the men just climbing off his 'bug. "Bey, go and fetch me the high and mighty Tey Varro."

"Yes, sir."

The one the leader had called Bey crossed the veranda and

stepped through the open doorway, disappearing into the relative gloom of the interior. Several minutes passed, and Bey's companions exchanged amused looks.

"Hey, you bastard—leave a little of that stuff for us!"

They chortled over that until Bey reappeared on the veranda, a spear tip protruding from his back.

"I . . . ah . . ." He turned around and they saw blood bubbles on his face and nostrils. He stumbled forward several steps before collapsing in a heap.

"Looks like the hellion's got some sharp teeth and claws," one of the others said with a smirk, the death of his compatriot arousing little sympathy in him.

"Yeah," Saare agreed. "Be more careful than Bey was, Yan."

Smiling, the man thumped his polyglas thoracic armor as if to point out his imperviousness to anything as puny as a spear gun. He approached the house and stepped inside, still smiling.

Several minutes passed before a blood-curdling scream erupted from the interior. The men's grins faded.

"Goddamnit!" Saare cursed, rubbing his hand over the short burr of his hair. "Can't anyone do this right?"

"I'll tame the bitch," someone said.

"No," Saare said. "I think it's time I take matters into my own hands." He checked his weapon's charge to make sure it was on stun, held out his hand, and said, "Gas grenade." Someone pulled one from his belt and pressed it into his palm.

Saare depressed and released the pin with his thumb and then hurled it through the open doorway. He nodded, and two more grenades followed the first.

The grenades exploded one-two-three, filling the interior of the building with acrid white smoke.

"Shouldn't be long now," one of the team said.

"Yeah," said Saare.

They waited. "Uh, I don't think she's still in there," a tall, thin man said hesitantly.

"We heard Yan scream, but maybe he wounded or killed her before he died," another of the team offered.

"I sure as hell hope not! That's not supposed to happen."

"Hey!" someone shouted, and they brought their weapons to bear on a figure coming around from behind the structure with its hands in the air. They immediately saw a second figure behind the first.

"Well, I'll be!"

It was Tey Varro. She had a resigned expression on her face. Behind her, a short but sleek woman whose brush cut was a flaming red had a small slug-thrower pressed against the base of Tey Varro's skull.

"We didn't know you was back there," Lyl Saare said, looking properly abashed.

"I figured you just might forget that every place has a rear door as well as a front one."

"What shall we do now?"

Aware of everyone's deferential attitude toward her captor, Tey turned her head slightly—feeling the woman jab the barrel of the pistol more tightly against the back of her skull—and asked, "Who are you?"

"Me?" The woman chuckled. "So much for fame. I'm Suo Hann."

II

The three Legion floaters came in across the sea, their approach silent and ominous.

"Look at the size of those things!" one of Varro's men said.

"Impressive, aren't they?" asked Galen. "Part of their function is to intimidate."

"It works," a voice said.

"I was not aware the Legion had such craft on Cousteau," said Varro.

"They didn't," replied Galen. "Not until things started to heat up."

"Things haven't 'heated up' as far as I can tell," said the man who'd voiced his awe at the floaters' size. "The conflict is confined to the other Council worlds, not Cousteau."

Galen watched the three huge floaters slowly come to a halt about ten or fifteen meters from the sea, settling down into the sand. Turning to the man who'd spoken, he said, "*I* am here . . . and so is Suo Hann." He couldn't help adding, to himself, *And how many others would phrase that "Your leader Suo Hann is here"?*

Just before the ramps were lowered and heavily armed Legion regulars quick-marched out to take up their positions, one of Varro's senior bodyguards warned, "Keep your hands in sight and away from your weapons. We don't want to give them an excuse to start something."

"Too bad. I was looking forward to a good firefight," Galen said.

The bodyguard stared at him before emitting an odd, barking laugh. "It would be a good one all right, but too short."

"Damned short!" added someone else.

"Everyone shut up and smile," hissed Varro through clenched teeth as several officers with self-important airs about them approached with holodrama seriousness.

"Good day, gentlemen," said Varro. "Although it is probably unnecessary, allow me to introduce myself: I am Gar Varro." He nodded slightly; it was an almost imperceptible bow.

"And I am Major Barlow," said the highest-ranking of the three Legion officers who'd come to meet them. "These gentlemen are Captains Litvinoff and Benning. We are pleased to meet you, Citizen Varro."

His eyes bore through Galen like laser beams. "And who is this gentleman with you?" he asked.

A small smile played across Galen's lips. *As if you didn't already know!* Aloud, he replied, "I am Galen Yeager, a scientist/journalist from Terra." He pointed to the small holocam one of Varro's men was pointing at them. "As you can see, we are recording these events. The signal is being transmitted back to a recorder for safekeeping."

"I see," said Barlow. "Then you can record that we performed our duty with absolute correctness."

"And what might that be, pray tell?"

Smiling a tight oh-come-now smile, Major Barlow said, "To place Citizen Varro under arrest."

"On what charge?" asked Galen.

"Why none, right now. The Magistracy and the Council have determined that a threat to Citizen Varro exists; we have come to place him in protective detention."

When several of his bodyguards shifted restlessly at Barlow's words, causing an equal reaction among the soldiers, Varro said sharply, "Remember your orders! No resistance."

"Thank you, Citizen Varro," Major Barlow said. "Your cooperation is appreciated."

"What about my people?" Varro asked.

"They are not at risk. My orders are to take only you into

custody." At those words, Galen relaxed a fraction. So he wasn't about to be arrested along with Varro!

"However"—*Uh-oh!*—"I have been instructed to see to it that Citizen Yeager accompanies us back to Midland as well."

"Oh, on what charge?"

"There is no charge," Barlow said smoothly. "You are merely to be questioned and released, that is all."

"That's enough!" Galen said under his breath.

"I'm not happy about this," Galen muttered to Varro as they sat in the detention cubicle in the rear of one of the large floaters.

"I'm hardly ecstatic, myself," Varro responded crossly. Galen didn't begrudge Varro his crossness: The older man sported painful wrist restraints, while his own hands were unencumbered.

"I don't mean it that way."

"What way did you mean it?"

"I mean, first they took away our comlinks—and *only then* did they disarm us, separating us from your security people."

"Isn't that what you'd expect them to do?" Varro couldn't understand what was bothering Galen.

"Well, no. I mean, you'd think they'd take away our weapons first, not our communications devices."

"Maybe they didn't want us calling for help."

"Calling who for help? Who could we whistle up in an instant to come and take on that many Legion regulars?" He shook his head. "Something smells fishy."

For the first time since his arrest, Varro smiled.

Galen caught his amused expression and, in spite of himself, grinned too. Then the smile faded and he added, "But you know what I mean—haven't you ever had a bad feeling about something when there was no reason to feel that way?"

"You don't think they plan to assassinate me? Use some pretense like I was trying to escape, do you?"

"No. Not you, anyway."

Varro's eyes widened, and Galen could see the Cousteauean's nictitating eyelids slide quickly across his eyes, keeping them moist. "Does that mean you think that Director Feller has ordered up that scenario for *you*?"

"I don't know what to think," said Galen, throwing up his

hands. "I guess I've just got the boogums for no good reason."

They both felt and heard the ship's skeleton creak as an indeterminate number of people boarded her. After the usual preparatory sounds, the floater suddenly rose into the air.

"I assume we're off to Midland," Galen said, his forehead creased by a frown.

"I would wager that we are both thinking the same thing," said Varro.

"You mean, 'What about Tey?' "

"Yes."

Galen rubbed his chin thoughtfully. "I can't see them sending another party to arrest her." When the floater lurched suddenly, he reached out to steady Varro and to keep him from bumping his head. "I can't see that, but—"

"But?"

"But has she been told about your arrest, I wonder?"

"My only concern is her safety."

"It's you the Principate wants out of the way, not Tey. I'm sure she's fine."

"I hope you're right," Varro said.

Me, too!

When Sam waded out of the sea and approached Varro's home, he found the area in an uproar over the lightning attack and abduction.

"What's happened here?" Sam demanded.

"And who might you be?" asked a broad-shouldered man Sam had never seen before.

"I am Sam Houston."

"Sam . . . *Houston*?" the man repeated dubiously.

"I am Galen Yeager's partner."

"Yeager's partner?" Sam rolled his eyes.

Before either of them could say anything else, one of Varro's people joined them and said, "He's all right, Jal. That's the artificial from Terra." Sam looked at the newcomer. Although the man knew Sam's name, Sam didn't know his.

"Oh, yeah?" The man stared intently into Sam's golden eyes. "From Terra, huh? Maybe he had something to do with all this."

"Please," Varro's friend, a security person, said wearily. "Go down to the beach; they can use your help there."

The beefy man scowled but did as he was ordered.

"Thanks," said Sam. "For a second there I thought we were going to play 'Do androids go to Heaven?' "

"I'm not in a mood to joke around," Varro's man said. Seeing the grim expression on the other's face, Sam had no trouble believing him.

"Forgive me; I shouldn't have tried to make light of the situation," Sam said. He shrugged and explained, "I wasn't, really. But, tell me, please: What happened here?"

"As you can see for yourself, we were attacked. We believe they came in from the north, crossing the barriers on waterbugs."

"Waterbugs?"

"Yes. They're lightweight craft that skim across the surface of the water," explained the shamefaced officer. "They are highly maneuverable on land or water."

"I see."

"When they got here, they came right up on the shore." The security officer made a sweeping gesture that took in the carnage surrounding them. "They . . . they were well armed. As you can see, they overwhelmed the few defenders in place." He shook his head sadly. "They killed practically everyone."

"Everyone?" Sam's eyes swept the area, searching for Tey Varro's now-familiar face. "Uh, where is Varro's daughter?"

"They kidnapped her and escaped the way they came."

"Kidnapped Tey Varro . . ." said Sam, unable to keep the disbelief out of his voice.

"Gar will never forgive me if anything happens to Tey," the man said, hanging his head.

Sam heard the catch in the man's voice and saw the unmistakable signs of someone trying to come to terms with sudden and frightening changes to his universe. He seemed disoriented and on the verge of crying.

"What is your name, please?" Sam asked. "I can't continue thinking of you as 'Varro's security man.' "

"I am Mon Cerro."

"I am sorry we had to meet under such circumstances, Mon Cerro."

Just then Cerro's comlink chimed. "Yes?" he asked. "Where? How many? I see. Yes. I said yes! Yes, goodbye."

When he saw Sam staring expectantly at him, Cerro explained, "There's more. They killed some fishermen not three klicks from here, out near the guardian reef. There was no reason for such an outrage," he said softly.

"Did the fishermen have communications devices?" asked Sam. "You know—radios, sat-phones, or walkie-talkies?"

"Why, yes. Yes, they did."

Sam nodded. "The reef's probably where they assembled for the attack. They didn't want anyone reporting their presence. The fishermen were just in the wrong place at the wrong time."

"Bastards! Rotten, murderous bastards!"

"I agree," said Sam without any noticeable inflection. "Now then, what about Gar Varro and my partner, Galen Yeager?"

Cerro looked at him with the oddest expression on his face, seemingly caught off guard by the question. "Gar Varro?" *No wonder these guys are in trouble!* Sam fumed to himself.

"Yes, you remember Gar Varro. There's a rumor he's your leader." Sam didn't bother to try to hide his disdain.

"I . . . ah . . . That is, he . . ."

"He and Galen Yeager were visiting the rim islands," Sam finished for him. "Have you heard anything from him? Were they attacked? Does he know about the abduction of his daughter?"

"I do not know," Cerro admitted.

"Follow me, then," said Sam, walking toward the house.

"What are you going to do?"

"I'm sure *someone* has tried to contact them already," he told Cerro. "Even so, I'm going to put my two centicreds in."

Inside, several people were photographing and palmprinting the dead men. Sam steered a wide berth around them and headed for the communications console in Varro's office.

"Hey, you can't go in there!" objected one of the new security people, blocking the way.

"I have a note from the Council," said Sam mildly. The real strength was in his grip on the man's upper arm.

"Ah-h-h!" grunted the man as Sam's fingers dug into his biceps. Sam maneuvered him out of the way.

"Thank you," Sam said, stepping past him as the man massaged his aching muscle. "Don't," advised Sam over his shoulder; he hadn't looked back.

The guard was reaching for his sidearm when Sam's warning brought him up short. Wondering if the android had eyes in the back of his head, the outclassed security person muttered something unintelligible and dropped his hand.

Sitting at the communications console, Sam tried every channel and frequency he could think of to reach Galen and Varro; he had no luck.

Staring out the open door at the bodies of the attackers, he wondered if what happened at the sea farm had been one half of a coordinated, two-pronged operation.

"Goddamnit!" He slammed his fist down so hard on the surface of Varro's desk that several faces peered in nervously. "Galen, Galen—what the hell's happened to you?"

12

WHEN SAM SAW THE EXPRESSION ON THE FACE OF VARRO'S aide, he knew the woman had heard something. "What is it?" he asked.

"Gar Varro has been arrested."

"Arrested!" Sam thought about that for a moment. Certainly, Galen had told him that Varro's arrest was being planned. But Sam hadn't considered that it might come so soon . . . and so unexpectedly. Galen and Varro had discussed the possibility of the latter turning himself in before the Legion acted. Well, it was too late for that now.

"Where is he?" asked Sam. Before the other could answer, he added, "And what about Galen Yeager?"

"They've both been taken to Midland, to Krow. From what I understand, your friend has not been charged with anything." She made a sour face. "It seems they simply wish to talk to him."

"Yeah, right." Sam's mind raced. "Why Krow?" he asked. "Why not Bandar?" Sam knew that while both cities were on the island continent of Midland, Bandar was closer to the Crescent and Varro's sea farm.

"While Bandar is the capital and the larger of the two cities, Krow is the most like Terra," Varro's aide explained. "It is more the sort of place offworlders would wish to spend time in, I think. It has restaurants, night clubs, theaters and the requisite sex zone visitors demand."

Sam nodded; the woman's explanation made sense. Sam turned on his heel and walked away purposefully.

"Mr. Houston . . . ?"

Sam turned back. "Yes?"

"Where are you going?"

"To Krow."

"Please don't do anything rash."

Sam lifted his shoulders. "Who, me? What can I do? I'm just an android."

The floater carrying Galen and Gar Varro landed inside the force-field-protected walls of the newly built Kubyshev prison. A certain amount of unconfirmed scuttlebutt about the place had passed up and down the PrinSecPol grapevine during the facility's construction. Even so, Galen might never have learned about the place had he not seen a filecube about it and its state-of-the-art security lying on Rob MacKenzie's desk at headquarters.

When MacKenzie had returned from an impromptu meeting with his boss Hashem Fedalf, Galen asked him about the new facility.

"Information about that place is 'for eyes only,' " MacKenzie had told him.

"Uh-huh. Is that why you left this cube lying face up on your desk where I was sure to see it?" retorted Galen.

"Oh, did I do that?" asked MacKenzie. Then he confessed to the charge by saying, "The old man thinks his agents—or at least you—should know what Consul Zajicek and his cronies are up to on the colony worlds."

"Council worlds," Galen said absently.

"Oh, *of course*," agreed MacKenzie with a knowing smirk. Both he and Galen knew the score, but it was best to use the euphemisms even in private, lest one day you forget yourself and be impolitic enough to utter the more accurate word in public.

Galen had picked up the filecube again and studied it. "I don't get it," he said finally. "Why is the Magistracy building new prisons on col—uh, on Council worlds?"

"Why does anyone build new prisons?" MacKenzie had shot back, challenging him to face the obvious. Before Galen could reply, however, the deputy answered his own question. "Because you expect to fill them up," he had said pointedly.

Now, sitting in the floater beside Gar Varro, Galen repeated softly, " 'Because you expect to fill them up.' "

"Did you say something, Galen?" Varro asked before yawning. He blinked, rousing himself from a brief catnap.

"No. It was nothing."

Varro would have none of it. "It was not nothing, Galen. What did you mutter to yourself?"

"I was just remembering something Rob MacKenzie told me about prisons. He said you don't build them unless you expect to use them. I think Feller, Peter Zajicek, and the other hard cases are getting ready to begin a crackdown." He grimaced, like a baby experiencing a gas pain.

Seeing the look on Galen's face, Varro pressed him with, "What? What else are you thinking?" He decided he had to ask, even if the answer might not be to his liking.

"You're right. There is something else on my mind. I think I made a mistake."

"What kind of mistake?"

"I don't think it was such a good idea to allow yourself to be arrested."

"Now he tells me!" Varro exploded. His reaction was a combination of real annoyance and a certain amount of calculated bluster. It made Galen feel even more responsible for Varro's predicament.

Galen closed his eyes and rubbed them with the heels of his palms, causing colored specks to dance across his retinas. "I'm sorry, Gar. I think I made a very bad decision. I'm afraid that something major is going to go down very shortly. I blew it. I shouldn't have talked you into this."

Varro's jaw dropped, and he stared at Galen with his mouth open. He snapped it shut quickly and said, "You didn't talk me into anything, Galen. This arrest business made sense when you proposed it. Otherwise I wouldn't have agreed." He shrugged. "And who knows, your first impulse could still prove to be the right one."

"I sure as hell hope so!" said Galen fervently.

II

Tey had always prided herself on possessing a marvelous sense of direction. She was also usually very good at guessing the passage of time. Now, held prisoner inside an unknown craft, she was preparing to use both skills to create a mental map of her eventual destination. *As long as my captors do nothing to interfere with my kinetic and chronological abilities,* Tey told herself, *I'll be able to figure out where they've taken me.*

Whether or not Suo Hann or the others knew of Tey's abilities, they quickly ruined any hope she had of memorizing the route. A hatch opened and a young man ducked low to enter without bumping his head on the plasteel frame. He was carrying a ceramic mug.

Blinking in the glare of the light that poured into her cell behind him, Tey stared at the mug in his hand. "I take it you have something for me?"

He nodded. With the light behind him, his face was shadowed, preventing her from seeing him as clearly as she would have liked. "Try it, you'll like it," he said, handing her the mug.

"What is it?" she asked suspiciously, sniffing at the clear liquid in the mug without detecting any odor.

"Never mind that; just drink it."

"And if I don't?"

He stepped aside just enough for her to see the barrel of an energy pistol protruding into her small compartment. "My companion's weapon is set on stun. I've never had my nervous system disrupted by one of those things," he said conversationally. "They say it hurts like hell for a while once you regain consciousness. They also say that the stuff in the glass does the same thing without giving you the nasty headache that comes with being stunned," he told her.

"I certainly hope 'they' know what they're talking about," Tey said, taking the mug from him. She put it to her lips.

" 'To be or not to be . . . ' " she said. Then she wished she hadn't. Weren't a high percentage of the deaths in Shakespeare's "Danish play" the result of poison? *Oh, well,* she thought. She quickly drained the mug's contents.

"Now what?" she asked, handing the mug back and wiping

her lips with the back of her hand. Although the mug's liquid had tasted metallic, downing it wasn't an unpleasant experience.

"Lie down."

She did as he requested and he added, "Good; you should be getting drowsy right about . . ."

Tey was swallowed by the darkness.

Tey Varro awoke an indeterminate time later in a new and nonmoving location. *I guess we reached our destination,* she thought.

The space she found herself in couldn't really be called large, yet it was spacious enough to contain a small pool. The water looked a bit brackish, but inviting nonetheless.

She was debating standing up and seeing if her legs could carry her that short distance when she heard someone approach the door of the small room they were keeping her in. Tey wasn't terribly surprised to discover that her awakening was immediately noted by her captors. They apparently had her under constant surveillance.

"Where am I?" she demanded loudly.

He or she stopped outside, and there was a faint scratching noise; presumably whoever it was was peering in through the peephole.

A man's voice, muffled by the door between them, answered, "We did not go to all the trouble of making sure you had no way of knowing how you got here—or where 'here' is—to present you with that information the instant you awoke."

"It was worth a try," Tey said, extending her arms and twisting her shoulders to stretch her stiff muscles. She was surprised by how few ill effects she felt from her drugging. Her mouth felt as if it was stuffed with cotton, but aside from that the young man had not lied about the drug's residue.

"I suppose so," the man's voice replied. "Do you see the small pool in the floor?"

"No," replied Tey sarcastically. "Where is it?"

"You will feel much better if you immerse yourself and relax for a half-hour or so. I imagine that you must feel as dry and uncomfortable as a mummy."

Tey glanced at the water gently lapping at the edges of the small pool. Looking at it made her realize how much she needed to have a long, satisfying soak. "Yes, I think I will use the pool."

"Good," the man told her. "Later you may speak to the chosen one."

Tey rolled her eyes. "Chosen one? You mean Suo Hann?"

When there was no reply, she rose awkwardly from the rude cot she had awakened on, and walked slowly and stiffly over to the pool. *Just like the mummy he mentioned,* she thought. As she stepped into the water, another thought occurred to her. *He is clearly an educated man. How many Cousteaueans would know what something as alien to our world as a mummy is? I would have thought Suo Hann's supporters were all rabble.*

Then she chastised herself for such wishful thinking. It was clear that the terrorist leader enjoyed wide support, presumably even among the intelligentsia.

Maybe wider and deeper than my father's.

Then all such thoughts were banished by her complete submersion in the water. It was heaven.

Galen and Varro were quickly separated inside the prison. Kubyshev prison was remarkable for how much it resembled the prisons of Old Earth, the hundreds or even thousands of archaic facilities whose special purpose was to humiliate and deflate their inhabitants, sucking the will to resist from their dispirited minds and souls.

Under the proper circumstances, Galen would not have necessarily disagreed with those aims. Only a fool believed that everyone in prison was innocent or that no one belonged in such a place.

Galen knew that certain prisons, the medieval fortresses like Kubyshev, built by corrupt regimes increasingly distanced from the people they supposedly represented, were also used to incarcerate more than human beings. They were also meant to imprison strong new ideas, confining justice and hope by taking away the freedom of those who dared challenge the rules.

"Keep hope alive," Galen muttered under his breath as he was led down a long, drab, institutional corridor.

Kubyshev was so new the paint had hardly had a chance to dry, yet already it looked and smelled as if it had stood for a century, its walls soaking up the fear and hatred of countless men and women—inmates condemned collectively to a hundred thousand years of prison time.

"What did you say?" asked one of the two burly guards flanking him. The man's appearance was cartoonish: He was broad-shouldered and massive on top like an old-time football lineman, but his V-shaped torso rested on short, spindly legs.

"Nothing," Galen spat out unwisely.

Without warning, the guard swiveled and sank his beefy fist into Galen's stomach.

"Oomph!" Galen said, doubling over.

"Maybe that'll teach you not to lie," the second guard said approvingly.

"Kiss my ass, dick-breath!" Galen managed to get out, realizing as he uttered it that it wasn't the wisest thing to say under the circumstances.

"A tough guy, eh?" the second guard said, bringing both his hands down on the back of Galen's neck, driving him to his knees and nearly knocking him unconscious. "Too bad we're not keeping you."

They grabbed Galen under his arms and began dragging him down the corridor. Galen tried to walk but found that he couldn't make his rubbery legs work like they were supposed to.

I used to know how to walk, he thought crossly.

Galen had assumed the prison staff would have been given orders not to harm him. *Uh-huh. Yet another thing I have been completely wrong about.* So far, he'd been perfect.

Thinking as clearly as he could with his head pounding like the galaxy's biggest drum, Galen decided that whatever the game was, it was being played for higher stakes than he'd first assumed. If he didn't wise up soon, he might contrive to get himself or Varro seriously dead.

"C'mon, tough guy, on your feet," one of the guards told him as they dragged him to the front of a desk behind which was seated a bemused noncommissioned officer.

Galen didn't have to be an Einstein to figure out that the unmarked plaswood door behind the crew-cut sergeant was the domain of some bureaucrat higher up the food chain. Probably the warden himself. Given his recent track record on predictions, Galen thought, it was probably actually an interrogation/torture room.

"What have you two boys got there?"

"A tough guy," the one who'd punched him in the stomach replied.

"Kinda short for a hero, isn't he?"

Galen raised his head, which had been exhibiting an alarming tendency to seek the floor in the last few minutes, and said, "I'm tall enough when I have a needle gun in my hand."

"Aren't we all?" laughed the sergeant good-naturedly. "Go on in," he told the two guards. "They're waiting for you." He reached under his desk, pressed something, and the door swung open.

What would Sam say in a situation like this one? Galen wondered. Remarkably, he came up with a Samlike remark. "You guys go ahead," Galen told the two guards. "I'll wait out here." They pushed him forward, propelling him through the open doorway. Galen was somewhat surprised that what he said jokingly to the two guards occurred in reverse. They stayed outside while he went in.

He found himself in a medium-sized room with a modestly comfortable-looking interior. A large oval rug lay in the center of the tiled floor. A huge chandelier hung from a chain in the ceiling. Then Galen saw a familiar-looking desk. And behind it . . .

For just an instant, Galen thought that Nevin Feller was seated at the opposite end of the room. He was and he wasn't. A second glance was all it took for Galen to see that the glowering presence of the director of the Legion was a holo, not the real thing.

Galen examined his surroundings more closely now and saw that in addition to Feller, there were several others in the room, off to one side as if in deference to the great man who was favoring them by his holographic presence.

A slender man dressed in civilian garb stepped forward from between two younger and fitter-looking men and announced, "I am Warden Dorn. And you, I understand, are Galen Yeager of the PrinSecPol." Galen observed that Dorn had a small crescent-moon-shaped scar over his right eye, and a shock of black hair laced with gray.

"I am Galen Yeager," was all Galen would admit to. He studied Dorn closely, frankly surprised to discover that the warden was a Cousteauean. *Perhaps I've met my first dry.* The man had exhalatory slits in his neck, but Galen knew that they weren't a true indicator; it was the underdeveloped lungs, and that was something you couldn't see with your eyes. And of course, Dorn's name was another indication of his status.

"I was correct, Warden Dorn," rumbled Feller's image. "I told you Yeager would not confess that he is a member of our rival's intelligence service. Not even to us, even though he has privately admitted his involvement with Fedalf to me. No, he will concede nothing, not even in the security of this room." There was a gleam of respect in his eyes. "Yeager is too much the professional."

Feller was correct: Like a philandering husband caught with his pants down and his briefs buddy at full alert, Galen was determined to bluff it out and deny the obvious—that he was an agent for Fedalf's PrinSecPol. Besides, his words and image were probably being recorded.

"Rival?" repeated Galen, pretending to be surprised by Feller's use of the word. "I always supposed that the directors of the Legion and the PrinSecPol were as close to each other as Castor and Polydeuces."

"I see now, Director Feller," said the warden, "that your earlier description of Citizen Yeager was accurate."

As if Galen was a callow schoolboy who needed to have the goings on in a Restoration drama explained to him, one of Warden Dorn's uniformed assistants leaned slightly in Galen's direction and whispered, "The director told us you didn't much like authority."

Don't these guys have anything better to do? Galen wondered. "Once again my reputation precedes me," said Galen, bowing his head slightly.

"Enough of this nonsense," Feller said as if he'd read Galen's thoughts. "I am a busy man." He briefly glanced down at something on the desk in front of him, looking back up almost immediately. "I will make this short and sweet, Yeager. Minutes before the *General Woodard*'s destruction, a craft of Cousteauean registry, a private yacht called the *Flying Dutchman* made a rather hasty departure from the spaceport. The *Flying Dutchman* is the property of Gar Varro."

"That's old news," Galen began. "Besides, I think you know as well as I do that Gar Varro was on Cousteau when the *Woodard* was sabotaged. Someone else got hold of his yacht and did the nasty deed."

Feller put up a hand and said, "I have not finished." He gestured at the surface of his desk. "I have here in front of me any number of documents. For all intents and purposes they establish compelling evidence of Citizen Varro's complicity and guilt in the *General Woodard* matter." He shrugged. "Whether he is in fact guilty is beside the point. We have enough material to convince the general populace that he was behind this heinous capital crime."

"Heinous?" repeated Galen. "That sounds like something out of a pop-cult holo."

Ignoring Galen's interruption, Feller said, "That is why I have had several other documents prepared."

"Other documents?" All of a sudden Galen felt like a cock-roach seeing the boot coming down.

"Yes, others. The final two orders require only my signa-ture." He theatrically affixed his name to one of the pieces of plaspaper. "I have just ordered Varro's transfer to Terra."

"Terra!"

Feller ignored Galen and continued. "If Varro refuses to freely confess his crime, I will be forced to sign the second document."

"And?"

"And he will then be taken from his cell and executed under the laws of the Principate."

Galen was speechless.

III

Sam Houston literally flew across the water in his one-man floater. With reflexes no mere mortal could hope to match, he kept the floater as close to the surface of the sea as he dared. More a Pacific than an Atlantic, the single, globe-encircling ocean was, for the most part, a placid and forgiving body of water. The few visible waves flashed beneath the floater like the blinking of a strobe light.

Sam accessed his internal clock and estimated that he would reach Midland in less than sixty minutes at his present speed and course. He consulted his map again, still unsure how best to reach Krow. He thought it odd that the port city of Bandar was on the northern coast of Midland and closest to the landing field at Nemo, while Krow, the center of so much offworld commerce and trade, was on the southern coast and farther away.

Before he had left, he had heard ominous rumors, rumors about a place called Kubyshev. *Why do so many prisons seem to have Slavic names?* he wondered. And was the original Kubyshev, if he was not presumptuous in assuming that there was an original Kubyshev, a person, a place, or a thing?

He berated himself for wasting time on useless thoughts and returned to considering how best to reach Krow. For reasons that had never been explained to him, Cousteaueans had restricted private floater flights over land. That meant that if he wished to remain a good, law-abiding visitor he would have to land at Bandar or some other destination on Midland's northern coast and take a commercial flight to Krow.

It didn't take long for him to decide to break the law. He determined that it would be foolish to give up the floater and leave himself at the mercy of the somewhat arbitrary schedules of Cousteauean commercial transportation.

"So I'll pay the fine," he muttered as he plotted a course that would take him on a north-south route over the western reaches of Midland. The area was mostly undeveloped, and if he hugged the contours of the land as closely as he was doing with the sea, he should remain below most radars.

"Now all I have to—Jesus!"

He'd come upon the fishing trawler without warning. Apart from the command superstructure, the ship sat low in the water. But it was the bridge that he'd found himself hurtling toward at nearly five hundred kilometers per hour. Had he been a human pilot, he would have smashed into the trawler with an impact that would have punched a massive hole through the entire ship, dooming it along with himself.

As it was, his inhuman reflexes were barely sufficient for him to change course by the tiny increment that saw him zoom past the trawler like a seahawk just missing a slow and clumsy gull.

He gulped and decided to pay less attention to his maps and possible routes and more to what might be in front of him. Feeling just a bit ashamed, as if he were letting Galen and Varro down, he also shed about fifty kph of speed to give him more reaction time if the same thing reoccurred.

I can't help anyone if I'm scrap metal, he reasoned.

They didn't go to the bother of forcing Tey to wear restraints. *Pretty sure of themselves, I'd say,* she thought. Then she looked at the rippling muscles on the two men who flanked her and silently laughed at the idea of trying anything so stupid as attempting to escape.

Her escorts led her through a series of low, narrow, and twisting tunnels. The bare rock glistened damply and the air was comfortably thick and moisture-laden; comfortable for a Cousteauean, that is.

Tey chewed on that for a little bit. *We're underground,* she thought, acknowledging the telltale evidence. *No, not underground,* she amended. *Underwater.* This place was probably a few meters offshore, perhaps an undersea cavern or series of caverns filled with air.

Tey wasn't sure what to think about her upcoming audience with the woman who had made her a captive. What was Suo Hann, anyway? A terrorist or a freedom fighter? A madwoman or a visionary? A destroyer or a builder? What if Suo Hann had the right idea and it was her father who was wrong?

Tey shook her head, exasperated by her inability to categorize Suo Hann in a way that made sense. *And what's the rush anyway?* she thought. *I haven't even met her yet, not really. Neither am I going anywhere in the immediate future. There is plenty of time to figure out Suo Hann and her agenda.*

"We're here," one of her guardian angels pronounced as he raised his hand to the metal door and rapped sharply on it with his knuckles.

Metal, not wood, observed Tey. Wood, of course, would rot in such an environment. *Better even than that, not even plasteel. Plain old Veissen steel or something similar.*

"Come," said a strong, authoritative woman's voice.

13

GALEN WAS UNCEREMONIOUSLY ESCORTED FROM KUBYSHEV prison by a squad of Legion regulars who looked like they wouldn't be good bets to try any of Sam's snappy lines on, so he kept his mouth shut.

As they walked him down a long corridor, he paid special attention to his surroundings, noting as many of the prison's defensive measures as his necessarily cursory examination could uncover. While the sentry weapons in the ceilings looked impressive, Galen could think of at least two or three ways to disable or bypass them.

The staffing of the prison also seemed suspect. The lack of guards in the corridors and at the various checkpoints made Galen wonder if they hadn't given Dorn and his people a million-credit facility with a hundred-credit budget to operate it.

Galen thought about that for a moment. What if, despite the rumors, this prison *wasn't* as high-tech, kiss-your-ass-goodbye, state-of-the-art as it was made out to be? *I mean, who's to say at least half of the money intended for this place didn't end up in some high-placed folks' bank accounts?*

Putting aside the question of graft and kickbacks, Galen decided that if more guards and warm bodies *were* planned for the future, the bureaucratic mills were probably grinding slowly indeed. It wouldn't surprise him one bit if the orders responsible for posting the necessary allotment of prison officers had gotten lost in space and were now slowly trying to extricate themselves from a black hole of red tape.

Still, Galen had to concede, getting in or out of Kubyshev certainly appeared to be no easy task. Every fifty to hundred meters one encountered a locked gate which required a key to open—an old-fashioned, actual hunk of metal. The cell blocks themselves were reached by passing through a small, polyglas guard station double-locked on both sides.

The guards inside the blast-resistant cubicle could open only one door at a time. The keys were kept on a meter-long chain—far too short for them to be used to unlock both doors simultaneously. Even nastier, neither door could be unlocked, even with the key inserted, if the other door was open or unlocked.

Entrance to the prison was through a massive molecular steel door. There was no alternative entryway; one either came in through the moly-steel door or through the three-meter-thick, reinforced plascrete walls.

Galen tried but he was constitutionally unable to keep his disdain for authority figures in check—even when it was wise to do so. "Are these walls to keep prisoners in—or to protect the outside from the likes of you?" Galen asked the officer in charge of escorting him out.

"Shut up."

"Hey, it never hurts to ask." Galen shrugged. One of his escorts whacked him across the back of his head with a rubber baton—a *hard* rubber baton. *That's another old wives' tale put to rest*, Galen thought. *It does hurt to ask!*

Two of the soldiers grabbed him roughly by his arms, their fingers digging into his flesh, and manhandled him down a short ramp. They stepped from the gloom and doom of the prison into the blinding glare of the late afternoon sun. The local stellar body was a white-hot disk hanging fat and lazily a few degrees above the horizon, its rays spears of light hurled directly at them.

Blinking like a hol-vee celebrity forced to confront a plethora of holojournalists, Galen averted his gaze from the sun. His escorts marched him though a gate in the wall that enclosed the interior courtyard and the main administrative building and cellblock.

After the spots stopped dancing across his retinas, Galen turned his head back toward the walls and observed the laser cannons and automatic slug-throwers positioned in the corner towers. If their function was to make anyone think twice about attempting to blast his way in, then they were effective, he was forced to admit.

<If you're an example of who they're letting out, I'd hate to see who they're keeping in,> a familiar voice said in his head.

<Sam!>

<How're you doing, partner?>

<Could be worse.>

<Give it time.>

"You all come back and see us again," the corporal in charge of the small contingent of soldiers said as his men let go of Galen.

"Thanks. Maybe I'll bring a friend," Galen said, rubbing his aching arms where the soldiers had gripped his biceps tightly.

Shading his eyes against the glare, the corporal saw the approaching Sam's telltale golden irises and barked, "Him? An android would be no help."

<He don't know me very well, do he?> Sam said.

"Oh, you'd be surprised," Galen told the corporal. He walked toward Sam, who was also doing his best to close the distance between them, hurrying across the open "killing zone" that surrounded Kubyshev.

"Sam, it's wonderful to see you!" Galen hugged his friend, wrapping his arms around him.

"It's relatively okay to see you again, too, Mr. Yeager."

"Don't burst into tears, big fellow," Galen said, shaking his head.

"I'm practicing self-control."

"What about—"

Sam held up a finger. "In a sec. First things first." He cupped his hands around his mouth and called, "Hey, Mr. Soldier guy."

<What the hell are you up to now?>

<You'll see.>

The guards, about to reenter the prison, turned back toward them. "Yeah?" said the corporal, his hand resting lightly on his holstered sidearm.

"I'll be back."

*   *   *

Galen clutched his glass tightly, staring into it a moment before taking a long, satisfying gulp. Wiping his mouth with the back of his hand, he said, "Okay, I've had the drink you insisted on."

"Sit down."

"What is it that you want to tell me that's so awful you want me to sit down?"

"Sit down."

Sam waited patiently until Galen was seated. He didn't relish delivering the news, so he got it out of the way as quickly as he could. "It's Tey. She's been kidnapped."

"What!" Galen shot halfway out of his chair. Getting control of himself, he dropped back down heavily. "When did this happen? Who the hell's responsible?"

"The when is: about the same time you and Varro were being picked up."

Galen took a sip of his drink, his face scrunched up in concentration. "The same time?"

Sam shrugged. "As near as I can tell."

"And the who?"

"Some of Varro's people think it was Suo Hann and her followers."

"Suo Hann? But why? I mean you'd think they'd want to get their hands on Gar Varro, not Tey."

"You'd think," said Sam noncommittally.

"What's that mean?"

"Nothing, I was just agreeing with you."

"You hardly ever 'just agree' with me," said Galen, making a face. It was true: He expected Sam to play devil's advocate. Galen already knew his own opinions and his prejudices, so he didn't especially see any value in having them fed back to him.

"All right," said Sam. "I think Suo Hann has changed her mind and decided that a live Varro is better for them than a dead Varro—*if* he could be convinced to do what she wants him to do."

Galen quickly saw where Sam was heading. "So if Suo Hann had Tey tucked safely away, then . . ."

"Gar Varro would agree to do whatever Hann and her people asked him to in order to get her back," finished Sam.

"Shit!"

"It's quite logical, but it's not necessarily the case," Sam pointed out. "It's just one possibility."

"But a pretty good one."

"There are others."

"Yeah? Give me another one, then." Galen drained the remainder of his drink.

"Aware that Suo Hann will probably be blamed, Feller's people, or his in-place Cousteauean agents, snatch Tey. Suo Hann *is* blamed, and Feller and the Magistracy tell Varro the only way they can be sure to get her back is if he tells them everything he knows—or can find out—about Hann's organization."

Galen shook his head. "That makes sense, but I don't like it."

"You got another one?"

"Try this on for size: Yes, Feller nabs both Varro and Tey. But rather than pretending that Suo Hann is responsible, he simply tells Varro the truth. Varro sees the light."

"Which is?"

"To become the Principate's lap dog or watch helplessly as his only daughter is tortured to death before his eyes."

"I dunno," said Sam. "If Feller has Tey, then why didn't she share the ride to Kubyshev with you two?"

Galen thought about that for a moment. "Maybe so I wouldn't put two and two together and realize that it was Feller who kidnapped her. Feller wants Varro to know the truth, but he wants me and the rest of the world to think it was Suo Hann."

"That could be," conceded Sam.

"Listen to us," said Galen wearily. "The truth is it could be any of these blue-sky scenarios—or none of them."

"What shall we do now?" Sam queried. "Where should we start?"

"How do you feel about a fast return trip to the Crescent and Varro's sea farm?"

"I thought you'd never ask."

II

The morning sun was direct and hot as Galen and Sam walked from the small plascrete landing pad where Sam had put down their floater.

Waiting for them were many of Gar Varro's family, friends, and associates. Galen's eyes narrowed as he inspected the group. If you took away Varro's relatives and employees, including his security people, it was a shockingly small assemblage.

And how many of these people are here because of Tey? Galen wondered. *If it was just Gar Varro, would anyone but his family have shown up to greet us?*

"How is Gar?" asked Dya, the Varro household's housekeeper and cook, her round face furrowed by concern.

"Gar Varro was in good health when I last saw him," Galen told her.

"And where and when was that, Terran?" asked Yas Tanna, one of Varro's advisors. Galen gave him a good long look. According to what Tey had told him, Tanna was a sometime rival for the leadership of the Liberation Party.

"Yesterday in Kubyshev prison."

There were gasps of shock and surprise from the crowd. There was no outcry from Tanna, Galen observed.

"Kubyshev prison?" someone repeated.

"Yes, Kubyshev prison."

Galen had never seen a planet where news traveled so damned slowly. Tugging on an earlobe, he saluted the stranglehold the Magistracy and the Principate had managed to clamp on Cousteau's information network. He had studied enough political science to know that to control the dissemination of knowledge within a society is to control its life's blood.

Anxious for word about Tey, Sam nudged Galen impatiently. *<What?>* queried Galen.

<Ask about Tey.>

<Did you really think I was going to forget to ask about Tey?> Sam shrugged. *<So ask, Mr. D.A.>*

"What about Tey?"

"She is still missing," Yas Tanna informed them.

"And?"

"We cannot be sure who is responsible."

"So that's it?" Galen asked incredulously.

"We are mostly simple people here," said a pregnant woman with two barefoot children hanging onto her skirt and staring at Sam in wide-eyed wonder. A third child was suckling enthusiastically at her breast. "We do not know what to do in times like these."

<And that, my friend,> Sam said to Galen, <is why the drys and the Council government have so little trouble keeping this planet under their thumb on behalf of the Magistracy and the Principate. And, paradoxically, why Suo Hann is so appealing. She says, 'I will set you free—give me the power over you that the Principate has over you and I will tell you what to do. Follow me.'>

"What would you have us do?" asked Yas Tanna. "We are not soldiers or secret agents—like in the hol-vee shows."

Sam was watching Galen as Tanna spoke. Galen blinked once at the words "secret agent," but that was all. Sam smiled at Galen's self-control and his mastery over his facial expressions.

"Right now?" said Galen. "Go home. Sam and I will think of something."

"But—" began Dya.

"Please, go home," Sam told the crowd. Without further argument, they began to disperse.

"Why do I feel so shitty?" Galen asked Sam.

"Come on, let's go back to Varro's place, raid his liquor supply, and figure out our next step."

"You talked me into it."

Galen had grown so cynical about Varro's people's loyalty and support that he was pleasantly surprised when he was able to recruit five men willing to risk their lives to help free Gar Varro from prison.

The first man to volunteer his services turned out to be the biggest surprise of all. When Oli Foore heard that Galen was soliciting men for a mission whose goal could not be announced until they were well out at sea, he wasted no time in letting Galen know that he wanted to come along.

"I wish to join you," Foore told Galen and Sam.

Galen couldn't resist saying, "Join me, an air-sucker?"

There was more to his question than twitting the young Cousteauean, however. If Foore was serious, Galen had to know his feelings.

"There are air-suckers and there are air-suckers," Foore said. "Whatever else you are, you possess a Cousteauean hunter's courage. You faced an orn with nothing but the traditional weapons."

Galen nodded. He was almost, but not quite, satisfied. There was something else in the intense young man's eyes. "But that's not the only reason you want to come along, is it?"

"Wye Hassa and Kar Brunn were friends of mine. When they stepped forward to join Gar Varro's security forces, they asked me to come with them. Because of my anger at Tey for choosing an air-sucker, I spurned their request." His eyes narrowed. "Had I been with them that day, things might have turned out differently. They might still be alive, and Tey might not have been taken."

"It's also very possible you might have been killed along with your friends," Sam said, speaking up for the first time.

Oli Foore turned his hard eyes on Sam. "I should have been with them. Whatever happened to them should have happened to me."

"This mission does not have anything to do with Tey's kidnapping," Galen told him. "Not directly, that is."

"It does not matter," Foore replied. "When it is over, I shall join you in seeking out Tey. That is, if I have not been reunited with my fallen comrades." Having said that, his eyes bored through Galen. "You *are* going to go after Tey eventually, are you not?"

"Yes."

"Good."

<Jesus Christ!> Galen transmitted to Sam. *<Suo Hann is clearly not an anomaly. I don't think the Magistracy knows what it's getting into on this planet.>*

<Maybe breathing water does that to you,> replied Sam. *<You've breathed water, too,>* he reminded Galen.

<Kiss my ass!>

<See!>

Galen and Sam returned to Midland with their volunteers. Since seven people were not nearly enough to do what needed to be done, Galen planned to make use of all the resources of the PrinSecPol he could.

With the others safely ensconced in a nondescript hotel until they were needed, Galen and Sam strolled into a furniture store. *<They could have picked something less, less . . .>*

< Something less likely to make people think we're soul mates

looking to furnish our love nest?> Sam twitted him.

<No, I don't mean that!> Galen protested. *<Well, yes, maybe I do mean that,>* he admitted.

They entered a back room through an unmarked door and took a hidden drop tube to an underground passageway. "I love all this cloak-and-dagger stuff," Sam said as they followed the passageway into a sublevel of the local PrinSecPol station.

"Then you're going to love the rest of this game."

Sam nodded happily. He wasn't being facetious when he said he enjoyed the subterfuge and the role-playing involved in serving the PrinSecPol. *Maybe I was an actor in my flesh-and-blood days,* he mused.

Within minutes they were in a heavily guarded communications room lined with G-28 to prevent any possible electromagnetic scanning from revealing the content of the messages sent and received inside.

"May I be of assistance, sir?" asked an earnest-looking young communications specialist when Galen showed him his special I.D. cube and dutifully recited a series of code words and numerals.

"I need you to refresh my memory concerning the proper procedures," Galen told him. "I haven't sent out a message from a field station in a while." The young man nodded. "After that, you could go get me some coffee."

"Coffee? Certainly."

After thoroughly briefing Galen on the correct procedures, the young comm specialist started to leave.

"One other thing," Galen said.

"Yes?"

Galen looked sheepish. "Don't come back with the coffee until I give you a buzz on the intercom."

"As you wish."

When the other man in the room, the duty officer of the day, also left them to their own devices, Galen cracked his knuckles, sat down at the massive console, and punched in a preliminary signal. After all that, he got a 'please wait' response.

"Do you think Fedalf will accept the charges?" asked Sam.

"He will when he learns it's his prodigal son Galen."

The wait was nearly thirty minutes, longer than they had anticipated. When the connection was finally made, several soft chimes announced that fact.

"Hello, Hashem," Galen said. Seeing a familiar face behind Fedalf, he added, "Hello, Rob."

Both Fedalf and MacKenzie were slightly disheveled and sleepy-looking. "Oh, did I get you two out of bed?"

"If you bothered to look up our local time, Galen," Fedalf told him, yawning, "you'd know it was four in the morning here."

"Sorry," Galen said. Leaning against one wall in his chair, Sam stared at the ceiling and shook his head. There wasn't a gram of "sorry" in his partner's voice.

"Of course you are, Galen." Fedalf leaned forward. "Is Sam with you?"

Since Sam's chair was on rollers, he wheeled into the center of the holo beside Galen. "Good morning, Director Fedalf. Good morning, Rob."

"Hello, Sam," both men said dutifully.

With a this-had-better-be-good-Galen look, Fedalf asked, "Why are you calling me at such an ungodly hour, Galen? And why do you need the super-security of a station linkup?"

"I need some readouts. Blueprints actually."

"Blueprints?" Fedalf said. "Blueprints of what?"

"Kubyshev prison."

"Kubyshev prison!" Fedalf and MacKenzie chorused.

"Yes," Galen said patiently.

"Is that all?" Fedalf couldn't keep the tinge of sarcasm out of his voice.

"As a matter of fact, no."

III

The day had turned out to be a particularly brutal one, even for equatorial Cousteau. It had begun hot and muggy and only gotten more so as the afternoon progressed. The sun had beat down unmercifully on the low, marshy wetlands outside of Krow, impacting the walls of Kubyshev prison like a blacksmith beating on an anvil.

The guards had just finished eating a typically institutional meal: light on vegetable and fruits, heavy on meats and fats. As a result of their dinner, everyone was sluggish and drowsy. Consequently, few of the sentries in the towers realized that the radar screen that showed the immediate area had gone blank. The first to notice the not-ready condition keyed her comlink to report the failure and was further annoyed when she discovered that it had gone dead as well. She sighed an I-might-have-known-it sigh.

On average, the radar, the motion detectors, the comm channels, and just about everything else had fallen below normal operation parameters at least once a day since the opening of the prison a scant four weeks earlier.

If Warden Dorn and the bureaucrats who insisted Kubyshev was sufficiently ready had bothered to ask their officers' opinions, they would have gotten an earful; the consensus among the men and women who had to make the place work was that the prison could have used another six weeks of i-dotting and t-crossing.

Today it was the force-field generators' turn to be balky and recalcitrant about maintaining operational status. Throwing up their hands at being unable to project a perfect hemisphere around the prison and its towers, the technical staff was content to throw up shields around the inner walls alone. With hardly anyone inside, they decided, there was little reason to worry about maximizing the field's performance.

"Sonofabitch!" was the guards' consensus concerning what they thought was this day's only glitch, their radar-blindness. Since they had nothing to do with the force field, the tower personnel were unaware that it was functioning in a truncated form only.

Without radar, the guards were forced to rely on their own eyes. And with the sun now lancing in from the horizon, this was easier said than done.

The guardposts in the towers were suddenly filled with the buzzing of furious bees: ropy streams of plasteel-jacketed slugs being spat out at high rates by rotary slug-throwers. Most of the sentries in the towers were shredded like paper dolls by the lethal enfilade.

The source of the onslaught quickly became apparent as two Nostromo A-21 attack floaters roared in out of the sun like World War Two fighters and dove toward the prison. They flashed by the now-ruined guard towers and swung around for another pass.

"Not bad shooting, if I say so myself!" Sam whooped.

Oli Foore nudged his own command mouthpiece into place and asked, "How the hell could you do that, android?" He reconsidered that, saying, "I mean Foxfire One."

"Foxfire Two, this is Foxfire One," replied a soft, feminine voice. That got Foore's attention. "The android—that is to say, Sam—just flies this craft. I operate the weapons."

"Who are the hell are *you*?" Foore had thought he'd met all the team's members. This was a new one on him.

"Never mind who she is," responded Sam. "Let's see if we can strafe the open areas inside the prison's walls."

"Roger, Foxfire One."

After making sure his mike was off, Sam said seductively in the female voice Foore had heard, "Who am I? Why, honey, I'm Samantha." Sam grinned and swooped low over the prison's interior courtyard, his Nostromo A-21's weapons spewing death and destruction.

"Throw the force field over the whole damn prison!" a Legion lieutenant shouted at the first engineer he could find.

"You heard the man," the tech told his startled crew.

"Sir, we haven't the power to throw up more than a level-three intensity. We'll be stretched thin."

When the tech looked beseechingly at the lieutenant, the latter insisted, "We have no choice, dammit!"

"Yes, sir."

While reinforcements rushed to reoccupy the towers, a great fire-breathing dragon climbed out of the sea and padded purposefully toward the walls of Kubyshev prison. It wasn't *really* a fire-breathing dragon. It was a John Henry, a massive fusion-torch mining vehicle powerful enough to cut through solid rock.

His arms up to his elbows in the John Henry's operating waldoes, Galen stared at the outer wall's gate. It was growing larger and larger in the machine's viewscreen as the mining vehicle approached it.

"What's that?" asked Arn Shero.

"What's what?" Galen was focused on the upcoming gate and precisely where he wanted to impact it.

"That noise."

Galen cocked his head. "That? Sounds like bullets." He shook his head. "Idiots." Plasteel bullets had no more effect on the John Henry than mosquitoes had on a rhinoceros.

There was a bang, and a shiver ran through the John Henry's structure. "Now, a laser cannon is a different matter," Galen told his companion. "However, since we're about to enter the belly of the beast, it's too little too late."

Galen rammed the nose of the John Henry against the prison's outer gates. The force field was so weak at this critical point that the mining machine's torch easily ate through the molecular-steel bars like they were licorice.

"We're in!" Galen shouted.

"Look at that!" Oli Foore transmitted to Sam as the two A-21s hovered over the prison, exchanging gunfire with the remanned towers and with defenders inside the prison walls.

"I see it, Foxfire Two. I see it." Then, in "Samantha's" voice, he added, "They're in."

14

WHILE THERE WAS NO DENYING THAT THE WOMAN WHO STOOD before Tey was impressive-looking, she nonetheless failed to live up to the few exaggeratedly heroic likenesses Tey had seen of her. That was one reason why Tey hadn't immediately recognized who had taken her prisoner after the attack.

Suo Hann was just beneath medium height and didn't appear to be especially muscular, certainly in comparison to Tey herself. But first appearances can be deceiving, and a more careful examination revealed broad, powerful shoulders atop a compact build. It was also clear, despite her name and her ancestry, that Hann was no dry.

Tey felt strangely warm, as if Suo Hann's return stare was white-hot. If a stranger avoided her azure eyes and the intensity of her gaze, he or she might say that Suo Hann's most striking feature was her fiery red brush cut. It was made more memorable for the fact that few Cousteaueans were natural redheads. If Suo Hann were to actually defeat the Principate somehow, Tey mused, there would be a lot of young women dying their hair blood-red to match hers.

"Do I meet your expectations?" Suo Hann asked, a touch of amusement in her voice. She nodded to the two muscleboys who'd escorted Tey; they withdrew, closing the metal door behind them.

"Yes and no," Tey admitted.

Suo Hann laughed a deep, throaty laugh that Tey guessed many men would find very attractive—that is, if they were able to overlook the single-mindedness that burned in her eyes.

Suo Hann turned to a wrinkled old woman whose breasts were flaccid flaps of skin that hung almost to her waist, and said, "She is truly the daughter of a politician, is she not, Pia?"

"Yes, chosen one."

Chosen one! Tey thought. Suddenly, she realized that she would have to be very, very careful. Someone who allowed herself to be called "chosen one" might react in wholly unexpected ways if you misspoke yourself by uttering even a single inappropriate word.

Suo Hann might very well be a megalomaniacal madwoman, but she was not stupid. She observed Tey's eyes widen slightly at Pia's homage. "It makes you nervous, does it, hearing me addressed by my people in such a . . . a *flattering* way?"

It wasn't really a question, but Tey decided to answer it as such. "No, of course not." When Suo Hann's bushy eyebrows rose in response to that, Tey added, "A little, I suppose."

"You suppose!" laughed Suo Hann. "Please, have a seat," she said, indicating a sofa and herself sitting down on a wide chair with slashing diagonal stripes.

Tey did as Hann suggested and was surprised to note that neither the sofa nor the chair was composed of living matter. She thought that more than a little peculiar. *How odd that this woman who would be our planet's leader should not follow one of our more basic customs.*

Taking closer note of the room, Tey saw that it was essentially utilitarian, with only a handful of personal touches, like beaded wall hangings and small objets d'art, tossed in as if someone belatedly recognized the need to humanize the place.

"Now then," Suo Hann said briskly, "I have disturbing news to share with you."

"Disturbing?" Tey felt a sinking feeling in the pit of her stomach. *Father!* she thought. Only later would she realize that Galen's name hadn't leapt into her mind immediately after her father's.

"Yes. Disturbing for us both. It seems that at the same time that we snatched you from your family farm, your father was himself being picked up."

Tey frowned. "What do you mean, 'picked up'?"

"He was arrested by Nevin Feller's Legionnaires." She studied Tey closely. "You *truly* had no knowledge of this?"

Tey shook her head slowly, still trying to digest this unsettling news. "I knew that my father was to be put under arrest. He and Galen both told me that much. But we had all agreed that it would be for the best if he were to give himself up rather than be taken by force."

"Galen . . ." said Suo Hann thoughtfully. "Ah, yes—the Terran spy." She looked sharply at Tey. "Your lover, so it seems, was not entirely truthful with you about your father's fate."

"What do you mean?" *Orn shit!* Tey thought a fraction of a second after she said it. *I know what she means, dammit!*

"I mean simply that as an agent for Feller, this Galen Yeager presumably knew what his superior's intentions were with regard to your father."

As if hearing her own words triggered something, some awareness, Suo Hann crooked a finger at her ancient companion. When the old woman leaned down, Hann whispered something in her ear. The crone shot Tey an evaluative look and nodded.

Me and my big mouth! Tey thought.

Seeing that the monstrous machine had eaten its way through the outer gate when the weakened force field proved inadequate to the task of maintaining its integrity, the chief field engineer ordered his people to go to a "code yellow" status. That meant withdrawing the force field from the outer wall and gates to the walls of the prison proper.

"But that will leave the sentries in the guard towers unprotected!" the lieutenant in charge of the generators protested.

"It can't be helped," the engineer said through clenched teeth. "If we're to have a prayer of holding off that thing, we've got to pull the field back."

The lieutenant just gulped and nodded. In a situation such as this, he had no choice but to accept the advice of the chief field engineer. He wondered how much that would count for at his court-martial if the engineer's decision proved to be incorrect.

While all this was going on, the John Henry was twisting and turning this way and that on its treads like an angry bull impatiently casting about for something to charge. While the huge machine was much more than a mere bull, Galen *was* searching for the perfect place to "charge" the prison wall to bore through and rescue Gar Varro.

Even though the mining machine's fusion torch was presumably more than a match for the thick molecular-steel door which was the only way in or out, Galen saw no point in putting it to the test when there was an easier way.

"Ah, there's the spot," Galen said. Wiggling his fingers and feet, he made the machine do his bidding. The sense of power that operating the John Henry gave him was exhilarating; he could easily get addicted to being a monstrous entity with the abilities of a god.

Galen approached the administrative building housing Kubyshev's high security cell block, gradually slowing down and then pressing the John Henry's nose against the force-field-protected wall with a surprising delicacy; the sensitivity of the waldoes made him one with the machine.

A shrieking, screaming, nails-across-slate sound promptly erupted as the fusion torch penetrated the constantly renewing stream of energy flowing protectively over the wall's surface. The hideous sound was sweet music to Galen's ears; it was the sound of success.

Secreted in their ceramic-lined control room a dozen meters beneath the prison, the force-field generators were sorely tested by the too-sudden increase in power required to maintain the integrity of the barrier. Whining in high-pitched protest like a wounded tyrannosaurus rex, the generators began to throw off blue-white arcs of electricity that threatened to incinerate anyone foolish enough to approach them in a vain attempt at a manual shutdown.

Galen had earlier refused to think negatively, putting his faith in the idea that the John Henry could slice its way through the prison's force-field barrier. Only now, after it had successfully done so, did he realize what an enormous chance he had taken. Where would he have been if the field had repelled his attack? He was thankful he would never know the answer to that question.

Glancing at the holographic display of the blueprints that danced above him, Galen made certain he was going in the right direction. He was. The blueprints confirmed that the cells containing the highest-security criminal and political prisoners lay directly ahead of the rampaging John Henry.

"My God!" exclaimed Arn Shero, staring slack-jawed at the damage the mining machine was wreaking within the prison.

A few soldiers and guards halted, set themselves, and bravely, if fruitlessly, unleashed the full power of their weapons at the inexorably approaching John Henry.

Galen mused that the mining machine was perhaps the perfect illustration of the old term "unstoppable force." It seemed unlikely that the John Henry would meet an immovable object unless they encountered a square-jawed, ebony-haired man in a blue suit with a red cape blocking their way.

"There it is," Arn Shero pointed. "The cell block you mentioned."

"Yes, there it is," agreed Galen. He suddenly found himself with a cottony mouth. There was no reason he should have that reaction, he realized. No reason at all, unless . . . *Things have gone too damn smoothly. I'm not sure I like it when things go according to plan.*

"You know, things have almost gone too smoothly," Shero said.

"Things can never go too smoothly," Galen remonstrated. Then he shook his head at both of them having the same thought at the same time. Shero wasn't the deepest thinker in the world, but he was an okay guy. It made Galen feel the tiniest bit ashamed for hoping their shared concern was uncharacteristic.

Galen halted the John Henry outside the cell block, stilling its relentless forward motion and shutting down its torch. "While I believe in the concept of a 'surgical strike,' this thing isn't a scalpel," he said, answering Shero's questioning look.

"Time for the boys in the suits?"

"Yeah."

"Jan and Zev—get into position," Shero told them, speaking self-consciously into his communicator.

"We hear you," came back the voice of one of the two battle-suit-clad men. Galen and Shero could hear their thudding footsteps as they clomped to the hatchway. Wondering why he didn't do it sooner, Galen activated the camera in the back. Both men looked like fat, rubbery robots.

Galen paused a moment before opening the hatch. "Be careful out there," he told the two men. "Sometimes wearing a battle suit can make you feel invincible. You're not. Someone might have a can opener."

"We'll keep that in mind," said Jan dryly.

"You do that. Good luck." Galen irised open the circular hatch, the two warriors exited, and he quickly closed the hatch again.

Zev and Jan stepped into a maelstrom of small-arms fire as the soldiers and guards directed all their anger and frustration at the only available targets. Their eyes riveted to the John Henry's external displays, Galen and Shero watched the two suited men waddle unceremoniously toward the cell block guardpost.

The ungainly Varro loyalists affixed a small, gooey mass to the plasmetal door and then prudently stepped back several meters. There was no actual need for them to do so, since the battle suits were protection against almost anything, up to and including field atomics.

The shaped explosive charge blew open the door and they stepped inside—and out of sight.

"Christ," murmured Galen. "I'd forget my head if it wasn't attached to my neck."

"Huh?" said Shero.

"Turn on your helmet cams," Galen told the team.

"Right," Jan responded, and Galen and Shero now saw what the battle-suited warriors were seeing.

Galen guided the dynamic duo down the corridors, telling them when and which way to turn. Almost ashamed of the "unfair" advantage the suits provided them, Jan and Zev tried to ignore the occasional attacks against them by the defenders. When compelled to respond, however, they struck back with appropriate force.

With no one or nothing capable of stopping their progress, the two battle-suited men took very little time to reach Gar Varro's cell.

When Jan pointed his flashlight at the small "E" on the heavy door, Galen told them, "That's it."

Zev detached a drill from his utility belt and approached the plasmetal door. It took him no more than thirty seconds to drill through the cell's lock.

"That's enough," Jan told him. "Let me try it now."

"Be my guest."

Jan yanked on the cell's door and it popped open. He hesitated for an instant before pulling the door completely open and stepping inside. Galen stared at the murky image returning from Jan's battle suit. He tried to swallow but found he couldn't.

The helm-cam served as Galen's eyes. As Jan swept the room with his electric torch, the cell's severity was apparent. There was really nothing in the room apart from the rude cot and the ceramic ring set in the floor that served as the sanitary facilities. There was no pool of water. For a Cousteauean, that truly was cruel and unusual punishment. *Unusual?* thought Galen. For the Legion it was SOP—standard operating procedure.

A scrabbling sound caused the battle-suited intruder to turn and catch the source of the sound in a circle of light. It was a rat, the largest rat Galen had ever seen. Its beady eyes shone red in the flashlight's accusatory beam while it stared defiantly back. Then, taking its time, it disappeared into an opening in the plascrete wall.

After sweeping the cell with the beam from his flashlight, Jan said, "There's nothing here."

"Nothing and no one," added Zev.

Galen shivered even though he wasn't cold. Nothing and no one: Gar Varro wasn't there.

II

Tey Varro's nostrils flared and she became aware that the warehouse smelled of the sea. That was hardly a revelation to her, since *everything* on Cousteau smelled of the sea. The others gathered within the warehouse probably would not have noticed the odor unless someone had pointed it out to them. Does a fish notice the water, or a bird the air?

Tey herself would not have noticed the warehouse's particular scent had not she been blindfolded. *It's amazing what taking away one of your primary senses does for the others,* Tey marveled. Her arms bound tightly to her sides, she sat stiffly in a chair against one of the walls. She had no idea why she was there, but she intended to absorb whatever she could.

The blindfold not only prevented Tey from seeing the faces of Suo Hann's fellow conspirators, it also kept her from seeing the warehouse itself and the hundreds of crates of fish meal filling it which were destined for the hungry cities of Terra and other overpopulated planets.

The restrictions on her vision denied her the opportunity to notice the intense lighting that illuminated every corner with relentless efficiency, the dirt and discolorations on the plascrete floor, and the many glo-signs and posters exhorting workers and visitors alike to wear hard hats and to observe basic rules of safety.

When a blinking **THINK** sign, its letters pulsating their crimson message, floated over Tey Varro's head, her primal sense of proximity alerted her that *something* was within her natural space. An air current caught the sign and carried it away.

While Tey could not see those in attendance, they could all see her, and her presence seemed to alarm them to the point where few could take their eyes off her.

Not so with Lee Perro. He was aware only of the face of the woman who had called them to this illegal and highly dangerous meeting. Perro sat unconsciously rubbing his wrists and staring at the red-haired woman's face, the face of Suo Hann. *How nominally nondescript she is,* he thought. *Or would be, if it weren't for the color of her hair and those luminous eyes. How the hate and fury she's bottled up inside her shines through!*

Watching her, Perro noted how her lithe figure shivered with barely contained energy as if some spring inside awaited explosive release. He knew that some of her friends, those closest to her, called her Ahkan Ai, after the great volcano on Horath. Perro thought her brilliant and shared her politics and her vision of a self-governed Cousteau but not her intensity of commitment. But then, few did.

"Why have you brought Varro's daughter to this meeting?" someone, a woman, asked Suo Hann.

"Because it is time this fool Varro was bypassed," Suo Hann said. "For far too long he and his friends have held back the revolution by preaching patience. But waiting has only served to continue our domination by the Principate."

"I agree," said Lee Perro. "We must do something now."

Mao Yanna, a labor leader, watched Perro rubbing his wrists and said, "So it's true. A friend told me he'd seen the police arresting you this morning. What did you do, spit in the street?"

"Something just as bad. I was distributing wet literature without a permit. My father got me out on bail so I could attend tonight's meeting." He glanced at the others. "Don't worry," he reassured them, "I wasn't followed."

"Well, enjoy yourself while you can," Yanna said. "With the courts controlled by Magistracy lackeys, you'll be sure to get at least thirty days in the Henley work camp."

"I'm getting too fat anyway. The exercise will do me good."

"More proof that the revolution is overdue," said Suo Hann.

"I suppose Suo's right," said Bor Tirro, "but a revolution is a one-way drop chute; once it starts there's no turning back . . . is there?" Her unlined face was furrowed by the earnestness of her question.

"By the damned godwhale! We've been all through that. Did we not say the same things before agreeing to destroy the *General Woodard*?" asked Yur Palio, a dark-skinned fisherman from Gasir.

"Oh, that's just terrific!" a not-quite-fat man muttered loudly, glancing meaningfully in Tey Varro's direction. For some reason, that made Suo Hann smile broadly.

"The hell with that jellyfish's daughter! I am not cowed by her presence and I did not come here tonight to argue over points we've debated into the ground." He looked at the faces staring at him from around the table, seeking confirmation. "We must act immediately. The revolution must begin here and now."

"Why?" asked Kea Wynne, a pale young woman with doe eyes.

"For the same reasons people have always overthrown their governments: The bastards won't listen otherwise. It's a guaranteed attention-getter. Orn shit! Why should I be denied my economic and individual freedom simply because I was born on Cousteau and not Terra?"

"There are other ways," said Wynne. Suo Hann shot her a look. Wynne stared back for a moment, then dropped her eyes, seemingly in shame for questioning their very purpose in coming together as a revolutionary action group.

Putting her hands beneath the table at which she sat, Suo Hann activated the comlink cube resting on her lap and keyed a string of coded commands into it. She waited a few seconds and then glanced down. The corners of her mouth turned up ever so slightly. Kea Wynne would return home to find someone waiting for her. The ethereal young woman's sudden reluctance for what was necessary would not be allowed to threaten their plans.

Unaware what had just transpired, Yur Palio continued. "Let me be more specific, in the way we're going to have to be if we're to win over full public support from Varro and his do-nothings: Our catch this year off Gasir was larger than ever— an aberration, really—but the air-sucking Principate bureaucrat who purchased it for Terra told me we were expected to exceed it by ten percent next year. Ten percent! Trust an air-sucker to ask for the impossible," he concluded amid bitter laughter from the others.

"I agree," said another attendee, his face hidden in the shadows. His uniform was visible, however, revealing him to be a highly placed member of the local police force. "We're being bled dry by the Principate, just like all the other colonies. We owe them nothing, nothing at all. That's all we're left with in return for our protein after all the taxes and 'privilege fees' are taken off the top!"

"Soon we'll be paying a privilege fee to take a leak in the ocean," joked Yur Palio.

"Sh-h-h," cautioned Mao Yanna facetiously. "Let's not give 'em any ideas if we're bugged."

Bor Tirro did not laugh. "What about the drys? What are we to do about them?" She looked about, her eyes avoiding contact with the others'. "My . . . my brother is a dry," she said softly, almost inaudibly.

They all knew this fact, of course, but this knowledge did not prevent an almost instinctive disgust from registering on several faces; it was not a subject for polite discussion. A few faces reflected pity and compassion. Suo Hann's face, however, remained impassive, revealing nothing of what she was thinking.

"I would not want there to be . . . reprisals," Bor Tirro added hesitantly.

Suo Hann's father was born a dry. After Suo herself was born, her father decided to cast his lot with other drys and Principate brown-noses and seek an office job, breaking his closest tie with the wets, the sea. A brilliant man, Tal Hann rose quickly within the ranks of Council planetary officials and, when Suo was eight years old, migrated from Cousteau for a high-status job on Terra and never returned. He severed all ties to the family he left behind.

For that ultimate betrayal, Suo had never forgiven her father— or the Principate that had drawn him away from her and her mother. Her father's rejection of her was her one great secret. Since she told no one, not even her lovers or closest friends, no one knew the source of her anger and hate.

"Assuming the drys cooperate," Suo Hann said, measuring her words carefully, "there will be a place for them in the new Cousteau. We will still need contacts with Terra and people who can work 'above.' They will have to swear allegiance to Cousteau and to the revolutionary government, of course," she finished, toying with her necklace of orn's teeth.

Nodding at Yur Palio and careful not to use the other's name in front of an outsider, the owner of the warehouse in which they were meeting, Tes Moore said, "I must agree with our friend from Gasir's earlier remark. This too is something we have discussed before. Are we all talk and no action? I want to know when we're going to *do* something, not just talk about it. Are we a revolutionary committee or a debating league?"

"You forget the *General Woodard*," a voice said.

"Hardly, since it was mentioned a minute ago," Moore said. "But all I hear is the *General Woodard*, the *General Woodard*! It has been weeks since we struck that blow. We talk about it like fat old veterans of a war remembering their one shining moment!"

"All right," suggested Suo Hann, "let's return to the subject we were discussing before we adjourned our last meeting. We had reached an impasse and—"

"We *always* reach an impasse," someone muttered.

Suo Hann smiled indulgently. "As I was saying, we had reached an impasse that had to be broken. I have since broken it by our attack on Varro's sea farm and the taking prisoner of his daughter."

"What is your plan, Suo?" Mao Yanna asked.

Suo Hann smiled. There was no warmth in her smile; it was just a curling back of her lips to show her teeth.

"I had thought to use Varro's daughter to bend him to our wishes. But he has been arrested by the Magistracy—by Nevin Feller's Legion." She shook her head. "He is a strong man and—"

Several voices angrily protested that characterization of Gar Varro.

Silencing the outburst with the raising of her hand, Suo Hann continued. "He *is* a strong man," she said. "Not as strong as he needs to be, nor strong enough to resist Feller's sophisticated methods of persuasion, I fear. For that reason, Gar Varro no longer interests me."

Her eyes shining, Suo Hann glanced around the room, making eye contact with her rapt followers and co-conspirators. "I have reason to believe that the Terran secret operative called Galen Yeager is *not* an agent for Feller and his Legion. He is, instead, an operative for the wily Hashem Fedalf and his PrinSecPol."

Tey sat absolutely still, listening. She almost forgot to breathe.

"This man is also Tey Varro's lover."

"You mean . . . ?" began Lee Perro.

"Yes," Suo Hann said. "She can be used to force one of the Principate's most dangerous and accomplished agents to do our bidding."

"And if he will not?" asked Bor Tirro.

Suo Hann turned to stare thoughtfully at the bound and blind-folded Tey. "Then she will die a slow and lingering death."

15

~~~~~

"ARE YOU RECEIVING OUR SIGNALS CLEARLY?"

"Clearly enough, Jan." Galen licked his lips nervously. *Where the hell is Gar?*

"Now what'll we do?" Zev's voice asked plaintively.

Jan put his hand to the side of his helmet, cocking his head quizzically. "Hey, hear that?"

"Hear what?" Galen and Zev asked simultaneously.

"It sounds like someone shouting," Jan said. Zev and Jan increased their suits' auditory levels.

"You're right," Zev told Jan.

Looking at the images the helm-cams were sending back, Galen saw both turn toward one another, their faces hidden behind the helmets' featureless visages. "It's Gar!"

Getting into the second cell proved no more difficult than getting into the first had been. As Zev drilled through the lock, Galen noted sheepishly that the cell door had a small "F" painted on its exterior. The cause of the confusion was obvious: In his haste, he'd simply mistaken the F for an E.

"Could have happened to anyone," Galen murmured.

"What?" asked Sharo. "Oh, that 'F' on the door. Yeah."

Once in, they saw Gar Varro sitting limply on the cot that was the cell's major feature. The cot was the largest, but far from the only, piece of furniture. There was a standard toilet, a tiny rectangular pool of water, a small upholstered chair, a writing desk, and—wonder of wonders—a nondescript but not entirely pileless carpet to cover the bare plascrete floor.

A part of Galen's mind noted subconsciously that it might be worth considering why Varro's cell was so luxurious when compared to the empty one Jan and Zev had first examined. It didn't occur to Galen, not even to his subconscious, that perhaps he *hadn't* misread the letter on the cell's door.

"Gar?" Jan said.

The Cousteauean leader was slumped against the cool plascrete wall, his legs splayed out across the bed. With what seemed to be great effort, he focused his eyes on his visitors.

"Who . . . who are you?" He slurred.

"We're with Galen Yeager," Jan explained. "We've come to get you out."

"Get me out?"

"Yes, get you out," snapped Zev, moving around the bed to grab Varro by the shoulders. Seeing what his companion was doing, Jan joined him and the two of them pulled Varro to his feet.

"Come on," Zev said.

The two battle-suited men half-carried, half-dragged the semi-conscious Gar Varro out into the corridor and back the way they had come. Watching their slow if steady progress was agonizing for Galen. While Jan and Zev were fully protected by their battle suits, Gar Varro was essentially naked.

"Come on, come on!" Galen urged the trio between gritted teeth. Fortunately, Zev and Jan had decimated or chased off any guards or soldiers in the vicinity on their way in, and they met no resistance.

When Zev's helm-cam showed them approaching the John Henry's hatch, Galen opened it just long enough for the three of them climb through. "Come on, come on," he muttered under his breath.

As soon as he was sure they were inside, he cycled the hatch shut and began the process of turning the gigantic piece of mining equipment around; it was no small task. While the John Henry was cylindrical—it actually resembled a stubby submarine on plasteel treads—it was hardly svelte.

The John Henry was as confined in the long narrow corridor as a locomotive in a tunnel would be. After a momentary feeling of being trapped swept over him, Galen realized getting out wouldn't be a problem. He didn't have to turn around. All he had to do was keep moving forward and "eat" his way out.

With the fusion torch vaporizing whatever it came in contact with, Galen deconstructed the end of the corridor. He plunged the nose of the John Henry into the hole, and then backed down a side corridor. The huge machine's treads spun momentarily until they bit into the rubble beneath them; then the John Henry surged forward, back again, and forward one more time. The mining vehicle was not intended to turn on a coin, and it didn't.

"That's done it," Galen said to Shero before he realized the other had gone back to attend to their three passengers. "Oh, right," he mumbled to himself. "He's helping Varro and the others." Sharo had taken charge of the disoriented Varro while Zev and Jan fumbled with the releases on their suits.

Actually . . . "Hey, Zev."

"Yeah?"

"I think it's a good idea if you and Jan stay bundled up until I give you word that we're out of here." Galen stared at the fast-approaching wall and added, "Things are about to get hot and nasty again. If I was in one of those things, I wouldn't shed it until I was absolutely certain no one was trying to give me a plasma enema."

"Gotcha."

"How *is* Varro, by the way?"

"He seems in pretty good shape physically," Shero said via the intercom from the rear of the vehicle. "But don't expect him to make sense for a little while yet. I think they drugged him or something."

"Okay. Thanks." Galen tensed as the mining machine approached the hole they'd punched through the wall on their way in. "I'm going to be too busy to talk for a while now."

"Do what you have to," Jan told him.

The John Henry plunged through the perfectly circular opening in the wall it had made just minutes before, exiting into the prison yard. As if its reappearance was the signal they had been waiting for, every soldier and guard who had a weapon rained laser beams and bullets on the mining machine—to no discernible effect.

"They never learn, do they?" Galen said, steering the lumbering vehicle toward the ruined gates.

Once through the smooth-edged opening it had burned through the steel bars, the John Henry was again bathed in the intense rays of the early evening sun. The system's yellow dwarf star—their unwitting ally during the initial attack—now became just as unwitting and impartial an enemy.

"Christ!" exclaimed Galen, averting his eyes.

Although the John Henry's cameras—its eyes on the outside world—adjusted almost instantaneously, there was a brief moment when Galen was hit full face by the blinding glare. Blinking his eyes to clear the massive red-orange blob that danced across his retinas, Galen failed to see the large half-track that had responded to the attack on Kubyshev by rushing to the prison site to shore up the defenses.

Poised to intercept the intruder when it attempted to make its getaway, the half-track instead became just another victim of the larger vehicle—albeit one that bit back. The John Henry's treads climbed up and partially over the half-track, its weight crushing the smaller vehicle. The flattened truck blew up with a devastating explosion that rocked the John Henry.

Concerned by the severity of the blast, Galen anxiously glanced at the readouts. "Piss and crackers!" He was horrified to see that the explosion had so weakened the John Henry's left tread that it had snapped in two and spun off uselessly.

"What's that?" asked Oli Foore nervously.

Sam Houston looked at his own holographic display. "Damn!" he cursed softly.

"Not good, huh?"

"Not good at all," Sam replied. "Our company appears to be two fighters as heavily armed as we are." Sam peered at the display again. "And it looks like there are two more on their way to join their buddies."

"*Four?* Christ, let's get out of here."

"We can't just turn tail and leave our people on the ground to the tender mercies of those fighters," Sam told the antsy Foore. "Their air-to-ground missiles would make short work of the John Henry."

"But—"

"Goddamnit!" Sam erupted.

As Sam was circling around to get into position to fend off their attackers, he had seen that the John Henry had gotten hung up on another vehicle.

The danger now was from more than just the fighters. If Galen couldn't free the John Henry, enemy ground reinforcements could show up at any moment. In fact, their appearance was almost a certainty, since the Legion barracks were no more than two klicks down the road.

"What's the matter now?" Foore sounded ready to cry.

"It has nothing to do with you," Sam told him. "Just help me gang up on the first two fighters before the other two get here. If we can take either or both of them out fast, we have a chance."

"How can two 'gang up' on two?"

"You forget that I'm not human, boy," Sam said, flipping over the Nostromo and dropping like a rock.

"While Sammy's playing 'air ace,' you continue flying straight at the first two floaters, Oli," the mysterious feminine voice told Foore.

"Yes, ma'am," Foore said, gritting his teeth and forcing himself to fly head-on at the attackers. "Just tell my folks I died bravely."

"I see our new arrivals are A-21s as well," Sam noted. "There must have been a no-money-down, manufacturer's special at the lot this week."

After the three floaters exchanged "Hi, how do you do?" weapons fire, Sam suddenly jerked his A-21's nose up, kicked in all the power he could, and climbed through the thick, sea-level air like a peregrine with his tailfeathers on fire. He rocketed straight up past the combatants, nosed over in a long, looping maneuver, and dove seaward again at his aircraft's top speed.

"I did my job flying this crate. It's your turn now," Sam pretended to say to "Samantha" for Foore's sake—if he was listening.

"Bye bye, babies," Samantha crooned, unleashing a devastating volley of energy bolts that overwhelmed the two ships' modest topside defensive shields and blew them apart in a multicolored pyrotechnic display.

"Damn good shooting, Foxfire One—whoever you are," Foore said.

"With two more fighters about to meet us for air-to-air missiles at twelve o'clock, there's no time for back-slapping," Sam said primly in Samantha's voice.

"Can't argue with that."

Sam and Foore made wide, sweeping turns out over the ocean and, hugging the tops of the waves, headed back toward the just-arriving attackers. Sam couldn't believe their luck had held true for this long; once again they were flying out of the dying sun.

"Shouldn't we be trying for height?" asked Foore. "I mean, it worked pretty good for you and your mystery gunner."

"Not with the sun at our back. We're so low to the water they can't really see us with the glare and the reflections."

Sam knew that even if their enemies' eyes were blinded by the sun, the attacking fighter pilots still had their inboard radar and other ranging devices to rely on.

The four Nostromo A-21s shot past in opposite directions like a quartet of medieval knights tilting at each other in the lists. While both sides gave as good as they got, no one suffered much damage.

As all four turned for second passes, Sam looked down and saw three armored cars speeding down the road to the prison. From the plume of dust the cars threw up behind them, he guessed that they would arrive in minutes and immediately begin slashing at the immobilized John Henry like hyenas attacking a downed water buffalo.

"Be careful, Galen!" he said in frustration.

The first blast from the armored cars' laser cannons shook the John Henry but did little real damage. Seeing the three armored cars in the external display for the first time, Galen cursed.

"I take it that's not opportunity knocking," said Shero from the back of the vehicle.

"Give that man a two-credit cigar."

Galen knew that the armored vehicles could do little against the John Henry with a few bolts of cannon fire, but not even the big mining machine could stand up to a continuous bombardment. Their attackers had another advantage—they only had to keep everyone inside until something heavier arrived, something that did possess the firepower to do the job properly. Or Legion combat engineers could simply plant charges against the John Henry's hull and blow the hatches open.

"Aren't you two glad I asked you to stay in your battle suits?" asked Galen dryly.

"We're delirious with joy," Zev responded.

Galen grinned to himself. *Are there finer people than these anywhere in the galaxy?* He answered his own question: *No. A person couldn't die in better company.*

"Hey!" said Shero.

Hey, indeed! Galen agreed. Patiently directing a steady stream of energy bolts at the John Henry's right-side hatch, the nearest armored car had seemed to levitate for an instant before blowing apart in a massive explosion.

Just as the fireball from the explosion was about to envelop the second armored car, it blew up in a similarly spectacular fashion.

"Overheated engines?" Galen asked, unaware that he had inadvertently opened the comm channel to Sam and Oli Foore's Nostromo A-21s.

"Hardly," said Sam's voice.

"I should have known it was you."

"Not this time. You have Foxfire Two to thank for pulling your beacon from the fire." Sam was too smart to use Foore's name on the airwaves.

"Foxfire Two . . . as in 'I hate all Terran air-suckers' Foxfire Two?"

"The same," Foore said, joining the conversation. "I had a couple of missiles I was dying to try out, so it wasn't that big a deal."

"I have to disagree," Galen told him. "Speaking of deals, what's the one with Foxfire One?"

"Since you asked I'll tell you," Sam said. "My gunner and I are in a dogfight."

"A dogfight . . . ? What the—"

"Sorry, no time to talk."

II

While Tey Varro passed her days in captivity alternating between despair and boredom, Suo Hann initiated a series of terrorist acts. Scaled to slowly ratchet up in intensity from industrial and commercial sabotage to mass murder on a grand scale, the campaign of destruction began at sea.

The huge cargo ship was twenty-eight hours out of Krow on Midland and headed for Gasir when the explosives hidden in its hold detonated. They were devastatingly effective and blew two holes, each the size of a small house, through the hull.

The ship slipped beneath the waves in less than eight minutes. A few survivors huddled together in one of the two lifeboats that were successfully launched in time. Other survivors swam to the second lifeboat. Since they were all Cousteaueans, meaning amphibians, they didn't really need the lifeboats to sustain their lives.

With the sails raised and supplemented by the small but adequate motor, however, the lifeboat would help them to reach safety much faster than if they had to swim the many kilometers to the closest port. Further, it was assumed that all this was made moot by the ever-vigilant communications satellites circling overhead.

Since most of the force of the two powerful bombs was directed at the hull, the ship and its cargo were really not much damaged by the blasts. In the cargo bay were several low-radiation, low-yield atomic weapons. Despite the Council ban on atomics, the Legion was secretly putting several dozen low-yield "clean bombs" in place in various locales around the planet.

When the Magistracy and Feller approved the bombs' deployment, everyone assured everyone else that sending the weapons to Cousteau was merely a "precaution"; there was no intention of ever actually using them. Not ever. Never.

What that *really* meant was that the weapons would not be used unless it became "absolutely necessary." The atomics would not be fired in anger unless the Cousteaueans "forced" their use.

As the now-orphaned weapons plummeted into the deep trench that traversed the sea floor, the pressure of the water caused the arming and detonating device on one of the small atomics to malfunction.

A Legion spy device aboard the same communications satellite circling overhead that received the doomed ship's distress signal also recorded that the resulting explosion was contained to a relatively compact area deep beneath the surface of the sea.

When the data was later examined by experts, they counted their blessings that the detonation not only happened well out at sea, but also in such an obscure and unpopulated area. After all, no one lived at the bottom of the Gasir Trench.

At about the same time the proscribed atomic weapon detonated at the bottom of the sea, Suo Hann's sappers were meeting the *P.S.S. Thaddeus Stevens Curtin* ten kilometers from the port of Ikton, on the knife-shaped island that was appropriately named the Dagger. Each sapper had a magnetic mine to attach to key places along the keel of the Terran-owned ship's hull.

The sappers finished their lethal work in less than five minutes and the ship sailed on, its crew oblivious of the six mines clinging to its hull. Each was inexorably ticking down to the moment when the timing devices would open the switches that would detonate the plastic explosives and send the ship to the bottom of the sea.

Their timers in perfect agreement, the mines blew enormous holes in the plasteel hull and the ship quickly filled with sea water and began to plunge toward the cold, dank depths of the ocean. Unlike the similarly ill-fated cargo ship, the *Curtin* was not carrying atomics or weapons of any sort. It was carrying something much worse: chemicals and toxins so foul and dangerous that they were listed on the manifest as "building supplies," lest the ship's owners be prosecuted for illegally transporting hazardous materials without authorization.

The freighter's captain, aware of what his cargo hold held, bobbed on the surface of the sea and thanked the gods that the poisonous liquids and powders his ship had been carrying would end up at the bottom of the sea—many kilometers below the surface where nothing lived except odd species of glowfish, giant squids, and misshapen monsters of the deep.

Slipping silently deeper and deeper, the ship resembled a harpooned whale of old. And like some fatally pierced Moby Dick, the ship "bled" all the way down, its toxic cargo seeping out of the wounds in the hull.

The ruined freighter finally came to rest on the sea floor. Still leaking its silent death, it was solemnly regarded by a massive shape that ventured no closer to the death ship than was necessary.

The shape moved off, found a thermoplane, and began its song. A song of discovery, of death, of apprehension. When the song ended, the gigantic shape looked upwards once, then swam silently away.

III

"Well, 'gunner,' " Sam said to his alter ego after closing the comm channels to Galen and the others, "think we have a chance?"

"Does Cerberus have fleas?"

"You bet—and why are you talking to yourself?"

"Good question," Sam said, applying full power and hurtling directly at the two A-21s trying unsuccessfully to catch his floater in their sights long enough to blow him out of the sky. They'd already exhausted their allotment of missiles trying to outdo Sam's nanosecond-sharp reflexes and his ability to pull high gees without blacking out.

When they finally broke off, peeling off to opposite sides, he killed the forward thrust, shed about seven hundred kph, and again allowed his Nostromo to drop toward the sea. As his opponents carved tight, circular turns through the sky to curve back on him, Sam accelerated at an inhuman rate and shot toward the slower of the two enemy fighters.

Their flesh-and-blood bodies unable to match acceleration and grav-pulls with Sam's mechanical one, the Legion pilots could only gape in a combination of awe and fear as Sam completed an impossible maneuver that left him hurtling at the exposed undercarriage of the laggard. His laser cannons spat fat, hot bolts of energy that burned through the doomed floater's belly like a fish gutter's knife opening up a carp.

Even as the destroyed Nostromo was disintegrating in a fire-ball composed of bits of metal and plastic, Sam was slamming on the brakes again and coming around to position himself like a matador preparing to lean over the horns of the bull in a ring of death and drive the tip of his sword deep into the beast's shoulder. And like the guest of honor in that blood "sport," the other fighter craft had two chances: slim and none.

The other pilot seemed to realize the futility of continued

engagement with whomever or whatever was flying the other A-21. Seconds before the bolts of energy Sam poured into the other Nostromo blew it apart, the pilot ejected.

"Smartest man I'll meet today," Sam said, watching the other man's chute open and begin carrying him down toward the sea. With some deft maneuvering, the Legion pilot manipulated his descent so that he was carried back over land.

"Now then, where were we?" Sam asked, reaching out to reestablish the hookup to Galen and the John Henry.

16

≈≈≈

"EVERYONE'S ON HIS WAY BACK TO THE CRESCENT?" GALEN asked Sam. Then he sipped his cooler.

Sam nodded. "Everyone. Well, not Samanthə, of course."

That made Galen smile. "You mean not a single one of 'Yeager's Heroes' wanted to stay and sample the delights to be had in the big city?"

"I guess you can take the boy out of the sea farm, but you can't necessarily take the sea farm out of the boy," Sam said.

"It's just as well. They'll be safer back where they belong. That's the best place for them now—away from here," Galen decided. "Away from the door-to-door searches and the curfews that are coming."

Sam agreed. "And they can see that Varro gets the medical attention he needs."

Galen stared into his drink as if the answers he was looking for could be found there. "I can't really believe it," he said softly, almost to himself. Sam, with his inhumanly acute hearing, had no difficulty picking up his partner's words. "We pull off the goddamnedest, craziest, hairiest stunt imaginable and don't lose a soul—don't even suffer a scratch—and we find out that the man we came to rescue is a zombie."

"Pisser, ain't it?" agreed Sam. "There is a bright side, however."

"Yeah, what?"

"Maybe you can sell the story to the sinnys."

"Sam, what would I do without you?"

"You'd have to find perfect strangers to drive you nuts."

"But seriously . . ."

"Seriously, what is the problem with Gar Varro?"

"Stop your damned kidding already!"

"I'm not kidding." Sam was all wide-eyed innocence.

"Oh, please," said Galen wearily.

Sam raised his right hand and said, "Scout's honor." Then a look of introspection crossed his face.

"A memory trace?" asked Galen. "Something from your previous existence?"

"I'm not sure," replied Sam, putting his hand to his head. "I think so. I must have been a Boy Scout."

"You mean a Star Scout, don't you?"

"No, they—we—were still called the Boy Scouts."

"That's amazing," Galen told him. He knew that in the bad old days there had been a lot of separation by races, nationalities, and sexes, but to hear that an organization could be so gender-specific was a bit unreal. "I'm talking to a human time machine here," he chided Sam.

"Be nice or I won't tell you how I gave Edison the idea for the light bulb."

Sam's words evoked a rare response: Galen laughed so hard that tears came to his eyes.

"It wasn't *that* funny," Sam said mildly.

"I know," Galen said, wiping his eyes. He was unable to stop giggling completely. "I'm so wired and tense that I'm about this far away from hysteria," he said, holding his thumb and forefinger a centimeter apart.

"Is that why you're still avoiding answering my question?"

"Gar Varro," Galen said in a voice that was hardly above the level of a whisper. He stared hard into Sam's golden-irised eyes. "You saw the condition he was in."

"Drugs?"

"Obviously, but there's more to it than that, I think."

"*More* than drugs?"

Galen's eyes darted about the room. "I don't know. It's just that . . ." His voice trailed away. He looked drawn and tired.

As if inspired by his earlier mention of Edison, Sam imagined a light bulb lighting up his own head. "You're worried about Tey, aren't you?"

"What do you think?" Galen asked a little more sarcastically than he intended.

Sam paid no attention to his friend's sharpness, aware that Galen wasn't himself. "I think we've got to do something. But what?"

Galen finished his drink. "I can't see that there's anything to be gained by either of us returning to Terra. For one thing, Fedalf can take care of what needs to be done on that end."

"I agree."

Galen put his hand around his empty glass. Sam watched in amazement as Galen slowly tightened his grip. When the glass shattered, Galen stared at the blood on his palm and then said, "It's time to go after Tey."

Sam looked at Galen's bloody palm and said, "Let me show you something first, okay?"

"Why can't you tell me what it is you want to show me?" Galen asked plaintively, eying the waiting exchanger with apprehension. He was surprised at how little time away from the sea it took for the idea of putting that sack of slime on his face to seem . . . well, *disgusting*.

"I'll speak slowly this time and use words no longer than two syllables: I made a promise."

"Yeah, but to the fishfaces," Galen said, using Sam's term for the silvery boka.

"Fishfaces . . . tee-hee-hee," chortled a boka, poking its head out of the water. "You funny as Sam."

"Oh, hi . . . um-m-m . . . Ariel," Galen said. He hadn't spent as much time with the boka as Sam had, so he was proud of himself for remembering the silvery animal's name.

Ariel was quickly joined by Nemo, Rachel, and Jacques. Seeing them again, Sam was struck by the fact that these four boka seemed to have adopted him—either that, or they came as a matched set that couldn't be separated.

"It's a gathering of fishfaces," Galen told the bright-eyed boka poking their heads out of the water. He had something to live up to—they thought he was as amusing as Sam.

"Sam come in water?"

"Yes, I'm coming into the water, Nemo," Sam replied.

"Gay-len come in water?"

"Yep, me, too." Turning away from the boka and staring at the exchanger waiting for him, Galen said, "Okay, Mr. Houston, let's get this over with."

Sam grinned and gathered up the exchanger, waiting patiently for Galen to lie down flat. "Here we go," Sam said. "Try not to think of drowned bodies and eels trying to wiggle into . . . well, you know."

"Al keel yah latah, yah sonuffabitch!"

"Kill me later? Tsk, tsk, you can't even talk right."

The sea made Galen feel at peace, despite his deep concern for Tey's safety. He knew there were many kinds of hydrotherapy, but wasn't aware of any that simply involved swimming in the ocean. It seemed the best kind, however.

With his human/android friend and partner at his side and the four friendly boka first ranging ahead and then gliding back to circle protectively around him, Galen wondered why his long-dead ancestors had ever given up the sea for the land.

"You look happy as a pig in a wallow," Sam told him after observing the slight crinkling around Galen's eyes that betrayed the big smile hidden by the exchanger hugging his face.

The crinkles increased, then vanished. "I do?" Galen sounded stricken.

"Hey, it's all right to relax and enjoy yourself, you know," Sam admonished him. "I'm worried about Tey, too. But worrying about her doesn't preclude a person—and that means you—from accepting whatever simple pleasures come his way."

"Yeah, I know," Galen said without conviction.

"You'd make a great mom," Sam told him. "That or a sheep dog. Yeah, that's it: I see you as a conscientious border collie."

Nodding toward Ariel swimming a few meters from his shoulder, Galen said, "You're forgetting where we are. Try a conscientious boka."

"I have no problem with that."

"Prob'lm?" asked Ariel, overhearing them. The four boka had seemed a little disconcerted when they'd learned that Sam intended to take Galen to view the "thing." Although communicating clearly with the different-brained boka was not always easy, Sam was pleasantly surprised that they appeared willing to accept the idea that he was not literally violating his promise of silence by *taking* Galen to the object instead of *telling* him about it. If they felt betrayed, they didn't reveal it.

"No, no problem, Ariel," Galen told the concerned boka. <*That's some kinda hearing these guys have, isn't it?*> he said to Sam.

<*Better than mine, even. They can probably hear the food digesting in your stomach.*>

<*Water's a great conductor of sound.*>

When Rachel and Jacques swam back for a quick look, Galen asked, "Is it far yet?" His arms were getting a little tired. When Sam began getting a sled for them before they left, Galen had told him not to bother. He wanted the exercise. Now he wasn't so sure how good an idea it had been to refuse the sled.

"Far, Gay-len?"

"Yeah, *far.* You know, is it going to take a while for us to get there or just a few minutes?"

"Hehhehhehhehheh," rattled off Jacques like a machine gun, flashing that sometimes endearing, sometimes grating perpetual grin that was the bokas' only real facial expression.

"What'd I say?" asked a confused Galen.

"Oh, I'd guess that the fishfaces were amused when you turned your question from one concerning distance to one concerning time."

"Yeah?" Galen stared at the grinning, silent boka.

"The distance thing they probably could have answered if you'd allowed them to, but I'm not sure they have a real good grasp of time."

"Five races," said Nemo suddenly.

"Huh?"

"Is five races to secret place."

"Um-m-m . . ." began Galen.

Sam laughed. "You asked and they've told you." He laughed again. "It's not their fault you don't know how far 'five races' is."

Galen had to join in the laughter. "I give up. I guess when we get there, we'll be there."

"Yes-s-s-s," chortled Ariel, lashing her tail up and down vigorously to propel herself back to the point.

"What now?" Galen asked.

"Glowfish," Sam said mysteriously.

II

"My God!"

"That was my reaction, too," Sam beamed, pleased by Galen's appropriately awed response.

"What is it?"

"The 'thing,' " Sam said, now pleased to hear the boka titter.

"What's so funny?"

"Private joke."

"Okay, it's the 'thing.' Now that we've all gotten our jollies from saying that out loud or hearing it repeated, what in the world *is* it?"

"It could be anything. It could be a really large oyster. Can you imagine the size of the pearl that—"

"Sam!"

"It looks to be what folks used to call a flying saucer."

"A flying saucer?" Galen had never heard the term before.

"You know—little green men from Mars." Sam stopped when he saw that Galen's forehead was furrowed by a frown. "Oh," Sam said unenthusiastically. "It's the old 'that was before my time' bit again, eh?"

"Sorry." Galen *was* sorry and tried to make it up to Sam by adding, "You don't look your age."

"Anyway, to make a long story short—though I suppose that's impossible now—that thing down there looks suspiciously like one of the twentieth century's most enduring myths: the flying saucer, an alien spacecraft."

"I don't remember alien spacecraft visiting Old Earth."

His equanimity restored, Sam just smiled benevolently. "That's because they were apocryphal. Flying-saucer sightings were a sort of mass hysteria that—"

"So when are we going down there?"

"Huh?"

"We can talk about it until we're blue in the face," Galen told Sam, smiling briefly at the off-base figure of speech, "or we can go down and check it out."

"Check it out," repeated Rachel.

"We can't do that now," Sam insisted. "At least you can't."

"Say that again?"

"I wanted to show it to you. That's all we can do right now, because of the depth it's at. I could safely descend that many fathoms, but not you or the boka."

"You mean you brought me all the way out here just to eyeball that thing?"

"Well-l-l-l . . . As I said, *I* can investigate it."

"Not with your mechanical head stuffed up your mechanical butt, you can't!" Galen said hotly.

"I'm taking that as a rejection of my suggestion," Sam said brightly, trying to jolly Galen out of his annoyance. When the storm clouds didn't lift, he added, "I suppose we could go back and have you fitted for an abyss suit."

"A-bis, a-bis, a-bis," sing-songed Jacques, swimming circles around one of the glowfish.

Sam had a sudden thought. Cocking his head, he looked oddly at Galen and asked, "What about Tey? Are you telling me now that you *don't* want to go after her immediately, that you'd rather come back here? I mean, this thing's probably been here a long time and I don't see any reason to believe it won't be here a while longer."

"It's crazy, isn't it?" agreed Galen. "Finding and rescuing Tey has been an obsession with me, yet . . ."

"Yeah?"

"Somehow I know that she's okay, at least for the time being." He looked confused. "And there's something else."

"Again—yeah?"

"This thing, this flying saucer or whatever it is, it . . ." He paused, groping for the right words. "I don't know how or why I know, but I sense that it *wants* us to go down there."

"You sense that?" Sam asked dubiously.

"Yes." Galen stared into the depths. "I also sense that our going there won't hurt Tey," he said confidently.

"Guh-bye!" trilled Ariel and the others.

"Goodbye," Sam said to the four boka. Since neither he nor Galen was good at regurgitating partially digested food to feed the glowfish, Sam had taken care to bring along several high-intensity, hand-held electric torches to provide whatever illumination was needed.

As fat and rubbery in his abyss suit as Zev and Jan had been in their battle suits, Galen didn't really require any additional lighting instruments. The abyss suit he wore came with everything a person would conceivably need on a visit to the bottom of the sea, including more than adequate sources of illumination.

"How do I look?" Galen had asked Sam after he had climbed into the contraption that would allow him to dive safely into the trench containing the strange alien object.

"Like a fat man whose body wasn't found for a week," Sam told him after taking a long, hard look at Galen's half diving suit, half diving bell getup.

"That's what I get for asking you."

While Galen's abyss suit would permit him to reach depths of up to nearly two kilometers, it wasn't meant to go all the way to the bottom. For that, one still needed a submersible like a bathysphere.

Still, the abyss suit was a marvelous thing. Galen would have compared it to a space suit but for the fact that a space suit normally only had to cope with containing one atmosphere in a total vacuum. The abyss suit didn't have it that easy. It had to maintain one atmosphere of internal pressure against the crushing weight of the water. At one hundred meters, the water pressure was an awesome ten times that of the surface—or one kilo pressing against every square centimeter of the suit.

The earliest models of the suit, Galen had learned, had come with a confusing array of switches on the shoulder yoke and on and in the helmet. While there were still a few such manual backups, most of the suit's functions responded to simple voice commands. The computer was an old Bathgate bubble-neuro grid whose CPU had all the charm of an insurance salesman with a level-three personality restructuring.

The suit's four-point lighting was a result of twin headlights on the helmet and one atop each of the shoulders. The helmet lamps were fixed, but the shoulder lamps could be individually swiveled and tilted.

The water bottle and nipple was the most archaic thing about the suit. While miniaturization and computerization had made remarkable progress over the years, there was still no substitute for the simple internal canteen that slaked the wearer's thirst.

Up to this moment, up to the time they said goodbye to the ever-grinning boka, Galen had been looking forward to his voyage to the bottom of the sea, thinking that a great adventure lay ahead of him. Only now, as he adjusted his suit and began to trade buoyancy for ballast, did he contemplate what sinking into the depths like a drowned giant might mean if anything went wrong.

<Ah, Sam.>

<Yes?>

<Is it too late to turn around?>

<No,> Sam replied, deciding not to joke about the possibility.

<Good.>

Sam smiled at that. He knew Galen was nervous. He also knew that his friend was braver than any three people you might point to. Galen just wanted to hear that there was a way out if one was needed. *Kinda like a kid who's scared there might be monsters under his bed when he's going to sleep in a darkened room. He's afraid, but he's reassured by the presence of his mom and dad just a few steps away.*

<Isn't this something?> Galen marveled as he slowly sank deeper and deeper.

<It's a whole other world,> agreed Sam.

The further down they sank, the more light became a curiosity. This was a realm untouched by the sun; a place of cold and continual midnight. Fish with long whiskers or antennae trailing behind them swam lazily by. More than a few fish of all sizes were attracted by the lights both men carried or wore. For that matter, the fish themselves were often the possessors of light-emitting appendages.

Something that looked like a meter-long log with gills "sniffed" its way up Galen's suit from his boots to his helmet.

<You must smell good enough to eat,> Sam laughed. *<Either that or some of the fish find you attractive. I don't understand it—you're not even wearing your codpiece.>*

<My what?> Galen asked, distracted. Then he added, *<Do you mind if we turn the lights off for a minute?>*

<It's okay by me,> Sam said, following Galen's lead in switching off their lamps and torches. After taking a moment to get used to the total blackness, Sam exclaimed, *<Wow!>*

<I was in a mine once,> Galen said. *<It was almost exactly like this. You don't know how dark 'dark' can be until you find yourself in place devoid of all light. Not just dim, utterly black.>*

<It is truly astonishing,> Sam said. Holding out a hand,

he sensed the increasingly cooler water flowing past him. He knew that was just an illusion. It wasn't that the water itself was moving, so much as he was falling through it.

That sense of falling became apparent to Galen as well, and he said, <*Okay, let's switch the lights back on.*>

<*Wait a second!*> Sam exclaimed.

<*What? What is it?*>

<*It's completely black!*>

<*I thought that was the point of turning out the lights.*>

<*That's not what I mean,*> Sam told him. <*Why isn't the object glowing? One of the reasons the boka were able to show it off to me—and me to you—was the fact that it was glowing, or at least being lit up by some source of illumination.*>

Galen looked down. It was true: The object was nowhere to be seen through the inky blackness of the water. Gulping, he said, <*I see what you're saying, but could we turn the lights back on now?*>

<*Sure.*>

<*What do you think it means?*> Galen asked.

<*Maybe they know we're coming,*> Sam said, igniting a flare and letting it fall from his hand into the depths.

<*They?*> Galen pondered Sam's usage of the word. He *had* told Sam he believed the two of them had been called to this place, but he wasn't as certain any longer. Things seemed different down here.

<*I don't know what to think,*> admitted Sam. <*You're the one who said you received an engraved invitation.*>

<*Yeah, I know,*> said Galen. He glanced into the utter void that lay beneath them. <*Have you considered the possibility that the thing—the ship, whatever—is no longer there?*>

<*That thought did cross my mind.*>

<*What a goddamned fucking development!*>

<*Please,*> remonstrated Sam. <*I told you I was once a Boy Scout. No cursing, please.*> He ignited another flare stick, sending it fluttering down after the first.

<*I'll give you no cursing. I'll—*>

<*Oh, good,*> said Sam. <*It is there, after all.*>

<*Huh?*> Galen looked down between his booted feet and confirmed that Sam wasn't pulling his leg. Before dying out, one of the flare sticks revealed that the missing flying saucer hadn't moved; it simply was no longer glowing.

<Just another hundred meters or so left to go,> Sam calculated.

<Great,> Galen told him. *<That means another kilo of pressure per square centimeter.>*

<Are you sure you'll be all right?> asked Sam, unable to hide his concern for Galen's safety.

<I can handle another hundred meters without any problems. But . . . > Galen looked down at what lay beneath his feet, making calculations of his own.

<But?>

<Do you think it's a good idea for me to plop right down on top of that thing? That's what's going to happen if I don't maneuver a little to the right or left.>

Sam glanced over at Galen and made a suggestion. *<Adjust your angle of descent so that you land right beside the object. There's more than enough room on the ledge that thing's resting on.>*

<All right.>

Galen did as Sam directed and he gently settled down not more than two meters from the saucer. A huge plume of mud and lightweight debris silently rose around him, all but obscuring him in a chocolate-colored cloud.

<Touchdown. The Eagle has landed.> When Sam gave him a funny look, Galen explained, *<I felt like Apollo 11 touching down on Luna and disturbing the lunar dust for the first time in billions of years.>*

The cloud was just beginning to dissipate when Sam joined him on the huge outcropping of rock that supported the massive saucer-shaped object. *<That's one small step for a man, one giant leap for an abyss suit.>*

<Well,> said Galen as the new cloud of dirt and debris thrown up by Sam's landing swirled around them. *<Here we are. Shall we go exploring?>*

<Before or after I carve 'Galen luvs Tey' into the side of this thing?>

<How about instead *of?>*

<Oh, all right,> Sam said crossly. *<You and mom never let me have any fun.>*

<That's not true,> remonstrated Galen. *<We let you throw the garbage into the disintegrator, don't we?>*

Sam stared at Galen, then checked his suit's readouts.

<What's the matter?>

<You made a funny. I'm just checking to see if you're getting too much oxygen.>

<Hey, I can say funny things too, you know!> Galen said hotly.

<So could Hitler—who was also a damned fine dancer.>

Having tired of playing verbal tennis with Sam—he was not unlike a teenager in that he had a short attention span when it suited him—Galen took stock of his surroundings. Barely two meters away was the smooth metallic-looking surface of the object that had drawn them to this hostile place.

17

≈≈≈

AFTER SLOWLY APPROACHING THE SAUCER'S SHELL AND CAU-
tiously rapping it with his knuckles—it made no sound whatsoever—Sam said, *<Let's circumnavigate this sucker and see if
there's a doorbell.>*

*<Did I happen to mention how goddamned big this thing
is?>* asked Galen as the two of them began slowly marching
around the saucer's perimeter. After seeing Sam's bravado, he
now boldly reached out and stroked the silky smooth exterior.
<Glossy, too.>

<It is incredibly smooth,> agreed Sam. *<That means it either
hasn't been down here long, or whatever it's made of is resistant
to a hostile environment like this.>*

<Check this out,> Galen said, attempting to bend over in his
semirigid suit. Because of the pressure, he could only get about
a third of the way down.

<What're you trying to do?> Sam asked.

*<I want to examine how completely the dirt and sand and
other crap that's floated down to cover this ledge has drifted
against the saucer's sides. It's a good idea, but the pressure has
made me too stiff.>*

*<Too stiff? I'll bet you never had any complaints about that
before,>* Sam said, reaching down through the detritus until he

touched bare rock. The layer around the saucer's bottom was easily fifty centimeters deep. *<I'd have to say this thing's been here a long, long time.>*

<I agree.>

As he often did when he was puzzled by something, Galen tried to scratch his head. His gloved fingers simply rasped against his helmet. Since he wasn't consciously aware of what he was doing, going through the motions was as satisfying as if he'd actually completed the act for real.

<What's that?> Sam asked.

<What's what?> Galen began, then stopped. *<Oh,>* he said, cocking his head. *<You're right—what* is *that?>*

It was an eerie, plaintive sound that sent shivers up Galen's spine. Low and mournful, it was repeated several times before fading away. Galen and Sam looked at each other. Whatever it was, it had nothing to do with the silent object beside them; the sound seemed to have been carried to them from a great distance.

<Do you think that might have been a whale singing?> asked Sam.

<A whale singing? There aren't any whales on Cousteau.>

<You're forgetting about the Berserkers,> Sam told him.

<I never *forget about the Berserkers,>* insisted Galen. *<But they aren't true whales.>*

<Sez who?> challenged Sam.

That made Galen think. Who *did* say the Berserkers weren't at least cousins to whales? They didn't breathe air and seemed unlikely to be mammalian, but almost no credible research had been done on them.

<You may be right,> Galen said finally. When another long, plaintive passage reached them, he asked Sam if the source of the sound seemed to have gotten any nearer.

<I don't think so,> Sam replied.

<Good,> Galen said. He was relieved to hear that, although he didn't know why. Shaking off an ominous feeling, he gestured toward the saucer and said, *<Let's get on with it.>*

<Fine by me.> Sam played his lamps' beams of light over the thing's outer skin and they continued their inspection. *<Well, this hunk of junk is clearly a craft of some sort—a spaceship, I suppose one would have to say,>* Sam observed. *<But I'm disappointed by the lack of identifying symbols—lettering, numerals, or images of any sort.>*

His gloved hand still trailing lightly over the saucer's skin, Galen said, *<Maybe there are symbols on the top or bottom.>*

<We'll never know about the bottom, will we?>

<I suppose not,> Galen said, nodding agreement. He glanced upward. *<But there's always the top of this thing. It looks like only twenty meters or thereabouts to get up on top.>*

<Only twenty meters or so?> laughed Sam. *<We're going to have to readjust our buoyancy to neutral and then haul ourselves up hand over hand.>*

<That's not going to work,> Galen said with a shake of his head.

<Why not?>

<As you yourself have pointed out, this thing's almost frictionless.>

<You've got a point,> conceded Sam. *<Tell you what; one of us will just boost the other right up top—throw him, really. After all, we're making it sound like we can't just float up.*

<Have we seen everything there is to see down here?>

<We can walk around it a few more times if you wish.>

<A simple yes would do—no need to be a wiseass.>

<Come on, then, you first,> said Sam, ignoring Galen's riposte.

<Why not you?>

<Because I don't move like a pregnant hippo.>

<Good point.>

Sam waited until Galen adjusted his buoyancy to a hair above neutral, and then made a step for him with his fingers interlocked. *<Here you go, Humpty.>*

Galen put his booted right foot into Sam's hands and felt himself being propelled upwards by the other's strength. With a few blasts of compressed air, he maneuvered himself onto the top of the saucer.

<Hey, it's nice and level up here, like being on a billiard table's playing surface.> Galen walked to the center, paused, and then walked to the other side to peer down into the void.

<The thing that gets me about . . . > Galen's voice trailed away.

<Galen?>

<Oh . . . my . . . God!> Galen bit off slowly but emphatically.

Sam quickly joined Galen atop the saucer and just as quickly exclaimed, "Jesus!"

Regarding them both with a large, blue eye turned their way was the largest living thing either of them had ever seen.

"Hello, Mr. Berserker," Galen said through his external speaker.

II

Tey fumed and fussed, striding back and forth in her small cell. She was upset and angry. Upset at what she'd learned of Suo Hann's plans to initiate an all-out revolt against the Principate; angry at herself for allowing Suo Hann to figure out that Galen worked for the PrinSecPol instead of the Legion.

How had Suo Hann put the pieces together in such a way that pointed her toward Galen's allegiance to Hashem Fedalf? "Pia?" she said softly, remembering Suo Hann's ancient advisor.

Could that old crone actually be a witch? Tey didn't believe in such nonsense herself, but she realized a touch of the Ability was often mistaken for witchcraft. And why not? The Ability gave one powers that were "magical" enough—the capacity to read other people's intentions, or to see into the near future, or to cloud the thinking of the weak-minded.

The weak-minded? Tey laughed a bitter laugh. *Like me?*

Suo Hann had returned Tey to her original place of imprisonment after the meeting at the warehouse, and the frustrated young woman now beat the damp, cold stone walls with her fists and cried out in rage, "Let me out of here!"

Suddenly exhausted, she slumped down and leaned against the unyielding stone. But instead of weeping, she raised her head. There was no one there to see the steely look of determination that now won out over the mask of despair that she had permitted herself to wear for far too long. *This is* my *world*, my *special environment, not Galen's or Sam's. I can't expect them to come to my rescue as if I were a fairy princess in a high tower.*

She remembered what Suo Hann had said about her. They were going to use her to make Galen do their bidding. Like hell they were! Tey made a vow: *I am going to get out of here or die in the attempt.*

<*I've got an underwater energy pistol tucked in my utility belt,*> Galen said, unable to take his eyes off the heart-stopping

behemoth hovering perfectly motionless in the water not five meters from them.

<*Don't even* think *about shooting that monster.*>

<*Why not?*>

<*You might just piss it off.*>

<*Good point.*>

"Hi, there. How'ya doin'?" Sam said to the Berserker observing them gravely.

When the Berserker didn't react, Sam added, "Nice weather we're having, huh? Kinda wet, though." Galen just shook his head and rolled his eyes toward Heaven.

<*If you're trying to*—> Galen stopped, his eyes widening. <*What's that noise?*>

When the high-pitched, pure harmonic increased in intensity, Galen put his hands to either side of his helmet, unconsciously trying to clap them over his ears.

<*Lower the volume on your suit's aural circuits before you ruin your eardrums, Galen,*> Sam advised.

Already in the process of doing just that, Galen said, <*It's too loud. It's too damned loud.*> His equilibrium gone, Galen stumbled sideways for a step or two before falling slowly backwards and landing on his back since his suit was too rigid to bend.

Sam watched open mouthed as Galen toppled over. <*Are you all right?*> Staring at his fallen comrade, Sam noticed that the top of the saucer was beginning to glow—at least a small area that enveloped the fallen Galen.

<*Yeah, I'm okay,*> Galen replied. As the high-pitched sound tried its best to invade his suit, he added, <*I just wish that damned sound would*—> To Galen's amazement, Sam, the saucer, and the Berserker disappeared in a flash of ruby light.

For Sam, it was Galen who disappeared.

When the glow faded, Sam was left all alone. Not completely alone: There was still the Berserker regarding him somberly. Sam's mind raced furiously as he tried to sort through the peculiar predicament he found himself in. Galen Yeager, his friend and partner, the man who had helped him be reborn, was gone in a brilliant flash of light, leaving him standing alone atop a massive alien artifact confronting a savage killer of the deep.

Apart from that, Mrs. Lincoln, did you enjoy the play? Sam smiled a tight, bitter smile; that was precisely the sort of border-line nasty comment that he liked to make for Galen's benefit—to keep his human partner's mind off the bad things that could happen. Speaking of Galen . . . *Where* is *Mrs. Yeager's little boy?* he wondered.

"So, big fella," Sam said to the solemn-looking Berserker, "would it help if I said I was a Pisces? I'm not—I just wondered if it would help."

He was aware how giddy and I-don't-give-a-rat's-ass his concern for Galen was causing him to act. Normally, Sam would be pissing in his pants—figuratively. As it was, he didn't much care that he was only a few meters away from one of the most vicious and merciless killing machines of this or any other world.

The Berserker's tail lifted and fell once, and that modest motion was enough to propel it slowly but surely toward Sam's position atop the saucer.

Although Sam's leg bones were made of the finest polysteel, they felt like rubber to him when he realized the Berserker was moving toward him like a giant locomotive bearing down on a small animal frozen with fear on the tracks.

"Jesus-s-s-s!" Sam hissed, retreating backwards across the top of the saucer as the Berserker glided toward him as inexorably as death and taxes. Its mouth began to open—a mouth full of picket-fence teeth capable of rending him into tiny bits.

Sam sensed the edge of the saucer behind him; he could edge back no further without falling off. The Berserker's mouth opened wider and wider. Sam threw his arms up across his face in an involuntary response to the monster's approach. One gulp and he would be swallowed whole.

"I'll see you in Heaven—or Hell. Galen."

Galen's chest rose and fell rhythmically and he felt himself swimming up to the surface of consciousness. Eyelids fluttering, he opened his eyes and saw nothing but white. He was lying flat on his back on a hard surface and staring at a white ceiling.

The room in which he had awakened was totally white and essentially featureless. Was it a cell? A holding pen? Heaven? He tilted his head and looked around. *Don't see any angels*, he observed. *And if this is Heaven, where's my double Jack Daniels on the rocks?*

He disrupted the sameness of the white background by raising his arm and interposing his hand between himself and the ceiling. What was it about his hand that made him frown in concentration? It was so obvious that he couldn't see it for a second—he was no longer in the abyss suit.

Sitting up, Galen dangled his legs over the edge of the hard, plastic rectangle supporting him. It was all of one piece with the rest of the room, seamlessly rising up out of the floor in a solid block.

Looking around the small room, he saw that it appeared to extend approximately three or four meters in every direction. And except for the floor and ceiling, it was completely circular.

That wasn't true, he decided. There was a single rectangular wall roughly three meters by three meters. He hadn't seen its angularity at first because of the white featurelessness of the room; it caused a sort of snow-blindness that obliterated detail. Or would have if there had been any detail to obliterate.

As soon as he slid off the slab supporting him and then turned around to stare at it, the slab was gone. *Did it withdraw down into the floor?* he wondered. *Soften and melt into the floor?*

"Sam?" he said out loud. He heard his own voice, but the sound was oddly muffled. He tried again and got the same disappointing result.

Despite his feigning total ignorance about flying saucers for Sam's benefit, he did remember a thing or two about them from the history and psychology cubes. One of the elements that seemed inseparable from the overall phenomena was the reputed kidnapping of human beings for study and experimentation. As paranoid and ridiculous as that delusion had seemed to him when he read about it, Galen could not keep a tendril of doubt from insinuating itself into his thoughts.

"So, little green men from Mars—or wherever—show yourselves, if that's who you are." Galen was not surprised when his invitation elicited no response.

Galen was deciding what to try next when a brief chime seemed to come from the square wall. Looking intently at the white surface, he was surprised to see an image forming. When it was complete, he tugged on one earlobe, then laughed out loud. It was childlike in its iconic simplicity.

The figure was this:

III

This is disgusting! Tey thought. *Throwing up is one of my least favorite things in the whole world, and here I am trying to make myself vomit on purpose.*

Tey had submissively retreated to the back of her cell when one of her jailers brought in her evening meal. "That's a good girl," the fat-bellied man said, beaming. Bearded and coarse, he set the tray down on the rude plaswood stool her captors had grudgingly permitted her to have on the third day of her imprisonment.

"What, nothing to say to your humble servant?" he asked with a leer. From the beginning, he had made it perfectly clear that he would enjoy nothing so much as to run his rough hands over Tey's body, kiss her face and neck, and thrust his moist tongue down her throat or into her ear.

"Thank you," Tey said, feigning shyness and awkwardness.

"That's better," he said approvingly. "Now you just let me know if there's anything else I can do for you. *Anything* else." He grinned and backed out of the room, pausing long enough to say, "I'll be back in twenty minutes for that, sweetheart."

Tey nodded as the door closed. "I'll be waiting," she said softly.

And so she was—or would be, as soon as she could induce herself to bring up the meal she had wolfed down, barely bothering to chew the spicy cubes of meat and the soggy vegetables.

Tey withdrew the spoon she had shoved down her throat as soon as the spasms began. "Ohmygod!" she moaned as she felt the gorge rising. Had anyone been watching and grading her performance, Tey was certain she would have gotten high marks for volume; it *all* came up.

As the convulsions diminished, she allowed a little bit to dribble down her chin onto her bare neck and chest. Doing something so revolting was easy: She simply thought of Galen

and her father floating lifeless in the sea—dead because of her—
scavenger fish darting in to tear away bits of flesh. Next to that,
soiling herself was nothing.

She arranged herself on the floor, taking special care to position herself in the far right side of the room, her head away from
the door. Her guardian would have to enter the cell completely
to examine her. As she lay waiting on the floor, she begrudged
the fact that she did not also have long, flowing hair to splay
out artfully for dramatic effect.

Hearing the key turn in the lock, she took a deep breath and
held it, hoping to keep her chest from rising and falling any
more than necessary.

"By the godwhale!" the fat jailer exclaimed when he saw
her. It was a measure of his lust for Tey that he bemoaned her
possible loss to his desires before he considered the blame that
would accrue to him if he had carelessly allowed her to consume
poisoned food.

He knelt down beside her with great difficulty, his rolls of fat
making it a challenging chore for him to get down completely.
He placed one beefy hand to the side of her head and turned her
face toward his.

"Please don't be dead," he moaned. "Please don't be dead."

He didn't see her hand close around the handle of the dull-
edged spoon. She brought it up without warning and drove the
stem into the side of his throat.

The fat man shrieked like a stuck pig, and bright arterial blood
spurted over Tey. Losing his balance, the stricken man fell over
backwards, writhing in pain on the wet floor.

Tey grabbed the cushion that padded the nearby plasmetal
chair and positioned it over the wounded man's face, hoping not
only to muffle his cries but also to choke off his air supply.

As she lay atop him, pressing the cushion down over his nose
and mouth with as much force as she could muster, the mortally
wounded man's hands sought and found her own throat, his
sausage-thick fingers sinking into the flesh.

With the strength of a wounded bull, he began to force himself up despite her best efforts. Rather than resist his superior
strength, probably a futile gesture at best, Tey allowed him to
rise to a sitting position. Then she used an old martial arts
move to break his grip on her neck. Free of his powerful

hands, Tey now hurled herself at him. Her momentum caused him to jackknife backwards and his head smashed on the stone floor with a sickening, dropped-melon sound.

He made some odd, grunting, porcine squeal, shuddered, and was still. Even before Tey removed the cushion to stare at his sightless eyes, she knew he was dead.

"Oh, God . . ." She stared in horror at the fat man's body. What had she done? She turned her head and heaved silently, but there was nothing left to come up.

When her shaking had subsided, she pulled herself over to the small pool of water and rolled in. The water washed the blood and vomit from her, and she quickly climbed out.

Looking at the puddle of thick, red-black blood that had spread out around the dead man's head, Tey covered her mouth with the back of her hand and swallowed. At the same time that she wanted to scream at what she'd done to a living, breathing person, she couldn't help noticing and marveling at how much blood the human body contained.

Tey forced herself to approach the dead body and kneel down beside it. She pulled a small needle gun and two full clips from his pockets. "Lucky, lucky, lucky," she repeated softly like a mantra.

Lucky, yes, but what lay outside the door? Surprising herself, she realized that she didn't want to find out. That was no good, she knew. "You killed a man to be able to walk out that door," she told herself. "His death will be for nothing if you don't follow through."

A determined look on her face, Tey Varro approached the doorway to her cell, hesitated an instant, then stepped through.

IV

When he wasn't gobbled up in one bite, Sam cracked open an eye and squinted through it, like a little boy checking for monsters in his bedroom at midnight. There was a monster in his bedroom, all right. Looming before him was the wide-open mouth of the Berserker, a pitch-black railroad tunnel to Hell. It was a sight no one on Cousteau had ever seen and lived to tell about.

Sam lowered his arms and gaped like a rube at a sideshow. "What is it?" he asked. "What is it you want me to do?" It slowly dawned on him what was expected of him. "Oh, no—not that!"

When the Berserker did nothing, Sam began to accept that "that" was exactly what he was supposed to do. "That" was to walk into the creature's hangar-sized mouth. "No way, José," he said firmly.

Then something occurred that had never happened to him before; he had a vision. Sam knew all about the Ability, and grudgingly accepted that certain people truly possessed psychic powers, that they could see wispy images of possible futures, maybe even *the* future.

Sam was a rationalist, but he couldn't deny that people with the Ability had powers he couldn't logically explain away. Perhaps it was because he was so skeptical about the unexplainable that his vision was especially startling to him.

What he saw in his mind's eye, as if caught in separate blinks of a strobe light, were two strong images. In the first, he saw himself entering the Berserker's mouth. This was immediately followed by a second image. In this one he was holding up and staring at a large rectangular shape. *Yeah*, he thought sourly. *Queequeg's coffin.*

Since it seemed like a lot of unnecessary effort to go to to make him choose the role of Jonah voluntarily when the Berserker could simply gobble him up, he decided he had little to lose by trusting the vision.

"I'm either the bravest sonofabitch that ever lived or the dumbest," Sam muttered, walking into the Berserker's mouth.

He felt his feet sinking slightly into something firm and spongy, and gulped when he realized he was walking on the monster's tongue. He stepped on something hard and aimed the beam from one of his hand-held torches down at it.

"What the hell?" It was a piece of polysteel, a refrigerator-sized hunk of metal with lettering on it. In the glare of his torch, it revealed its origin. It read: *P.S.S. Thaddeus Stevens Cu*

Even before he opened his eyes, Galen realized he was flat on his back once more. And what was the cause of that strange yet familiar sensation? "Hey, I'm in my abyss suit again!"

<Welcome home, partner,> Sam said, eying him curiously.

<Where did you go?> asked Galen.

Sam shook his head. *<I didn't go anywhere. The real question is, where did you go?>*

Galen considered that, recalling the white room. *<I guess you're right. Well, it's a long story.>*

<Okay, I can wait, especially since you're back.> He regarded Galen curiously. *<I would like to know one thing now, however.>*

<Sure.>

<What's that?> Sam pointed at Galen's gloved left hand.

<Huh?> Galen looked down at his hand. He was clutching a crystalline object just slightly smaller than an ostrich egg.

PART FOUR

ALFIE

18

TEY BREATHED A PRAYER OF THANKS THAT THERE WAS NO ONE
outside her cell. There were also no lights. That wasn't exactly
true; the ceiling of the underground and undersea passageway
was covered by phosphorescent algae. It was as bright as the
light from a full moon, but no brighter. Tey shrugged; it was
enough.

Tey took several steps to the left. Through the semidarkness
she saw a heavy metal door, not unlike the door to her cell, bar-
ring entrance to a room not five meters from her own. Another
cell? She looked at the keys she held in her left hand and then
at the door. None of the small bits of plasmetal looked like they
fit the lock.

Beyond the room, further down the corridor, the tunnel curved
left. With nothing but her intuition to rely on, Tey decided that
was not the way to go. She turned right and followed the tunnel
until she came to an intersection. She could go straight, turn
right, or turn left.

She sniffed the air, her broad nostrils flaring, and peered left.
If the scent she smelled wasn't wishful thinking, the sea lay in
that direction. Unfortunately, there were probably more than a
few of Suo Hann's people in that direction as well. She peered
down at the needle gun in her left hand and wondered if she

could use it on a complete stranger, despite what she had just done to her fat keeper.

"Wye . . ." Tey whispered. When Tey was captured, Suo Hann and her people had marched her past Wye Hassa and Kar Brunn. With the image of their mutilated bodies burned indelibly into her memory, she looked at the needle gun in her hand a second time.

Forcing herself to remember her murdered friends' bruised and battered faces had changed something inside her, and she knew now that she would not hesitate to use the weapon when the need arose. Shoving the keys into a pants pocket, she turned down the corridor that she hoped led to the sea and freedom.

She came to a second intersection and repeated her earlier sampling of the air. The smell of the sea was stronger now, and she was almost certain that she was heading in the right direction. Immediately, she rebuked herself for her optimism, noting that at times the floor of the tunnel was covered by as much as ten to fifteen centimeters of sea water. How could she trust her sense of smell under these circumstances?

Hearing voices coming her way, Tey stopped short. She glanced around the tunnel frantically for a place to hide. There wasn't any. She backtracked until she came to a small alcove carved into the rock. Filled with buckets, ropes, and other odds and ends, it was some sort of janitorial area. She squeezed in, crouched down, and tried to make herself inconspicuous.

The voices became louder and louder, and the two speakers approached her hiding place. Peering over a box, Tey saw one of them waving his hands in the air to make a point. After they passed without seeing her, she gave thanks for the weak illumination provided by the algae; anything stronger and she'd have felt like someone standing under a street light. She waited until their voices trailed away before rising from her place of concealment and slipping back into the corridor.

Another sixty meters down the tunnel, she came to a set of metal rungs set into the damp rock wall. Aware that the way out involved going up at some point in her odyssey, she shrugged, slipped the needle gun into her belt, and began climbing.

She emerged into a tunnel remarkably like the one she left. It was the same but different—the sea smell was stronger yet. *I'm getting there,* she told herself. *Slowly but surely I'm getting there.*

Tey thanked whoever was watching over her for her good fortune in not encountering anyone so far. No sooner had she expressed her gratitude than she rounded a bend and came face to face with a man and a woman.

"Hey!" the man shouted, reaching for a sidearm.

"Damn!" Since Tey was expecting trouble and the other wasn't, she was quicker on the draw. She pulled her needle gun from her belt and fired in one fluid motion. The first ceramic shard stuck the man in the shoulder, and the second passed straight through his breastbone and out the back. He tumbled lifelessly to the floor of the tunnel.

The man's companion, a blonde woman, opened her mouth to scream, and Tey calmly swung the needle gun's barrel to point directly at her. The woman somehow was able to choke back what would have been a fatal outburst. Blinking rapidly, her chest heaving, the woman stared the killer of her comrade in the eyes with an unspoken plea for mercy.

"Don't say anything," hissed Tey. "Not one word." She crossed the space between them and struck the terrified woman's temple a short, sharp blow with the butt of the needle gun. A clipped "Ah-h-h!" escaped from the woman's lips before her legs folded under her and she collapsed.

Staring down at the already purpling wound on the motionless figure's forehead, Tey hoped she'd only rendered the ashen-faced woman unconscious. Although she wasn't a professional like Galen, Tey realized that it wasn't as easy to "knock out" a person as the hol-vee shows made it appear.

There was a fine line between knocking someone unconscious with a blow to the head and killing him. Any blow sufficiently violent to knock someone out was easily capable of fracturing his or her skull.

However serious the injury she had caused the other, Tey had tried her best not to take the woman's life unnecessarily. It was time to put the unfortunate woman's condition out of her mind and move on. She had a father and a lover to worry about.

The shuttle carrying Mao Yanna, Lee Perro, Yur Palio and four other volunteers made the jump to the home system by snuggling up to a massive cargo freighter and being transported along with it inside the larger ship's hypersphere.

"Where are you guys going?" asked Perro.

"The United States—South Dakota," a member of the second team said.

"Shut up, Lee," his team leader barked. "They don't need to know where we're going any more than we need to know where they're going."

Lee Perro winced at his stupidity. If either team was captured, they couldn't be forced to reveal information they didn't know. Thinking about the possibility of capture made him run his tongue over the molar in the upper right rear of his mouth. Just touching it with his tongue made him shiver. He prayed he wouldn't be taken alive if things went wrong.

Once in Terran space, the shuttle's pilot allowed the craft to drift aimlessly away from the freighter it had piggybacked inside Terran air and space defenses. When he was just a few thousand kilometers from the planet's surface, the pilot expertly mimicked the flight path of a small, nondescript shuttle that had taken off from Belém in Brazil a scant sixty minutes earlier.

It was a straight switch: The Terran shuttle was outward bound with contraband and a dozen fugitives from Terran justice, and the self-styled freedom fighters' shuttle was headed planetside, carrying the seven of them and Suo Hann's campaign of terrorism to the evil heart of the Principate. To Old Earth itself.

Had someone in authority expressed sufficient interest in the flight to make a close reading of the radar records, it would have become apparent that the shuttle craft that had gone up from Belém was not the same one that circumnavigated the globe and came down again in Spain, in Barcelona.

Routine discrepancy reports were filed by the Equatorial and Euro-Russo central navigational/defense air-space web computers and just as routinely ignored by their human overseers. No one even went so far as to bother justifying his inaction by reminding his peers that such anomalies were all too frequent occurrences.

Even if he'd taken the time to explain himself, the air-space traffic controller's co-workers probably would have laughed and reminded him that similar inconsistencies occurred too frequently to waste time and energy investigating even one such incident out of a hundred.

Unaware of the bureaucratic inertia favoring the success of their bold maneuver, Mao Yanna and his six companions didn't allow themselves to even begin to relax until they were off the shuttle craft. So far, so good, but they weren't out of the woods just yet.

They found the rental vehicles their people on the ground had provided them. As Yanna and Perro watched anxiously, Palio keyed in the series of numbers he'd been ordered to memorize. A member of the four-man team did the same.

The right sequence of numbers unlocked both cars' doors, and they scrambled in and activated the power cells. That was the last contact the two groups would have until they'd completed their missions. If all went well, they'd meet at a spaceport in India in three weeks. If things didn't go well, they all had poison-filled false teeth.

Less than ten minutes after they'd landed, the seven terrorists' cars had made their way onto the correct feeder/exit road leading to and from the spaceport and joined the flow of traffic streaming up and down the coastal E-Mag highway. In minutes Perro, Yanna, and Palio were occupants of just another anonymous car traveling toward the French border.

"Now what?" Lee Perro asked Yanna, wiping his heavily perspiring hands on his trouser legs. Palio regarded the nervous youth with serious eyes; he hoped Perro was up to the tasks ahead.

"Now we grab the Magistracy by the balls and squeeze until they holler 'Uncle.' "

II

<Where did this come from?> repeated Galen slowly, staring wide-eyed at the object he was clutching.

<No fair. I asked first,> Sam chided him.

<It . . . ah . . . >

<Lemme try this one instead—what is it?>

<I . . . ah . . . >

Sam sighed and held up his middle and index fingers. *<How many fingers do you see?>*

<Two.>

<Whew,> said Sam, feigning relief.

<Hey!> protested Galen, cradling the crystalline egg in his arms like a newborn baby. *<I'm okay. There's just a lot I'm fuzzy about right now. I could ask you a thing or two as well.>*

<Ask.>

Galen looked around. *<For starters, where's the Berserker that was right here?>*

<Berserker? What Berserker?>

<Don't try to be cute. You know what Berserker.>

<He/she/it left.>

<It did?> said Galen. *<That's strange. I wonder why it was even here in the first place?>*

<I think it was to deliver this,> Sam said, picking up the jagged piece of polysteel and showing it to Galen.

<What the hell's that?>

<What's it look like?>

Galen stared at the piece of plasmetal and read, *<P.S.S. Thaddeus Stevens Cu . . . What does that mean?>*

After biting his lip, Sam simply said, *<Maybe this is a wild leap of speculation, but I think it's from a ship.>*

<So?> asked Galen, ignoring Sam's sarcasm.

<So it would appear that this ship came to a bad end.> Sam turned the hull fragment around in his hands to stare at it himself. *<I think the Berserker was sending us a message.>*

Galen seemed to twitch at Sam's words. *<A message? Maybe you're right,>* he said. *<We can check the ship registry when we get back to shore.>*

<That's what I thought.> Sam shot Galen an evaluative look and then decided he had to ask the question. *<Uh, why were you startled when I said that the Berserker was sending us a message?>*

<Startled?>

<Come on!>

<All right.> Galen relented. He proceeded to tell Sam about the white room and the rectangle—the teaching screen—and its first symbol, the simple whale outline.

<You said first symbol. There were more?>

<I think so, but I can't remember now.>

<How'd you come by your going-away present?>

Galen put up his hands helplessly. *<That's one of the things I'm hazy about.>*

<Okay. We can figure out what it is later. Just hang onto it for now.>

<Good idea.>

<*Whatever you do, don't drop it,* cautioned Sam. <*It could roll off the saucer and disappear into the depths just like that.*> He snapped his fingers, albeit clumsily because of his swimming gloves.

<*Don't drop it?*> repeated Galen. <*You mean like this?*> he asked, letting the object fall from his hand.

<*Jesus!*> exclaimed Sam, too far away to do anything but watch as the object fell toward the saucer. It came to a halt a centimeter from the unknown substance that comprised the saucer's skin. <*Why'd you do that?*>

<*I . . . I don't know,*> Galen replied. <*I just knew it wouldn't allow itself to be damaged.*>

<*Wouldn't allow itself to be . . . Hoo boy! Have we gone through the looking glass or what?*>

<*It has been an eventful day,*> agreed Galen.

Sam watched Galen pick up the crystalline egg and slip it inside one of the abyss suit's many storage pockets. Staring thoughtfully at the saucer, he said, <*Um-m-m, Galen, old buddy . . .* >

<*Yeah?*>

<*Our friend is glowing again.*>

<*I think that's a signal for us to go. We need to be hundreds of meters from this thing as soon and as safely as we can get away.*>

<*I won't bother asking why,*> Sam said. <*You 'just know.'*>

<*That's right.*>

Safely cocooned inside the abyss suit, Galen didn't have to worry about getting caisson disease from rising too quickly from a great depth. And Sam, of course, had no blood to be affected by crippling and potentially fatal pressure-induced nitrogen narcosis. Since neither of them had to concern himself about pressure sickness, an ailment more commonly known as "the bends," they made good progress, rising steadily through the water.

<*I appreciate you waiting around for me, Sam,*> Galen said as they ascended toward the surface. <*Was I gone long?*>

<*Oh, days and days,*> deadpanned Sam.

<*Really?*>

<*Oh, c'mon, you goof. You know you weren't gone more than four or five minutes.*> Seeing the look on Galen's face through his helmet's polyglas visor, Sam added, <*You did know that, didn't you?*>

<I'm kind of hazy on a lot of things. Time duration is just one of them.>

<Forgive me for asking this, but I'm compelled to,> Sam said. *<You didn't happen to see Amelia Earhart, JFK, or Elvis, did you?>*

<Of course not!> said Galen hotly. A beat, and then: *<Who?>*

"Sam . . . an' Gay-len," chirped Nemo as the boka swam down to meet them. Seemingly unmindful of the pressure, the boka met them a few fathoms deeper than was prudent.

"Hi, guys," Sam said, more than a little relieved to see the four playful boka and touched by their willingness to take a risk to join them.

"Where the thing went?" asked Rachel.

"Huh?"

"The thing, where it went?" repeated Rachel.

Galen and Sam looked back down into the depths. It was true. The saucer was gone.

Tey stopped and cocked her head, listening. Was it her imagination, or had she really heard something? No matter. If it was something that might affect her, she'd find out about it soon enough. And if she was imagining things, there was no need to worry at all.

No need to worry . . . *Yeah, right!* She was an escaped prisoner at loose in an underground labyrinth with no clear knowledge of the way out and with who knew how many people on her tail with blood in their eyes after what she'd done to their comrades.

"What would Galen do in a situation like this?" she asked herself. While there was no way of knowing the answer to that question, she allowed herself to feel a smidgen of pride at how well she'd managed things so far. "I seem to have a talent for this," she muttered as she crept around a corner, aware that it was a vulnerable moment. Then she rebuked herself. "A healthy self-confidence is one thing, girl—but don't get cocky!"

She stopped and again tilted her head to listen. There it was again. It sounded like . . . like . . .

"Ohmygod!"

For a long, terrifying moment she was paralyzed by fear. If the high-pitched squeaking sounds she heard were what she thought they were, she was trapped underground with an unknown number of carrion crabs.

Tey was right to be worried—very worried. She knew that the nearly meter-long crustaceans were not only remarkably agile and fast on land for creatures that normally made their homes in the water, but were also equipped with powerful claws to tear bits of flesh from their victims.

Galvanized into action by the increasing volume of the clicking, chittering sounds the crabs made when hunting, Tey hurried down the tunnel at a half-walk, half-jog.

She pulled out the partially depleted clip in the needle gun and replaced it with a full one. If the crabs caught her, she'd need every ceramic needle she had, and then some. Would the needles even have any effect on the hard-shelled crustaceans, she wondered? She wished the fat man had been toting a slug-thrower instead.

Arriving at a junction in the tunnel, she decided to take the left branch. In less than three minutes she realized her mistake, as the tunnel dead-ended in a wall of rock.

"No, no, no!" she shouted, pounding on the bare rock with her fists. Having gotten at least some frustration out of her system, she turned and hurried back the way she'd come. No longer allowed the luxury of conserving her energy by continuing her half-running, half-brisk-walking mode, she moved out at a full trot.

By the time she reached the junction and started down the other tunnel, the sound of the crabs was growing louder and louder.

Click clack. Click clack. Click clack.

Abandoning any pretense of maintaining a steady pace, she ran down the tunnel, her heart in her throat. She'd seen what a half-dozen of the carrion crabs could do to a sea calf in just minutes of frenzied feeding.

Click clack. Click clack. Click clack.

Looking nervously over her shoulder, she turned a corner. "Hey!" someone shouted, and a bolt of energy from a Legion-issue Matsusoni K-90 just missed blowing her head off; it made the wall of the tunnel behind her sizzle.

When she started to raise her hand with the needle gun in it, the man pointing the K-90 at her barked, "Hold it right there or you're dead!"

Tey held it right there.

She chided herself for being so concerned about the crabs that she'd walked right into the midst of a handful of Suo Hann's people. Noting a stack of weapons in the center of the large natural cavern the tunnel bisected, Tey assumed this group was cataloging the results of a raid on a Legion armory.

"Drop that little piece of nasty business in front of you and kick it over here before I decide to give you a tickle with my ninety."

Tey looked at the three men and two women. They clearly hadn't heard her coming. If they had, the one with the energy rifle would have shot her dead the instant she turned the corner.

The image of the crabs tearing and ripping the flesh from her still-living body terrorizing her, Tey decided that such a painless death might have been for the best.

Making up her mind that she would definitely rather be killed by a white-hot bolt of energy than be torn to bits by a horde of angry carrion crabs, Tey refused to acknowledge the rifleman's order to give up her needle gun. Instead, she told him, "There are God knows how many carrion crabs just behind me. If I surrender my weapon, you'll have one less person to help hold them off."

"Ana, take the gun from her."

One of the two women stepped forward and put her hand on the needle gun's barrel and gently but firmly pulled it from Tey's grasp.

"Good," the man with the rifle said. "Now, back against the wall." Tey did as he ordered.

"Shouldn't I at least check out the tunnel?" one of the other men asked. "Maybe she's telling the truth."

Like the rest of them, he was young. The fringe of lank brown hair that lay limply across his forehead made him look even younger.

Kids, Tey thought. *Suo Hann's leading a children's crusade.* There was nothing new in that, she admitted. All wars were fought by the young. That startled her. *How can I possibly be thinking of stuff like that when I'm about to become fish food?* The workings of the human mind were strange indeed.

"I don't hear anything," the one with the gun said. Tey saw that he was a big man. Her experience running the sea farm had taught her that big men too often mistake respect for their size as respect for their abilities. "But suit yourself and take a quick look-see if you wish."

The lank-haired youth grabbed an energy rifle from a small pile of weapons and headed down the tunnel. "I won't be long."

"Not long for this world, you mean," Tey muttered under her breath.

Tey cast a look of longing at the group's cache of weapons. It appeared that they had an anti-personnel, stedigrav shrapnel gun. That's the weapon *she* would have chosen to take with her, had she been the one walking down a darkened tunnel to an uncertain fate.

"Christ!" the big man swore when the tunnel was lit up by bright, hot flashes. The flashes were immediately followed by the longest, most bone-chilling scream Tey had ever heard come from the mouth of a human being.

"What—"

Click clack. Click clack. Click clack.

A wave of boiled-red crustaceans scurried around the bend of the tunnel. Everyone screamed—which seemed the only possible response to the horrifying appearance of so many flesh-eating scavengers clicking and clacking their claws.

While the others stood rooted in place, unable to move because they were frozen with fear, Tey flung herself at the stack of weapons, snatching up the shrapnel gun.

While Tey slipped the safety off and activated the gyros that helped balance the shrapnel gun, the others awoke from their dazed state and made a run for it. That was the wrong decision; the crabs cut their legs out from under them and then stifled their screams by crushing their windpipes.

The woman who'd taken Tey's needle gun from her was the first to be overwhelmed. The angry red horde quickly and efficiently brought her down by reaching out and snipping her leg tendons with their strong, sharp claws.

As she lay on the cavern floor, at the crabs' level, they ripped her open as easily as if she had been a rag doll. What flowed out from the wounds wasn't colored sawdust, however.

Firing steadily into the roiling mass of fast-moving, hard-shelled bodies swarming toward him, the rifle-toting leader couldn't target individual crabs quickly enough to halt their inexorable advance.

A squat, ebony slug-thrower was fired once in all the confusion, then flew from its wielder's grasp and skittered across the floor of the cave toward Tey. She gave it a quick glance but was content with the shrapnel gun.

One of the doomed men activated a grenade and took a lot of crabs with him when he blew himself to bits. Fortunately, since the grenade went off beneath him, the explosion was muffled and contained by the man's body and by the mass of carrion crabs that had swarmed over him.

Tey stumbled backwards, and as soon as she felt the rough tunnel wall behind her, she held the clumsy stedigrav apparatus out in front of her, centered the weapon, and threw switches. The crabs were scurrying toward her, their claws waving in the air and their mandibles clack-clack-clacking, while she fumbled for the firing stud. *Damn! This thing's more complicated than the cockpit of a starship!*

Tey gulped as the crabs' claws reached out for her. "I tried, Galen. I really tried." She felt the cold stone digging into her bare back. She had nowhere to go.

Click clack. Click clack. Click clack.

19

TEY FINALLY LOCATED THE FIRING STUD.

"Eat this, you little fuckers!"

Yellow-green flame shot from the end of the shrapnel gun and the massive, barrel-shaped cylinder spun as it began spewing out a nearly solid stream of jagged projectiles. The crabs literally exploded in a shower of crab gunk and shell. Tey now swept the corridor like a firefighter hosing down a burning hallway.

At the edge of her vision she saw the big man with the K-90 go down beneath a pile of crab bodies. "My God!" he screamed as they swarmed over his face. Tey averted her gaze when she saw them tear out his eyes.

"Kill me!" he shrieked.

Her face hardened into a grim but resolute mask, Tey turned the gun on the fallen man and the crabs that covered him like a chitinous blanket. Bucking and shaking in her grasp despite the stedigrav effects, the weapon spat pellets at an unbelievable rate.

The torrent of shiny metal stars and pebbles pummeled the blinded man's body like the blows from a thousand fists. His corpse and the bodies of the crabs on and near him were pulped and shredded by the gun's projectiles. Bits of blood, brain, and crab shell spattered against the walls.

Tey had no idea how long she stood there, the gun's cylinder spinning madly, the smell of hot metal and blood filling the air. Relentless in her maniacal decimation of the carrion crabs, Tey might have remained at the eye of the hurricane of death and destruction all day, screaming obscenities at the top of her lungs, had not the gun finally exhausted its supply of shrapnel.

Her chest heaving, Tey stared dumbfounded at the havoc she'd wrought, and threw the now-useless weapon aside. She'd killed them; killed them all.

Almost all.

One of the crabs had managed to climb the wall behind her and it leapt onto her neck and shoulders, driving her to her knees. "Argh!" Tey gasped as the crab's walking spines first whipped around her throat and then tightened.

She used her left hand to try to pry loose the attacker's fingerlike appendages and to fend off its claws while her right hand scrabbled around on the tunnel floor in search of the slug-thrower.

As a claw brushed her face, her frantic fingers finally found the slug-thrower and scooped it up. She pointed the gun over her shoulder, thrusting the barrel against the crab's chitinous body, and fired.

The slug ripped through the crab but seemed to have no effect. She fired twice more, each shot rewarding her with a spray of liquescent gore. Entwined in her short hair, the crab's rodlike antennae ceased moving and probing. The crab's hold on her throat loosened, and she was able to pry its lifeless body from the back of her neck.

She stared at the blood and dirt on her clothes and on herself and began to laugh hysterically. In seconds, she was crying.

When she regained her composure, she looked around at the horrific sights surrounding her. *Poor Galen,* she thought. *He felt shame for his past acts. He needn't have—the demon is in all of us, just waiting to be unleashed.*

Hashem Fedalf looked up from the field reports he was studying when Rob MacKenzie rapped on his partially open door and stuck his head inside.

"Yes?" Fedalf asked, slightly annoyed. He'd told his deputy he wished to be undisturbed for at least sixty minutes.

"Better turn on the hol-vee," MacKenzie said, entering and

handing Fedalf a fresh cup of coffee as a peace offering.

"What channel?"

"Doesn't matter."

"It doesn't *matter*," Fedalf said. He didn't like the implications of that. "This isn't about Paris, is it?"

MacKenzie shook his head. "It's something else."

"Hol-vee on," Fedalf told the computer.

A young black woman, so carefully coiffed and made up that she looked like a mannequin, was speaking directly into the camera. As she spoke, a graphic identified her as special correspondent Hillary Zolow.

". . . and with reports coming in from the park rangers and from the local disaster authorities, it now appears that the first estimates put the number of dead and injured at thirty-nine." The director cut to stock footage of Mount Rushmore taken from a floater that had circled slowly around the mountain to provide a breathtaking panorama of the sculptures of the five American presidents.

"What the hell happened?" asked Fedalf.

"Just watch and listen," said MacKenzie, pointing at the hol-vee image.

A new angle featured the massive sculpture as a backdrop for correspondent Zolow. "We have unconfirmed reports that the bombing of this quintessential tribute to the American character was the work of a terrorist group from the water planet of Cousteau, recently the scene of numerous acts of sabotage against Principate and civilian targets."

"Hillary, this is Daywatch anchor Nader Krupanidhi in the newsroom in Brussels," interrupted a distinguished-looking man seated in a chair fit for a monarch or a pope.

"Yes, Nader?"

"Is it true that the bulk of the damage was done to the recent addition to the mountain, to the image of Susan Buchanan, the fifty-third president of the United States of America?"

"That seems to be the case, Nader. It's ironic that the terrorists' bombs did their worst to the first woman to be elected president of the United States." Behind her, the image changed to a live floater shot of the front of the massive sculpture.

"We're seeing that right now, Hillary," Krupanidhi informed her. "Tell us, do the authorities on the scene—"

"Hol-vee off," ordered Fedalf.

"What now?" asked MacKenzie.

"Let's see what Feller and his people are up to," Fedalf said, putting his coffee cup down on the table and telling the computer to open a cryptex line to Legion headquarters.

The hol-vee image of one of Feller's senior staff appeared in a corner of the room. "Tomás, this is Hashem Fedalf—as you can plainly see. May I speak to your boss, please."

"I'm sorry," the droopy-eyed Tomás Almeida replied, "Director Feller is not here right now."

"Where is he, if I may ask?"

"He is on his way to a meeting with the Magistracy," Almeida said with a hint of satisfaction in his voice.

"I see," said Fedalf, breaking the connection. He understood the pleasure Feller's deputy took in giving that particular piece of news. It meant that he was at least temporarily excluded from the inner circle, cut out of the decision-making loop.

"They're meeting without you?" said MacKenzie incredulously. Then: "It's that prick Yeager's fault! If he hadn't been dicking around out there with Gar Varro's daughter instead of doing his job, we wouldn't be in this position."

"Let's not panic until we have to," Fedalf said, sipping his sweet, black coffee. "Something big is playing out on Cousteau and I have a feeling that Galen Yeager is in the thick of it."

"Do you say that because of your touch of the Ability?"

"The Ability?" Fedalf frowned. "No. As one of my fictional sleuths might say, it's a hunch."

Sam sat passively while Galen paced nervously around the Varro living room. "I just don't get it," Galen was saying. "What the fuck am I doing here?"

"What the . . . *fuck* . . . are you doing here?" repeated Sam, raising an eyebrow.

Sitting laser straight on a rigid-backed chair, his raven's-wing hair perfectly coiffed, his legs crossed at the knee, and his hands in his lap, Sam looked every centimeter like a poised and polished C.E.O. of a successful galactic enterprise. When Galen considered how formal and statesmanlike Sam appeared, it was like hearing the King of England break wind when he dryly and formally repeated his own use of the "F" word.

"You know what I mean," Galen insisted. "Why am I wasting

time playing around with flying saucers and crystal eggs when I should be trying to find Tey?"

"Pardon me if I'm a tad confused," Sam told him. "When I raised this point a little while back, you were adamant that you *had* to visit the saucer, that you *had* to go down to it and find out what it was all about. Was this all a dream on my part?"

Galen gritted his teeth. "No, you weren't dreaming. But maybe I was. I *did* feel that way when we were at the saucer."

"But you don't now?"

Galen carefully sat his drink down and then threw up his hands dramatically. "I don't know." He glanced at the crystalline object resting on a pillow on the coffee table. "I'm not sure that thing's big brother—or mama, or whatever its relation is to the saucer—didn't cloud my judgment when I was there. All I know now is that, away from its influence, I feel differently about events."

"We've waited this long," said Sam. "Would taking a little longer before going after Tey make that much of a difference?"

"What do you want to do?"

"Talk about what that thing might be," he said, pointing at the egg-shaped object. "Then talk about what happened to you inside the saucer—if that's where you were."

Sam got up from his chair and came over to where Galen was standing. "Then there's the little matter of the Berserker making me a present of that fragment of a ship's hull. Face it, Galen, something's going on and it's damned important."

Sam laid a hand on Galen's shoulder. "I don't like saying this any more than you like hearing it, but duty is calling—shouting at the top of its lungs, actually—and Tey is going to have to wait."

Galen walked over and stared into Varro's aquarium, envying the fish their dull, uneventful lives. He turned back to face Sam, putting one hand to his forehead and rubbing it gently. "God damn me to hell if my choosing to play secret agent instead of going after Tey results in something bad happening to her!"

"I'm not just saying this because I want you to follow up on this ship thing and forget about Tey for the moment—but she's a tough cookie. She can take care of herself."

Galen sat staring silently into space for a long time. He realized that a defining moment was at hand. If he acted like an agent for the PrinSecPol instead of like a friend and lover, his relationship with Tey would probably never be the same. If somehow she did come out of all this unharmed, they would both know that he had put her second to his duty.

Galen picked up the cup of coffee he'd allowed to cool on the table in front of him and drained it without tasting it. He stared into Sam's golden eyes. "I suppose you're right," he said finally, his voice betraying his weariness. "We've got other things to do before we can go after Tey."

Sam looked immeasurably sad, but said nothing.

Glancing toward Varro's study, Galen said, "Come on—let's use Gar's communications console to pick the brain of the nearest PrinSecPol computer to see what we find out about this mysterious ship."

"Sounds good to me."

Ten minutes later they had it all: the *P.S.S. Thaddeus Steven Curtin*'s registry, its last known port of call, and the time and location of its sinking. While there was precious little to be found in any of the "official" documents, the computer pretty much confirmed that the freighter's cargo had been literally too hot to handle.

"Toxic waste!" whistled Sam. "No wonder they couldn't submit a manifest listing the real cargo."

"Yeah, just reading the list of suspected chemicals this old tub was transporting is enough to give you cancer."

"It's the rest of this report that gives me the willies," Sam said.

"You mean the part about Hann's people sabotaging it and sending it to the bottom of the sea like a rock?"

"You got it."

"No, they got it," said Galen cryptically.

"*They* got it?"

Galen pointed to the screen. "It sank in the middle of the ocean, above one of the deepest trenches."

A look of awareness crossed Sam's face. "The Berserkers!"

"Uh-huh. That's where your ocean-liner-sized friend got the fragment of the ship's hull."

"God almighty!" exclaimed Sam. "If it's true that those monsters live at the bottom of the sea, and if a war breaks out on the surface that invades their home with contaminants—"

"Then we're in deep shit with them," Galen finished. "Don't

forget that simple representation of a Berserker the saucer's screen showed me."

When Galen got up from the console, Sam asked, "Where are you headed?"

"To get myself a drink. I know you never touch the stuff, but I sure as hell could use a stiff one."

"Okay, go ahead. I'll power down Varro's equipment," Sam told his partner. He had just turned off the last switch when he heard a loud "Jesus Christ!" from the other room.

Hurrying there, he asked, "What is it?"

"Look," Galen said, pointing. Sam looked—the egg was glowing.

II

Peter Zajicek looked around the conference room with grim satisfaction. "Then I take it we are in agreement on this matter?" There was a chorus of assent.

"Consul Zajicek?"

Zajicek recognized Consul Doerfler, a florid, red-faced man who always looked like he was about to explode.

"Thank you, Peter," Doerfler said, putting aside the report cube he'd been studying while the conversation swirled around him. "I just want to make sure that we have the people behind us on this thing"—he paused suddenly, looked around, and then grinned and added—"not that it matters." When the laughter died down, he continued by asking, "Are the polls to be trusted?"

Zajicek nodded, saying, "I understand your concern, but after the fire-bombing at the Louvre and the botched attempt to destroy the Eiffel Tower, even the professional apologists have had to concede that these terrorists from Cousteau have gone too far. No one on the planet wishes this campaign of terror against Terra's cultural heritage to continue—or to spread to more populated targets."

"Have the three so-called freedom fighters been executed yet?" asked Doerfler.

"They have only just been captured, Arnold," Consul Somoza chided him. "They certainly cannot be executed before their trial." The third member of the Magistracy, and the only woman, Consul Somoza believed it her role to be the voice of moderation in matters such as these. She viewed men as hostages to their testosterone.

Her comment made both Doerfler and Zajicek smile. "Yes, of course, Ramona," Doerfler said in a mock-serious voice. "We cannot execute them until they have a proper trial."

Annoyed, but not wishing to make the situation worse by responding to her colleagues' comments, Consul Somoza turned to Feller and said, "They have confessed?" It was more statement than question.

"Yes, they have—to everything," Feller told her. "They admitted their connection to this Suo Hann and her revolutionary council, and they even named the target of the second team of saboteurs. While we could not respond in time to prevent this morning's bombing of Mount Rushmore, we were able to capture the terrorists almost immediately thereafter."

"Tell me something, Director Feller—and please be completely frank," said Consul Doerfler, a peculiar gleam in his eye.

"Certainly, Consul."

"Could you *really* not respond in time, or was it a matter of deciding it was in our best interest to allow their terrorist attack to be successful?"

"Consul Doerfler, I can assure you—"

"Tell him the truth, Nevin," said Zajicek.

"You are correct, Consul Doerfler," Feller admitted. "Consul Zajicek and I agreed that the people would support what needed to be done only if we permitted these people to show their true colors. Therefore, we allowed the attack on the monument to go forward."

"I see," said Doerfler. "Very good, Director Feller. Very good indeed."

"Thank you," Feller said, dropping his eyes modestly and then turning to look in Zajicek's direction.

Zajicek felt Feller's gaze on him. Feeling slightly put off by the Legion Director's clumsy prompting, Zajicek nonetheless played along. "I believe it is time for Director Feller to reveal what our response to these atrocities is going to be. Nevin?"

"Thank you, Consul Zajicek. Here is the plan that I and my people have worked out and have had ready to go for the past two weeks: In thirty-six hours the battleship *San Paulo* will come out of hyperspace at a distance no farther than a few days travel from the Cousteauean system."

"Why so far away?" asked Consul Somoza, her brow furrowed by a frown.

"The *San Paulo* is no mere starship. She is a battleship, one of the four 'planet destroyers' remaining after the destruction of the *General Woodard*. The gravity tides and other complications attendant when such a massive jumper emerges from hyperspace are so enormous that to come out any closer to the target planet runs the risk of an incident."

Feller smiled a cat-with-a-canary smile. "A delay of a few hours or even days makes no difference to the outcome. There is nothing in the Cousteauean system to challenge the power of the *San Paulo*. A brief bombardment from the battleship will bring the planet to its knees. Then we can land a full contingent of shock troops to occupy the major cities, crush the rebellion and arrest its leaders, and restore Cousteau to its rightful place in our colonial hierarchy."

Consul Somoza nodded and then said, "Assuming that the courts of the provisional government do not disallow the forfeiture and seizure of the traitors' property"—again, the others chuckled at the courts doing anything except what the Magistracy wished them to do—"there will be a lot of money to be made by acquiring those properties."

"Not that any of us is influenced by such considerations," said Doerfler, a huge grin spreading across his visage.

"Of course not," said Zajicek with a straight face. "Now then, if there are no other comments or questions, I think we can bring this meeting to a close."

"What about Hashem Fedalf?" inquired Doerfler.

"When the matter of this rebellion is resolved, the head of the PrinSecPol will need to answer some questions concerning the activities of his agents on Cousteau. If his answers are satisfactory, then he will again have the confidence of this governing body."

"And if they are not?"

The feral expression that twisted Zajicek's face sent a shiver down Feller's back.

III

Galen held onto his glass as if it was the only thing in the world whose existence he could believe in. He was resting his chin on his forearm, staring balefully at the alien object.

<<*Hello, Galen Yeager. Hello, Sam Houston.*>>

"Who said that?" Galen asked, knowing full well where the "voice" had come from.

"No one 'said' it," Sam told him. "That thing spoke in our minds."

<<*That is correct, Sam Houston.*>>

"That's it, I'm leaving," Galen said, pretending to get up.

"Sit down, partner. I think we're about to get some answers to our questions," Sam said. Then he added, "At least I *hope* that's what's going to happen."

<<*You are correct again, Sam Houston.*>>

"You can call me just Sam, everyone does."

<<*All right, just Sam.*>>

"No," Sam said, shaking his head. Then he wondered if the egg-shaped thing could "see" his action. "Sam—not 'just Sam.' "

<<*Sam.*>>

"Now you got it."

"And who might you be?" Galen asked. Sam gave him a "thumbs up" for posing the question.

<<*I might be Alfie.*>>

"Alfie?" Galen and Sam blurted out simultaneously. Galen looked at Sam and Sam just shrugged, saying in effect, "Don't look at me."

"And where did you come by that particular name?"

<<*I came by that name from you, Galen Yeager.*>>

"That's just . . . ah, that's Galen, not Galen Yeager." He pulled on his earlobe and noticed Sam scratching his head. "Anyway, what do you mean that name came from me?"

<<*Several times, when you looked at me, you called me Alfie.*>>

"I did?" Galen said, frowning in concentration. "Oh, yeah— I guess I did think of you as an Alfie once or twice."

"It is a very human trait to give names to inanimate objects," Sam explained.

<<*I see,*>> Alfie said.

"Ah, do you mind . . . ?" Galen pointed to his glass and then nodded toward the liquor cabinet.

<<*Please, refresh your beverage.*>>

As Galen poured several fingers of the amber liquid into his glass, he said casually, "You know, Alfie, I never called you that out loud. And just now, you knew what I wanted to do."

<<Yes.>>

"Well, want to explain that to those of us who are hard of thinking?"

<<I have been conformed to your brain patterns.>>

"Conformed to our *brain* patterns?" said Sam.

<<Yes.>>

"Who are you?" Galen asked.

<<I am Alfie,>> the voice in their heads said infuriatingly.

"Let's try that again," said Sam. "*What* are you? Who made you?"

<<I am an artificial intelligence. I was created to serve you.>>

"Created by whom?" persisted Galen. "By the same ones who made that flying saucer?"

<<No. I was made by what you call the flying saucer. The Old Ones have been gone for many, many years.>>

"What can you tell us about it?"

<<I can tell you nothing.>>

"Nothing?"

<<I know only that I was created to serve you.>>

"And that's it?" queried Sam.

<<There is more,>> Alfie conceded.

"Now we're getting somewhere," Sam said to Galen. Returning to his line of questioning, he asked Alfie what else he had to tell them.

<<I am to deliver a message.>>

Galen took a sip of his drink, then asked, "This message, it's from the . . . ah . . . 'Old Ones'?"

<<No.>>

"No?" repeated Sam. "Then who the hell is it from?"

<<It is from the ones you call the Berserkers.>>

20
≋

THE CAVERN'S HIGH AIR PRESSURE WAS THE MOST OBVIOUS clue that the small pool in the center of the floor was the link between Suo Hann's undersea headquarters and the sea itself.

Tey couldn't believe it. She had made it.

All she had to do was dive into the pool, swim down and through a narrow tunnel, and then out into the waiting sea. The sea. She shivered with anticipation. Freedom.

"Hold it right there," commanded a strangely familiar voice. "Put down your weapon."

Tey did as ordered and then slowly turned around.

"Yes, it's me," Suo Hann said. "Or should I say 'us'?" She indicated her two male companions with a nod of her head.

The flame-haired revolutionary leader stared at Tey and then emitted a low whistle. "You're a mess, girl."

"I'm no girl," Tey said levelly as Suo Hann approached her until she was just two meters away. Hann's two escorts were content to remain where they were.

"No, I guess you aren't. Maybe you were when you arrived here, but I'd say this has been a finishing school for you. That's my fault. I should have had you killed immediately instead of bringing you here."

"Yes, it would have been better for you," Tey said. "Now I'm going to have to kill you."

"Hm-m-m, hear that, boys?" Suo Hann said, shaking her head. "We've been feeding her too much meat. From now on the prisoners won't get anything except gruel." One of the men snickered.

"Very funny," Tey said crossly.

"One other thing," Suo Hann reminded her. "In addition to my loyal twosome, I have a nice big slug-thrower and you don't."

Tey stared over Suo Hann's shoulder and beyond her two flunkies, her eyes widening. "That's fine," Tey agreed, "but any slugs you waste on me are ones you don't have to use against that horde of carrion crabs sizing us up."

"You must believe me a fool if you think that old hol-vee trick is going to make me turn around."

"Too bad," said Tey. "It's already too late for your guardian angels. They're as good as dead right now."

Click clack. Click clack. Click clack.

Hearing her two bodyguards' shouts turn into screams, Suo Hann whirled and fired almost in the same motion. Tey had to give her credit—the woman was quick. The first slug slammed through a crab advancing on them with its claws in the air. Her second and third shots similarly skewered the next two crabs, and she emptied the gun firing into the others, the crabs that were ripping apart her bodyguards.

When Hann's slug-thrower clicked uselessly, Tey said, "Gee, ran out of bullets." Hann backed away from the crabs and turned toward Tey—who promptly crashed a fist into the side of her head. "Surprise!"

Suo Hann staggered back a step or two, her eyes dulling for a second; then she regained her senses and threw herself at Tey, wrestling her to the ground. The two women rolled across the floor of the cavern, the remaining crabs scrabbling after them, and plopped into the water.

Thrashing and kicking, trying furiously to tear each other's eyes out, Tey Varro and Suo Hann pushed and pulled each other through the pitch-black underwater passageway to the waiting sea.

Still flailing away at each other when they emerged from the tunnel, they tumbled onto the ocean floor. Even though the water slowed and softened their blows, that didn't prevent the two women from going after one another savagely.

"I'll kill you for destroying my father's life!" grunted Tey, delivering a perfect—albeit water-retarded—roundhouse to Suo Hann's jaw.

Shaking off Tey's weak blow and replying with one of her own, Hann spat out, "You and your Terran-loving, Magistracy-ass-kissing father are two of a kind, princess! Cousteau won't miss either of you."

"You bitch!" Tey pushed off from Hann and then kicked her in the midsection.

"It's time to end this farce," said Suo Hann, reaching down toward her right foot. She withdrew a wicked-looking knife from inside her pants leg.

Tey gulped water, bubbles streaming from her exhalatory slits, as she examined her alternatives; they didn't appear promising. The best choice seemed simply to turn tail and make a run for it, hoping she was a stronger swimmer than Hann.

Accepting that as the best alternative, Tey opted for a strategic retreat, allowing herself to touch the bottom and then kicking off with her muscular legs.

"So much for killing me, eh?" mocked Suo Hann. The terrorist leader shoved the knife into her belt and gulped water before beginning to swim after Tey.

Glancing over her shoulder from time to time, Tey quickly understood her pursuer's lack of concern about the lead she had built up. Suo Hann was a powerful swimmer. Propelling herself through the water with practiced efficiency, Suo Hann began to narrow the gap separating them.

Once, when Tey looked behind her, Suo Hann told her matter-of-factly, "Yes, I'm slowly but surely gaining on you, Varro. Soon I will be ten meters behind you. Then five. And then I will catch you and drive this knife into your heart. I owe you that much for what you've done to my people, my followers."

Unwilling to give Suo Hann the satisfaction of a response or to waste precious oxygen, Tey said nothing. She knew, however, that the madwoman pursuing her was correct. It was only a matter of time.

Tey didn't know how long they had been swimming when she became aware that she had been angling ever deeper and deeper, following the sea floor as it plunged into the local trench. The water began to grow colder and denser, making it more difficult to extract its precious oxygen.

Suddenly, like a shock scene in a horror sinny, Suo Hann's hand seemed to come from nowhere and grab her by the ankle. Tey twisted to meet Hann's attack, hoping to fend off her knife hand and somehow wrestle the weapon away.

It was not to be.

Suo Hann closed in and forced the knife down and down until it plunged into Tey's chest between her collarbone and shoulder. Tey screamed and kicked out viciously, knocking Suo Hann backwards by the violence of her reaction.

With blood streaming from the wound, Tey half-swam, half-tumbled deeper into the abyss. If she was to die, she wanted her final resting place to be her planet's depths.

Following this fatal line of reasoning, she kicked with her strong legs and webbed feet, propelling herself downward. She was damned if she was going to give Suo Hann the satisfaction of seeing her die.

Oh, Galen, Galen, she said. *Why didn't you ever come for me?*

Through the translucent nictitating membrane protecting her eyes she saw a massive shape rising like a phantom from the depths. Instinctively, she knew what it was: a Berserker.

She watched with apparent disinterest as its gigantic mouth, a void darker and more ominous than the trench that lay beneath the behemoth, began to open. She closed her eyes and smiled beatifically as if in prayer.

Goodbye, father. Goodbye, Galen.

She was instantly swirled around and around dizzyingly, an insignificant speck in an infinite ocean, its water agitated by the passage of a creature of biblical proportions.

Dimly aware that she hadn't been swept into the monster's maw, she opened her eyes to see the enormous entity's mouth closing on Suo Hann. The terrified woman's screams ended abruptly when the Berserker's jaw snapped shut.

The Berserker lifted and dropped its huge tail several times and plunged back into the depths from which it had emerged.

"I'm dreaming," Tey murmured.

<<*You are not dreaming,*>> said an oddly soothing voice that seemed to originate in her head.

"Who are you?" Tey asked, now aware of a dull ache in her chest and shoulder.

<<*I am Alfie.*>>

"Alfie?"

<<*Yes. And these creatures have come to help you.*>>

"Creatures?"

"Tey! Tey!" burbled several boka voices.

"Rachel! Nemo! What are you doing here?"

"We comed for you, Tey. Gay-len an' Sam sended us."

Tey was too wracked by pain to say anything beyond, "Help me, Rachel. Help me, Nemo."

Then she passed out.

II

"How do you feel?" Galen asked Tey, unable to hide the concern in his voice.

Floating half in and half out of the water, buoyed by flotation rings, Tey looked more dead than alive. She sounded better than she looked, however, when she replied, "Not bad, considering."

"Yeah," agreed Galen. "Considering."

"I think I'm up to hearing a few explanations," Tey told Galen and Sam. "For starters, where's my father?"

Sam and Galen exchanged meaningful looks. "He's in his room right at this particular moment."

"In his room? Why isn't he here beside me?"

"He's with Dya," Sam explained. "She looks after him now."

"What do you mean, 'she looks after him'?"

"Your father is . . . ah . . . a changed man since we rescued him from Kubyshev prison," Galen said, squirming.

"Is he . . . ?"

"He was subjected to intensive psychochemical interrogation while in the prison," Sam told Tey. "He has not been the same since; he may never be the same."

"You said Dya looks after him." She blinked. "He is . . . impaired?"

Galen nodded. "I'm afraid so." Rubbing his forehead with his hand, Galen continued. "As I told you, Tey, my family has a very special relationship with the Voorhees Foundation. I will use all my connections to see that your father gets the most up-to-date care provided by the finest specialists Terra has to offer."

"Thank you, Galen," Tey said. "That is very generous."

All of them, including Sam, were aware of the awkward and strained relationship that now seemed to exist between Galen and Tey.

"Tell me something else," Tey insisted. Pointing at the small leather carrying case Galen wore over one shoulder, Tey asked, "Is that Alfie?"

"Yes," confirmed Galen. "I mean, Alfie's inside."

"May I see him?"

"Of course." Galen undid the pouch's fasteners and removed the crystalline egg from inside—gently, even though Alfie was impervious to anything this universe could throw at him.

"He's beautiful."

<<*Thank you very much, Tey.*>>

After waiting a few seconds, Galen rapped on Alfie's side with his knuckles. "I'm going to have to teach Alfie some proper manners before I can take him out into polite society."

<<*I did wrong?*>>

Tey laughed for the first time since they'd brought her home more dead than alive. "Alfie, I think Galen means that when someone compliments you, you are expected to return the compliment."

<<*I see,*>> Alfie said. <<*Forgive me, I did not think it necessary to point out Ms. Varro's great beauty. It is apparent to anyone who can see.*>>

"Fast learner, ain't he?" grinned Sam.

"What is he?" Tey inquired.

"Ah, now it's you who are being rude," Galen pointed out to her.

Tey understood immediately. "What are you, Alfie?"

<*I am an artificial intelligence constructed to conform to the mental patterns of the humans Galen Yeager and Sam Houston.*>

Tey frowned at that, glancing curiously at Sam. "Sam is not a human being," she said. "Sam is—"

"Better than a human being," Galen finished smoothly. "We'll straighten Alfie out on that little matter later."

"Who made you, Alfie?" Tey asked next.

<<*The 'flying saucer,'*>> Alfie said, having learned from Sam and Galen to put the quotation marks around those two words when he used them to describe the alien object.

"The flying saucer?" asked a confused Tey.

"It's a *very* long story," Galen told her, "and you only have time enough to hear the highlights before you need to get more rest."

"Does this 'flying saucer' have anything to do with the Berserker that swallowed Suo Hann while sparing my life?"

"Yes," Galen confirmed. "The saucer—or whatever it really is . . . ah, was . . . apparently helped the Society—"

"The Society?"

Galen raised a finger sternly. "No interruptions, please." He picked up on the look Sam was shooting him and relented. "All right: The Society is what the Berserkers call themselves. The Berserkers are . . ." He paused to consider just how to describe them.

"They are members of a complex society of whalelike beings living at the bottom of Cousteau's deepest trenches. They have existed there peacefully for hundreds of thousands, or possibly millions, of years.

"The Society is composed of gentle creatures"—Galen raised a hand to quiet Tey's exasperated protestations—"which never venture to the surface except under extraordinary circumstances."

"Like madness," Sam told Tey. "Those 'savage killers,' those 'monsters' your people call Berserkers, are really mentally ill members of the Society who have been driven to the surface by their insanity."

He paused as if unsure how to proceed. "It is because their brains are so large, and so well developed—the legacy of the alien object and the changes it induced in them and their anatomy at the dawn of their history—that they are so susceptible to mental illness. They experience so much more than we do."

"They have the Ability?"

"Yes. That and much more. According to Alfie—and what I have been able to remember of my 'lesson'—they have many mental powers, including psychokinesis."

Tey's own mind was spinning. "You mean they can manipulate physical objects through the power of their minds?"

"Exactly," Sam said.

"What do they want?" Tey asked.

"Maybe we ought to let Alfie answer that," Galen said.

<<Certainly,>> Alfie agreed. <<It is, after all, the message I was asked to convey to those who live 'above.'>>

"Well?"

<<The members of the Society wished to be left alone.>>

"That seems easy enough to accomplish," Tey said.

"Maybe, maybe not," cautioned Galen. "But there's more."

"More?"

<<They wish the war to cease and all weapons of mass destruction to be withdrawn from the planet. This must happen, or else.>>

"Or else?" Tey didn't like the sound of that.

<<Or else they will be forced to cleanse the surface.>>

Galen shivered, marveling at the power of three words to chill one's blood so completely: "Cleanse the surface."

"But that's in the hands of the Principate, the Magistracy and the Legion to decide!" sputtered Tey. "Tell them, not me!"

"That's the whole idea," Galen told her.

"Huh?"

<<Varro must negotiate the withdrawal of the hostile forces and objects,>> Alfie said. <<They were most emphatic about that: 'Varro' must be the one to speak to them.>>

"But if my father is too ill to—" Tey began. Then her eyes widened and she said, "Oh, no. Oh, no!"

"That's why this Varro must get all the rest she can," Galen said. "You are heir to your father's authority and position. You are the one to deliver the ultimatum to the Magistracy."

"They laughed at Tey's message?" Galen asked the holographic images of Hashem Fedalf and Rob MacKenzie, not believing his ears. It was agony waiting for MacKenzie's response to warp across space.

"Well," said MacKenzie after a glance at Fedalf, "perhaps 'laughed' is too strong a way to put it. Let's just say they were less than impressed by this contention that they or their people are in any danger from some large fish."

"Large fish?" repeated Galen. "Large fish!" he shouted.

"Put yourself in Zajicek's and Feller's place," said Fedalf mildly, speaking up for the first time since they'd made the connection. "They can't withdraw Principate forces—not the Legion and certainly not the San Paulo—on the word of the daughter of an opposition leader, a man who's gone stark raving mad."

"He hasn't gone stark raving mad," fumed Galen.

"Of course not," agreed Fedalf. "But that's how it looks to the Magistracy."

"Then everyone on the surface of the planet may be doomed, if . . ."

"*If* the Berserkers really have these amazing powers they're supposed to have," MacKenzie said. "Powers attested to by a talking crystal egg made by a flying saucer."

Galen sighed. "Yeah, it sounds pretty crazy, I admit. But, damnit, what more can we do? What do they want?"

"Proof," said Fedalf simply.

The captain of the *San Paulo* had just taken off his boots, put his feet up, and settled back with a drink when the first officer paged his private quarters. "Sir, you better get back up here on the double."

"What is it?" he asked, irritated at this intrusion.

"It's the singularity engines."

"The singularity engines?" The captain shot bolt upright.

"Yes, sir. Unexplained null-pulse signals are rapidly increasing in number and intensity inside the chambers. Helsing particles are proliferating beyond the capability of the de-graffers to process them. If this buildup continues, we're in serious trouble."

"Null-pulse signals? That's impossible."

"Yes, sir. I understand that, sir. But if you please— Ohmygod!"

"What is—"

The brilliant flash of light was many times brighter than that of a nuclear explosion and lit up the sky all across Cousteau's adumbrated hemisphere. Living creatures across an arc of fifteen thousand kilometers raised their eyes to the night sky in wonder and awe.

The destruction of the *San Paulo* went into the history cubes as the initial fireworks display celebrating Independence Day.

III

"How is he?" Galen asked.

"Father? Better. He knows my name now," Tey said. "He even asks for me when I'm not here."

"Remember my offer."

"I do—and I will almost certainly take you up on it."

"Good." Galen played with his glass of omo, then cleared his throat. "Ah, ummm, Tey . . . I . . . ah . . ."

She reached across the table and cupped his face with her hand. "I know," she told him. "If it makes it easier for you, I must say many of the same words."

"You mean . . . ?" He removed her hand and held it between both of his.

"Yes, of course. While Cousteau has gained its freedom, I have lost mine. I am no longer the same woman I was. I have responsibilities—to Cousteau and to my father."

"They say you will be the first president."

"Perhaps."

"I think there is no perhaps about it," Galen said. "May you be as successful a 'mother of your planet' as George Washington was a 'father of his country.' "

"Who?"

"Ask the computer to tell you."

"Dear Galen, what happened to us?"

"Fate. Fate and history."

"Fate. Things were never the same after the raid that took me away from my old life."

"I'm sorry if you ever felt that I abandoned you. It wasn't that, it was just . . . just . . ." Words failed him.

"It is I who am abandoning you now," she insisted. "I cannot marry an offworlder—a Terran—and expect to take my father's place and lead my people. Not after what has happened."

Galen's eyes shone with pride. "You're so different now, so much in charge. I guess I'll never know everything that happened while you were in Suo Hann's custody, but it changed you."

"Yes," she said simply.

"What the two of us had together was something special while it lasted, wasn't it?" Galen asked.

"Very special, darling Galen."

Shyly, they took each other's hands and leaned across the table until their lips touched.

21

〜〜〜

GALEN PUT DOWN HIS BOW IN DISGUST. "THAT WAS AWFUL, simply awful!" he exclaimed.

"Hm-m-m," said Sam. "It *did* sound a lot like a cat getting its tail caught in a fan."

Despite himself, Galen laughed. "It sure wasn't anything resembling what Mozart intended, was it?"

"Oh, I don't know: 'Quartet for the Academy of the Deaf,' " Sam deadpanned.

"End and save program, please," Galen told the house computer. He and Sam watched as their two VR partners disappeared. "I'm sure glad they aren't real people," Galen told Sam. "I couldn't stand the looks they'd have given me."

"I'm glad you admit the problem's with you."

"Yeah, it's with me, all right." Galen sighed. "Ever since we got back to Terra, things haven't seemed the same."

<<*You must not rush things, Galen,*>> Alfie told him. <<*It will take time for your emotional wounds to heal.*>>

"You're right, I suppose."

"There's one bright spot," said Sam. "Well, a number of bright spots, actually, but the one most applicable to you is your decision to go ahead with the divorce from Adrianna."

Galen nodded. "It's certainly made the lawyers happy."

Just then a chime sounded softly but insistently. Galen and Sam looked at each other. "Hashem!" they both said simultaneously.

Galen opened a secure comlink. "Hello, Hashem," he said to the image of the director.

Fedalf put his small cup down and replied, "Hello, Galen—and Sam and Alfie."

"What's up, chief?" Galen asked.

"Nothing, really," Fedalf told him. "I'm simply checking up on you, seeing how your vacation is going."

"Same as usual."

"That poorly?" laughed Fedalf. "In that case, we must see what we can come up with for you two."

<<*Ahem!*>> Alfie said in Galen and Sam's minds.

"Alfie says not to forget him," Sam reminded Fedalf.

"Oh, yes. Sorry, Alfie," Fedalf apologized.

"Aren't you too busy to be calling us?" asked Galen. "I mean with running the PrinSecPol as usual, *and* serving as the acting head of the Legion until the new Magistracy can find someone to replace Feller, it's a wonder you can find time to read your old mysteries."

"There is always time for my mysteries," insisted Fedalf.

"If you say so."

"Oh, before I go, there's one last thing," Fedalf said, unable to resist bragging a bit.

"Yes?"

"My old teacher's prophecy that a storm was coming and would begin with the 'ancient and end with the young' was on target."

"Your old teach—oh!" Galen said. He had forgotten their meeting before he and Sam went to Luna.

"My hunch that Luna was the 'ancient' he mentioned was also proved correct."

"That's right," agreed Galen. He smiled. "And the 'young' turned out to be Cousteau, didn't it?"

"Yes."

"The Ability is a strange and wonderful thing," Sam said, recalling the vision he'd had at the saucer site.

"Yes," said Galen slowly, thinking of the Society . . . and of Tey.

Seeing the expression on Galen's face, Fedalf said, "Well, I am more busy than I let on. I must be going."

"Goodbye, Hashem," Galen said as the mustachioed man's image dissolved.

"It's hard, isn't it?" said Sam. It was more an assertion than a question.

Galen made a face. "It seems that everything makes me think about Tey."

"Everything?" asked Sam, gesturing toward the chessboard in the den.

"As distracted as I am, you'll kill me!"

"That's what I'm counting on."

They were just pulling out chairs to sit on when the holophone chimed in the living room. "Set up the board," Galen said. "I'll be right back."

Sam arranged the pieces carefully, taking care not to eavesdrop on Galen's conversation.

"Life is amazing," Galen said, shaking his head as he returned to the den.

"Oh? Who was that?" asked Sam casually.

"That was Stan Raab, from headquarters."

"Yeah?"

"He heard I was back in town for a while. He's going away for several weeks."

"And?"

"He asked me if I could look in on his apartment and take care of things while he's away."

"What kind of things?" Sam asked.

"He wants me to see to his aquarium for him while he's on assignment. Keep an eye on things, feed his fish."

Sam was going to make a smart remark until the words Galen had spoken registered with him. More so than what he'd said, the expression on Galen's face betrayed his feelings.

As casually as he could, Sam asked, "So, what did you say?"

"I told him no." Galen looked at the floor, blinking rapidly.

Sam nodded and reached toward the board. "King's pawn to . . ."